The Prada Plan 2: Leah's Story

The Prada Plan 2:
Leah's Story

Ashley Antoinette

URBAN
BOOKS

www.urbanbooks.net

Urban Books, LLC
78 East Industry Court
Deer Park, NY 11729

The Prada Plan 2: Leah's Story Copyright © 2011
Ashley Antoinette

ISBN 13: 978-1-60162-611-0
ISBN 10: 1-60162-611-8

First Mass Market Printing October 2011
Printed in the United States of America

10 9 8 7

*This is a work of fiction. Any references or similari-
ties to actual events, real people, living, or dead, or
to real locales are intended to give the novel a sense
of reality. Any similarity in other names, characters,
places, and incidents is entirely coincidental.*

Distributed by Kensington Publishing Corp.
Submit Wholesale Orders to:
Kensington Publishing Corp.
C/O Penguin Group (USA) Inc.
Attention: Order Processing
405 Murray Hill Parkway
East Rutherford, NJ 07073-2316
Phone: 1-800-526-0275
Fax: 1-800-227-9604

Dedication

I dedicate this to the new little man who came along and stole my heart. I never knew I could love so deeply until I helped create you. You bring out all the best parts in me. I want to be better because of you. This one is for my new joy, my son. Your father and I prayed for you . . . our dream baby . . . our first child . . .

Quaye Jovan Coleman

I also dedicate this to my husband and soul mate, JaQuavis Coleman. We've been through a lot . . . more than the average couple could withstand. Good thing we aren't average, huh? We are extraordinary together.

I LOVE YOU . . . wholeheartedly, without apology, and through controversy. There isn't anyone or anything that can tear us apart. Nobody! Many have tried, but no one has succeeded because they have no idea how strong the glue that binds us is. Only we know the type of love we share. We are two halves of the same puzzle; one doesn't make sense without the other, and I am so honored to be the leading lady in your life. In addition to so many other things, you are my very best friend . . . always have been, always will be. Other people don't have to understand it. They don't live on our planet anyway. It is you and I against the world, fuck everybody else. Oh yeah, I guess we have to add Quaye into that equation now too, lol. It's all about our family. No one else matters. Every time you tell me you love me, I know that those words and your heart belong only to me.

"Many waters cannot quench love, neither can the floods drown it . . . "
—Song of Solomon 8:7

Acknowledgments

I have to thank God, because only He knows the challenges that I have faced along this literary road. Writing this one was a miracle, considering all the obstacles I had to go through, and although I don't understand why certain things happened in my life, I know that He will never give me a test that I cannot pass. This gift that He has given me, this amazing life that I have been afforded, and the beautiful husband and son that I was blessed with are enough for me to always be grateful to Him.

I would like to thank all of the fans that continue to support me. I do this for you, and I appreciate all of you who have been on this ride with me since my *Dirty Money* days. I hope you enjoy this new Ashley Antoinette classic. You are the best, and I will do this for you until I can't do it any longer. I read your e-mails, and I appreciate your positivity. Know that all of you are my inspiration.

Acknowledgments

I would like to thank my mom for her constant and unyielding love and support; my daddy for his strength, wisdom, and heart; my siblings for their purity and motivation. I love you all so very much. I'm blessed with an amazing circle of unending love, and the more I experience life, the more I appreciate how genuine you all are.

I would like to thank Carl Weber, of course. You are truly family, and you have taught me so many things about this business. This is a partnership, a team, and I know that I would not be where I am without the intricate part that you play in my success. I appreciate your belief in me and in my ability as a novelist. Thank you for your patience with this one. Forty weeks of pregnancy definitely slowed me down, but I'm back and better than ever! Time to take it to the next level . . . no ceilings.

Speaking of which, I would like to thank our super agent, Mr. Marc Maguire, lol. You are truly the best at what you do. I am so thankful to have you on this Ashley & JaQuavis team. You single-handedly took me into a crazy tax bracket, lol, and you have turned what I once considered a hustle into a lifelong career. I can't wait to see what the future has in store for us. I see big business ahead. Of course, I have to include Ms. Sasha in this acknowledgement for all of her hard work as well.

Acknowledgments

You two are a pleasure to work with. *Murderville* is next on the *New York Times* list, guys. Just wait and see. It is going to be epic!!!

I would also like to thank Natalie, Brenda, Denard, Martha, Walter, and the entire Urban Books/Kensington family for your hard work, for all of the feel-good e-mails throughout my pregnancy, your dedication to our brand, and for your support. You guys are the best in the business. It is all in the family, so my success is your success as well. We're in this together.

I would like to thank some of my dearest friends for being authentic and for being true even when it is not easy: Ashley Mustafaa, Shonda Gaylord, Charlynn Mi-dock, and Christine Love.

Last but most certainly not least, I would like to thank Cash Money Content for choosing Ashley & JaQuavis as one of the starters for your new book line. We're going to knock this thing out of the park. I promise! Can't wait to get started.

You can visit me at readerordieonline.com or ashleyjaquavis.com

Previously in *The Prada Plan*

Disaya sat straight up in the middle of the night and looked around the darkened room. She was in a cold sweat and her heart was beating erratically. She looked at the clock. It read 4:45 A.M. She held her breath as she listened silently.

"Indie," she whispered as she shook him out of his sleep.

"What's wrong, baby?" he asked.

"Something's not right," she said, her eyes wide and alert.

"Everything's fine, ma. You just got to get used to the new house," he urged as he kissed her lips. "Go back to sleep."

Disaya threw the covers off of her body. "She usually wakes up, Indie. Skylar doesn't sleep through the night yet. She wakes up around three every morning." She stood up and raced out of their room. Her panicky mood made Indie follow her into their daughter's room.

The sight of the empty crib brought Disaya to a halt as she stared into the darkness in anguish. "She's gone! Indie, she's gone!" Disaya screamed as she fell into his arms crying. "Where's my daughter, Indie? Where is she? Who would take her, Indie? Who would do this?"

Her terrified screams only intensified as the situation sank in and the shattered heart of a mother awoke the neighbors and pierced through the still of the night. She had no idea that her worst enemy was lurking around her. She had left New York in hopes of leaving her horrid past behind her, but trouble always seemed to follow. It was the story of her life.

Leah looked down at the tiny child in her arms. She was so gorgeous that Leah couldn't help but imagine what her own baby might have looked like. The child in her arms was still asleep, but the crying in her ear was as loud as ever.

Waaa! Waaa!

"Shut up!" she yelled. Baby Skylar whimpered, but settled down without so much as a peep. Leah was confused. *Where is the crying coming from?*

As she stood in the back yard of the house that Indie had built, her eyes darted around frantically until she found the source of the ear-piercing sound. It was coming from the grave where she had buried her dead baby. He was screaming, taunting her . . . haunting her.

Leah then looked at the tiny grave she had dug next to her baby's, and a smile crept across her face as she looked down at Baby Skylar. Indie and Disaya were going to pay for fucking her over. They were going to pay for all of her pain.

"Your mommy and daddy should have never fucked with me. Now, their precious little baby has to pay."

**THE WAIT IS FINALLY OVER! THE
PRADA PLAN 2 IS HERE.**

Prologue

I know you want to label me the bad guy. Every story needs one, right? The conniving bitch that is only out for self, the crazy one with nothing to lose. That's how you see me. Every pair of eyes that's scanning this page would love to see this bad girl die slow, but I'm used to that. It's the story of my life. Leah Richards has always been spoiled goods.

But you all are looking through a jaded lens. If you knew the true story behind my rage, you would understand. Little Ms. Prada Plan isn't as perfect as she seems, and I'm not as cruel as you would like to make me out to be. Rivalry, betrayal, friendship, rejection, loneliness, jealousy—those were the ingredients that brought me to this point. All of that mixed with rage contributed to the deterioration of my mental health. Now I'm teetering on the edge, and depending on which direction the winds of life blow, I could be pushed over.

I should have never opened up my life to YaYa. The greedy bitch just took and took from me until I had nothing left. Emotionally, she drained me. She left me on E, and now it's payback time. It's my turn to watch her suffer.

You've already chosen teams, and I get it, because you have only heard YaYa's side of the story thus far. *The Prada Plan* made that bitch look like a saint, but by the end of *Part 2,* you just might change your mind about me. I'm not a fake bitch, so I'm not saying you are going to love me; because frankly, I don't like any of you Indie and YaYa fan club members either. All of those Amazon.com reviews were sickening. Damn, I mean they are a far cry from Barack and Michelle. Get off their jocks. So no, I don't care for y'all that much, and you for damn sure don't like me, but let's just say that after my story you will understand me, and you most definitely will know it's not a good idea to cross me.

My life has been one constant struggle, and one exhausting tale of survival. When nobody wants you, envy can easily corrupt your heart, and when you have no loyalties, no one is indispensable. I've always done what I had to do in order to get by, and the people who got in my way always felt my wrath. Fuck a mother, a father, and a friend; all I've ever had was me, and I *refuse* to lose—especially to Disaya Morgan. I'll let my body hit the dirt before I let that bitch beat me.

I had learned to control my anger. Years of therapy and padded rooms had snapped me out of my vindictive nature, but YaYa brought me back. She unlocked the devil in me, and from the very first time I looked into those green eyes, I secretly hated her. She had what I wanted, everything that I desired. She was so beautiful and loved, yet was clueless as to how blessed she actually was. She was who I wanted to be, who I should have been.

Befriending the bitch was easy enough. Getting rid of Mona's tag-along ass was simple, because she was a weak ho from the beginning. Being close to YaYa fulfilled my need for attention, but after I helped her Baby Phat—wearing ass sleep her way to the top, she forgot that we were a team. I introduced her to real money and a completely new lifestyle, then the bitch fell in love, and she had the nerve to turn her nose up at me—like lying on her back hadn't just been her way to get paid too.

She acted like what we had didn't mean shit to her, as if Indie could offer her so much more. The bitch was stupid, because the way I see it, he was using her. At least my love was genuine. My love had been there all along. It was based on a much deeper connection, not just on the sex. Indie didn't decide to wife her until she gave him some pussy. I, on the other hand, appreciated her for so much more. YaYa's dense ass couldn't see that, though, and her brand new attitude turned me off completely.

I don't get clipped; I clip bitches. She should have known that there could only be one queen B, and now I have to teach her a lesson. It's time for her to kneel at my feet and know what it feels like to be second best.

I know I'm rambling. It is so easy for me to get caught up in my emotions and vent about this situation all day, so before I take it there, I'm going to hand this story over to someone who can do it justice. If I kick it to you, you are going to be biased. You already hate me, so you won't judge it with an open mind, so Ms. Ashley Antoinette is going to deliver it for me—raw and uncensored, the way that only she can do it.

I'm about to flip this entire shit upside down. Fuck a Prada Plan and the bitch that created it. It's Leah's turn. Welcome to my story.

Chapter One

YaYa's ears went deaf to everything around her as the explosive sound of her frantic heartbeat rang loudly in her ears. The sight of her daughter's empty crib incited a fear within her that she had never known. Her stomach instantly went hollow as she bent over in disbelief, and the agonizing thought of someone hurting Skylar broke her down to her knees. The lonely tears that cascaded down her delicate face were every indication that her grief was too much to bear. Her mouth formed in an O of horror, yet no words came out. Her cries were so heavy that they plagued her in silence. Her soul hurt so badly that she couldn't register the emotion in her brain. The torment that she felt was one that only a mother would know. A missing child is like a missing identity. She didn't know who she was without her daughter, and now that she was gone, YaYa felt as if the air had been knocked from her lungs.

Indie knelt with her in an attempt to console her. His strong arms wrapped around her fragile frame as she melted into his embrace. Tears plagued his own eyes as a jumble of emotion built up inside of him. He felt so many things at once as his mind kicked into overdrive. He immediately thought of any and everyone who he had ever had problems with. YaYa was a mother. She had birthed Skylar, but it was Indie who had created the little angel. Skylar was his seed, and the fact that someone had trespassed against his own sent Indie over the edge. Through all of the confusion, the sadness, the grief, his most prevalent emotion was rage.

"I'ma take care of it, YaYa. I'm going to find out who did this," he whispered as he held her, pulling her head into his chest.

"Who would take her away from me? She's a baby, Indie. She's my baby," YaYa cried.

"I don't know, ma," he replied truthfully.

YaYa sprang to her feet and rushed out of the room as she headed for the phone. "I have to call somebody. We need to call the police. She hasn't been gone that long. They can help bring my baby back." YaYa's hands shook violently as she picked up the cordless phone, but before she could dial one number, Indie removed it from her grasp.

"We can't call the police," he stated.

"What?" YaYa responded incredulously as her eyes squinted in confusion. "Indie, we have to."

Indie was trying his hardest to hold onto his logical reserve. The situation was threatening to cripple him at any moment, but he knew that he had to stay strong. Panicking would only cause more chaos, and chaos would ultimately lead to his daughter's demise. He had to remain focused and think. The weight of the world was on his shoulders. YaYa needed him. His daughter needed him, and he had to be the man they had come to rely on. It was up to him to make everything okay.

"This is federal, YaYa. If we report Sky missing, this place will be crawling with the feds within the hour, and they'll want to know everything. Everyone will be a suspect, including me. What I do and how I get my money will come under scrutiny."

YaYa shook her head in total disbelief as she stormed toward Indie, her eyes ablaze with anger. "I don't give a fuck, Indie! She's our daughter. They can take both of our asses to prison as long as they get her back. Give me the phone!" she demanded as she lunged to grab it from his hand.

Indie held the phone away from YaYa's reach, which only made her cry harder as she wrestled him for it. With a lack of someone to blame, she began to turn on him. He became her enemy.

"Give me the fucking phone! I hate you!" she screamed. Inside, she knew that she could never mean those words, not when it came to Indie, but at the moment, he was making her feel so helpless that they just slipped out. Her love for her daughter surpassed that of any man, including Indie, and she was reacting the only way she knew how.

She pushed Indie with all of her might, taking her frustrations out on him as she hit him repeatedly in the chest. "Somebody took her! How can you just stand there? I need that phone!" she yelled as snot and tears mixed on her face.

Indie grabbed her wrists and turned her around so that her back was facing him, and he restrained her gently as he hugged her to his body. "Shhh. . . . Everything is going to be okay. Calm down for me, ma. Just breathe," he whispered in her ear as sobs caused her to tremble.

She gasped for air as she began to hyperventilate, but Indie continued to hold onto her. For the past half hour, she had been falling into despair and fear had taken over her, but Indie had caught her. He was her rock, and he was slowly soothing her nerves and bringing her back to sanity. His baritone was like therapy to her as she closed her eyes and let her tears fall.

Indie was glad that he was holding her from behind. If she were facing him, she would have seen the tears forming in his own eyes and the uncertainty that lingered in his heart. He loved his family more than anything, and seeing the love of his life so broken was crushing. He could feel the tension leaving YaYa's body as she stopped fighting him.

"What am I going to do?" she asked.

Indie slid the phone into her hands and said, "You're her mother, YaYa, but she's my daughter too. They're going to have to put me in the ground to stop me from finding her. I need you to trust me, ma. I'm going to handle this, but if you feel like you need to call the police, go ahead. Do what's in your heart, I won't be mad. But if you trust in me, ma, put down the phone. I'll bring her home."

YaYa's mind spun as she contemplated her options. If she called the police, then she would feel peace of mind, but could they really help her? She had seen all of those news specials about children who had been abducted only to never be heard from again. There was a good possibility that even law enforcement would not be able to bring her baby home. Indie, on the other hand, had never let her down. She trusted him more than she had ever trusted anyone else in her life, and she knew that there was no one safer to put her faith in than him. She didn't know shit about Houston, but she knew that Indie ran the city. Her daughter's chances were better if she allowed Indie to hold court in the streets.

YaYa dropped the phone at her side and turned to face her man. "I'm scared," she said as she stared at him through glistening, tear-filled eyes. "But I trust you. Please, Indie, bring our daughter back. If something happens to her, I don't know what I would do."

Indie kissed the top of her head and then put both of his hands on the sides of her face. "I have to go out for a minute, ma. Will you be okay here by yourself?" he asked, genuinely concerned.

She nodded as he released her. He raced up the stairs and disappeared into their bedroom and dressed quickly.

"What are you going to do?" she asked as he came back into view.

"I'm going to handle it, ma. Try not to worry yourself sick," he said as he pecked her cheek quickly. He was trying to play it cool and keep it calm in front of YaYa. The last thing he wanted her to see was his panic, but if she could see inside of him, she would know his true fear. His insides were boiling, and his heart was beating so quickly that it felt as if he were having a heart attack. "I'm going to make everything okay," he assured with opaque confidence.

She wanted to believe in him, but the feeling that gripped her when he walked out of the door was haunting. Chills of doubt crawled up her spine, and the little bit of hope that Indie had left her with quickly abandoned her as soon as she heard the lock click behind him. She hoped that she had made the right choice, because her entire existence depended on it. Even in her darkest hour she had never felt so lost. To be responsible for the protection of such an innocent life was a daunting task.

I'm her mother. I was supposed to keep her safe, she thought dismally as she allowed the blame to fall on her shoulders. Her spirit was heavy with burden as she closed her eyes and imagined her infant's face in her mind.

Placing her hand against her chest, she gasped for air as she began to pray. *Please, God, protect my baby. Just don't let them hurt her.*

This blow weakened her, but there was one thing that she knew for sure—if anything happened to her daughter, there would be hell to pay.

The cocaine-colored Maybach ripped through the streets of Houston leaving burnt rubber on the pavement as Indie raced to Mekhi's house. He didn't even waste time parking the car when he pulled up to his partner's crib. He pulled his vehicle directly onto the grass all the way up to the front porch and then hopped out. His hand was fixed and ready on his waistline as he knocked the hinges off the front door. He could smell the aroma of the pungent weed smoke that was filtering out of the house as soon as the door opened.

Indie was viewing the world through a murder-filled haze, and when Mekhi opened the door, he immediately became the focus of Indie's wrath. Mekhi's smile of welcome was instantly replaced by confusion as Indie placed a pistol in the center of his forehead and grabbed Mekhi's neck with his free hand. Indie didn't give a fuck that they were on the same team. In the past there had been shade between them—a hood rivalry, a street beef—and Indie wasn't playing games.

He had just acquired the townhome that he had put YaYa in. Only a select few people knew its location, and amongst those who knew, Mekhi aka Khi-P was the only nigga he had ever had beef with. It was loyalty or death, and he wasn't one hundred percent sure that Khi-P was content with his current position in the game.

"Nigga, where the fuck is my shorty?" Indie asked through clenched teeth as he backed Khi-P into his own home. It wasn't until he was fully inside that he noticed his young gunner, Chase, was present, along with his li'l cook-up crew, Trina, Miesha, and Sydney.

"Whoa, my dude! Fuck is up, my nigga?" Khi-P protested with wide eyes as his hands shot up in his own defense.

"You still got beef with me? Huh, Khi? After all the money I've helped you get. After putting you on, you come into my home . . . what? You ain't seen me put my murder game down so you think it's a game, nigga?" Indie stated.

"Indie . . . fam, let's put the gun down and talk about this shit like brothers. I don't know what the fuck you on, but I don't appreciate the disrespect. We on the same team, fam. Where you coming from with this shit?" Khi-P asked, his eyebrows raised in concern from the fear of the unknown.

Nothing about Khi-P was soft. He didn't have a sweet bone in his body, but real recognized real, and the look of passion in Indie's eyes let him know that this was not the time for macho games. Safety off and hell-bent on revenge, Indie would not hesitate to pop a nigga. From one killer to another, Khi-P conceded respectfully.

"You on some foul shit right now," he stated with displeasure. He made sure that his tone was diplomatic, but still stern. They were both men, and gun or no gun, Indie was out of order. They should never be a target in each other's crosshairs.

"They came into my crib and took her! Right out of her bed. They got my li'l girl," Indie stated coldly.

"Indie, fam, put your gun down. Khi has been here all night, baby. Ever since we left your spot after dinner. We've all been right here," Chase reasoned. "This ain't on him."

Indie knew that Chase's word was bond, and if Chase was willing to vouch for Khi-P, then Indie was indeed out of pocket. He withdrew his weapon and balled his fists as he paced back and forth. The stress and heartache was written all over his face, and everyone stared at him sympathetically as they silently searched for the right words to speak.

"I'm sorry, fam. I'm going crazy right now. They got my baby girl," Indie stated sincerely.

Mekhi's disgruntled disposition lightened when he understood the seriousness of the situation. Any other nigga who came at him would have encountered problems, but he knew when to stand down. He had to remind himself that they were shooters for the same squad just to get himself to calm down. The tension level was on high as they all observed Indie cautiously, but remained silent.

Khi-P held out his hand and the men embraced as Indie gained his composure.

"How is YaYa?" Trina asked, finally speaking up to break up the apprehension that had clouded the room.

"She's out of her mind," Indie stated. "I need y'all over there with her right now. Make sure she's okay and keep her calm for me until I make it home." Indie went into his pocket to retrieve a stack of money, and he peeled off a few stacks to hand to each girl.

"Don't insult us. We're family. We got you. We'll make sure YaYa is okay," Trina replied. She stood on her tiptoes and kissed his cheek before she and the girls exited.

When the three men were alone, Indie turned toward Chase and Khi-P.

"We ain't got no beef like that out here. It's all love in Houston 'cause we letting everybody eat. The only mu'fuckas I can think who even got the balls to pull some shit like this are those Tallahassee boys," Chase stated seriously.

Indie immediately regretted sweeping them under the rug. He had not viewed them as a serious threat, but obviously they weren't playing games.

"Then those are the niggas I need to see. Put your ears to the street to see who's talking. It's time to start lacing pockets. I need to speak to any and everybody who can give me any information," Indie replied.

Leah's stomach twisted in excruciating pain as she drove away from her homemade cemetery. Her hands shook uncontrollably and her bloody fingertips gripped the steering wheel in desperation as she thought about what she had just done. She couldn't stop the devious smile that crept across her face. She didn't want to be so cold, but she was too good at it. Ruining the lives of other people was like a narcotic for her. She was addicted to misery and chaos. An evil dwelled inside of her that she could not control. Every time she tried to lock it up, it only grew stronger.

As a little girl, the good parts in her outweighed the bad, but with every new sin that she committed, her soul rotted more and more. She no longer remembered what it was like to be a moral person, and after the heinous acts she had committed, it was way too late to turn back.

Her blood-soaked car seat was a clear indication that she needed medical attention. She was bleeding from her womb and infection was an imminent threat, but she blocked the pain out as she pushed forward, determined, crazed over revenge.

The crying . . . the wailing . . . the screams of her dead baby tormented her, causing tears to flow from her disengaged eyes. It was as if the baby's spirit was haunting her, providing a deafening soundtrack as she sped through the country roads. Her conscience was begging her to stop the madness, but she couldn't. Leah was too far gone and hell bent on settling the score. She could not stop herself if she wanted to.

Waaa!

Waaa!

She turned up the radio to drown out the sounds, but they only grew louder. There was no erasing the bricks of burden that weighed heavily on her shoulders. She was haunted, and the shrill screams in her head were a constant reminder of the monster she had become. Her hands shook violently against the steering wheel as tears wrecked her. The thought of the things that had brought her to this point were sickening.

Mediocrity and rejection had plagued her since childhood. The people that she put her trust in were always the same ones who let her down. She had never been enough; she was always second choice. Her cold heart was no fault of her own.

People bring pain on themselves. YaYa made me do this to her. She made me the way that I am. Fuck her, Leah thought. The events she had set in motion were about to ruin Disaya, and she felt no inkling of remorse. YaYa had made her hurt in more than one way. Leah was intent on showing Ms. Morgan that karma was real.

As Leah drove, flashes of her past plagued her, and she was taken back to the place where her lunacy began . . .

Chapter Two

"Oww," Leah complained, cringing in pain as the sharp bristles of the hairbrush pressed against her tender scalp. "Mommy, that hurts."

"Girl, hush. I told you today is a big day. We're going back to New York City. That's where Mommy's from. That's where your daddy lives," Natalie stated. Seven-year-old Leah could see the stars in her mother's eyes, and an infectious smile spread across her young face.

Natalie had regaled Leah many times before with stories of her father and the magnificence that life with him in NYC had to offer. She had waited for this day to come, and finally her mother was taking her to meet him. Dressed in her best Sunday dress, Leah couldn't stop her eager heart from racing. Usually, she would complain about the itchy stockings and extremely tight hair bows, but she wanted to look her best. From the very first day Leah was born, she had been groomed for this reunion.

"You have to be perfect, Leah. Everything has to be perfect. Your father only loves the pretty girls," Natalie would say. "We can't go back for him until you are flawless. Everything about you has to be just right, so that he will fall in love with you as soon as he sets his sights on you." Her mother had drilled the ideal of becoming the perfect daughter into her for so long that Leah rarely made a mistake. From her appearance to her grades to her speech, she did everything without error.

Despite her youthful innocence, Leah was well aware of what her life was missing. Every little girl in Durham, North Carolina had a daddy to call her own. Sadness filled her when she saw fathers with their daughters on the playground. Envy ate away at her when she saw her classmates get dropped off at school by the big men who loved them so much. She yearned for the missing piece in her life. She wanted a father to take her fears away and make her the center of his world. She dreamed of meeting her daddy every night, and now her mother was finally granting all of her wishes.

"What is he like?" Leah asked excitedly as she turned to face her mother, only to receive a hard pop to the top of the head with the wooden hairbrush.

"Quit asking so many questions, Leah, and be still. I've told you about your daddy a million times. Turn around so I can finish. I don't have all day to get you dressed. Mama got to look good for Daddy too," Natalie stated with seduction in her tone. It had been eight long years since she had seen Leah's father, and the thought of him still caused her southern lips to cream in anticipation.

Messing around with a taken man, she had known that she was simply a little girl playing adult games. At seventeen, her heart had been stolen by someone she could never truly have, but he made her feel so good that she didn't care that she would never come first. When Natalie popped up pregnant, she thought that a baby would be the answer to all of her prayers, but when she was dropped off at the abortion clinic instead of accepted with loving arms, she decided to flee. Moving down South was the only way for her to have her baby in secrecy, but as she looked at Leah, she knew that it was time for the dark truth to come to light.

I'm not the same little girl who ran away all those years ago. I'm going back to get my man and embrace the life that I was supposed to lead. I'm supposed to be his number one . . . his only. I have his baby. He can't turn me away, she thought with renewed determination.

It took the twosome all day to prepare themselves for the reunion, but when they finally dragged their heavy bags to the car, they were perfect from head to toe. Dressed in their Sunday best, they climbed into the car to make the thirteen-hour drive up North. The overwhelming smell of perfume and hair grease filled the interior of the vehicle as they prepared to make the uncomfortable trip. Despite the miles of road ahead of them, they felt closer to home than they ever had before. New York City was where they both wanted to be. It was where they belonged. The man that they loved the most was unknowingly waiting. Whether he was ready or not, they were coming to claim him.

Natalie drove the entire way. Too eager to stop, she pushed forward until she could see the skyline of Manhattan's tall buildings. Eyes heavy from fatigue, she wanted nothing more than to drive to the nearest hotel, but she was too excited to delay the inevitable. The man she was searching for was one of predictability. He had been making the same moves on the same corners, frequenting the same spots for years. Being his young mistress in the past, she knew exactly where to find him.

An exhausted Leah looked up at her mother. The sandman was personally tugging at her eyelids as she struggled to keep them open.

"Are we there yet?" she asked with a big yawn. "Mommy, are we there? Is this where he lives?"

Natalie smiled and replied, "Yeah, this is NYC."

Leah's lazy smile was lopsided as her sleepy head rested against the seat. Natalie sighed. Knowing that Leah needed some rest, she reluctantly decided to stop at a motel. Seedy and in the worst part of Queens, the dilapidated neighborhood was no place for a single woman and child. She had used all of her finances to make the trip to the city, and luxury wasn't an option.

She went inside and quickly put Leah to bed, but found that sleep was evasive for her. Her mind was spinning with thoughts of her former love, and like a HEMI engine, her heart raced, unyielding and unforgiving, as it took over her wild emotional state. Natalie couldn't go to sleep—not before doing what she had come to town to do.

I've got to go find him, she thought restlessly. She peeked over at Leah, noticing her daughter's contentment as her tiny chest rose and fell. *I can just leave her here. She'll never know I'm gone. By the time she wakes up, I'll be back . . . and hopefully her daddy will be with me,* Natalie thought as she rushed to the mirror to refresh her makeup. She smoothed out the baby hair that rested along the edges of her neat, long ponytail, and brushed the wrinkles out of her skin-tight red dress before creeping out of the room. At that moment, it didn't matter to her that she was leaving a seven-year-old child alone.

Leah was just an accessory anyway, a pawn in a game of bait and hook. Natalie needed Leah to bait her daddy and convince him to make a home with them. *With me is where he belongs,* she thought as she drove off into the night.

Natalie walked into Jimmy's Bar, and although eight years had passed, everything about the place was unchanged. From the old jukebox that sat in the corner to the busty bartender behind the counter, the atmosphere was exactly as she remembered it. Cigarette smoke painted seductive pictures in the air as Leah stood in the doorway, nervous energy consuming her. Her eyes scanned the patrons in the joint. It was Saturday night, ladies' night, and all of the working girls were out on the prowl as they flirted with the men who frequented the spot.

At twenty-five, she was a far cry from what she used to be. Her memories were bittersweet. She remembered the long nights of tricking on the cold streets, but the mere thought of one man's warm embrace brought the corners of her mouth up into a small smile. As she reminisced, she set her sights on the back of the man she so desperately sought—Buchanan Slim—her old pimp, and the father of her child.

Although his back was turned to her, she still recognized him. His dominant demeanor could be spotted from a mile away. With his magnetic swagger, Natalie couldn't help but be drawn to him. She stepped over to the bar and sat right beside him.

Poison, his favorite scent, graced her body and piqued his attention immediately, causing him to look her way. The little girl he once knew was now a grown woman—a gorgeous vixen—and although she looked familiar to him, he didn't immediately place her face.

She pulled a cigarette from her purse and lit it as she wrapped her lips around it.

"Can I buy you a drink?" he asked as he spun on his barstool and turned on his charm.

Seducing a woman was instinctive to Buchanan Slim. He knew all the right things to say and do to get inside a woman's head, but whether he knew it or not, matters of the heart were sensitive. He had played with the emotions of many, and his manipulation was damaging. He owned the hearts of every lady in his stable, but he was only one man. He didn't realize that he was incapable of keeping up with the demands of their affection.

Greed and arrogance pushed him to pursue the pretty thing to his right, but he had no clue that they had already crossed paths. She knew him inside and out.

She gave him a slight grin as she shook her head from side to side. "You haven't changed one bit, have you, Slim?" she asked.

Caught off guard by her forwardness, he leaned back smoothly on his barstool to get a better look at her face. Her tight body, thick thighs, and long legs had mesmerized him, but now he zeroed in on her face.

"I know you, don't I? I can't quite place a face so pretty, but you look very familiar," Slim stated.

Natalie leaned into him seductively, her bosom pressing against his firm chest. Her hard nipples poked him, letting him know that she was turned on. "Maybe you'd remember me better with my clothes off," she whispered as she traced her long fingernail across his lips before she strutted off toward the bathrooms.

His eyes opened wide, but he kept his cool visage as he downed his drink before inconspicuously trailing behind her. The sway of her hips and the criss-cross pattern that her high heels left on the wooden floor caused his manhood to stand at attention. He adjusted himself in his slacks and cleared his throat as he followed her into the ladies' restroom.

Lifting her dress, she revealed the lace garter and thong she wore underneath. "Come over here and let me remind you, Slim," she moaned with the huskiness of lust in her tone. The music from the bar spilled into the bathroom, and Natalie began to dance slowly, winding her hips from side to side as her hands roamed her body.

An inexperienced man would have been flustered by her forwardness, but Slim leaned against the door and watched as her fingers crept inside her panties. Slim licked his lips as he imagined tasting her. The faster she massaged her clit, the harder he became. She was the aggressor, and for the first time in his life, Slim allowed a woman to take the lead. The mystery surrounding her identity intrigued him, but he could feel her familiarity.

Natalie's eyes never left his, and the moans that slipped from her lips beckoned him forward. When he was within arm's reach, Natalie grabbed him by the front of his slacks and pulled him to her. She grinded on his girth as he fucked her through his clothes. The friction from his hard dick was almost enough to send her into orgasm and he hadn't even entered her yet. Dry humping was enough to give her the shivers. Her swollen pussy lips left wet spots on the front of his slacks as he placed eager kisses on her sweet neck.

"Take it out, baby," she whispered as he lifted one of her legs, causing her wetness to stretch into a long, wet smile. Slim placed himself inside of her, and like a long lost key, he fit perfectly. She hadn't had another man inside of her in so long that her muscles formed a custom mold around his manhood.

"Ughh," he grunted as he pressed inside of her while cupping her ample behind in his hands. A pussy connoisseur, he immediately knew that he had sampled her before, and he beat it up as if he owned it.

Lust filled the dirty bathroom as she arched her back and closed her eyes while taking the feel-good train to ecstasy. His thick eight inches split her juicy peach in half as she bucked on him. He was smashing it, driving her insane.

"Say my name, Daddy. You know this pussy. It's yours, Slim. Say my name, baby," she whispered as she bit into her bottom lip to keep from screaming aloud.

The melody of her voice sent flashbacks into Slim's mind. He remembered hearing it before. He recalled being inside her, and before he knew it, he was calling her name. "Nat . . . baby girl,

Daddy's home. Damn, Nat, work it for Daddy," he groaned as he picked up his pace, his organ vibrating inside of her. The confirmation of her identity was all it took to bring them both to an explosive orgasm.

As they scrambled to dress, Slim eyed Natalie. Many moons had passed since the last time he had seen her. She used to be his li'l mama, the youngest worker in his stable of bad bitches, and he had groomed her well. Like all of the other women he oversaw, she was well versed in the language of sensuality and pleasure. She could make every man think he was the best she had ever had. There was only one who could resist her, only one who could see through her game and outperform her. That one man was her teacher, and she was his pupil. She couldn't resist Slim. He was the only man she had ever loved, and for eight long years she had waited for the right moment to make her reemergence.

"Long time no see, baby girl," he said as he buckled his pants.

"I've missed you, Slim," she replied with a sincere smile. She lowered her eyes insecurely as she continued. "It's been too long."

"That means we've got a lot of catching up to do," he stated. There was nothing better in the world to him than having control. Natalie had left him years ago, but still she couldn't help but find her way back home. Like a trained dog, she had come back to him whether she wanted to or not. It was instinctive in all his bitches. He was Daddy, and the only place that could ever be home was with him.

"There's something I need to talk to you about, Slim. Something important," she admitted. "I have a room out in Queens. Will you come there with me?"

"Don't need a room to do no talking," Slim stated. "Unless you got something else in mind?"

"I got everything in mind, baby. Everything," she insisted as she licked her lips.

Chapter Three

Natalie pulled up to the hotel with Slim following directly behind in his Cadillac Seville. Nervous energy filled her as she thought about Slim meeting Leah. She wondered how he would react. Hopeful that he would take his place as her child's father, she stepped out of the car and hurried over to him.

"Give me a minute to straighten up inside. I won't be long," she promised. She grabbed his stiff dick and rubbed it gently to keep him on ice.

With a cigarette hanging from his mouth, he leaned against his car door and nodded his head. "Go ahead and handle your business," he stated with authority. "Slim don't fuck with a dirty bitch."

Natalie ignored his arrogant nature and rushed into the motel room. Leah was sleeping soundly just as she had left her, and Natalie couldn't help but smile as she thought, *She's such a good girl. She's going to reel that man right in.*

Natalie was so close to making their family complete. The man that she desperately wanted was within arm's reach. All she had to do was close the deal.

She didn't want to throw Slim off by bombarding him with the news of his daughter. She needed to ease him into the idea of being a father.

"Wake up, Leah. Get up, baby," she said as she urgently shook her daughter out of her sleep.

"Hmm, Mommy, I'm tired," Leah whined, but still opened her eyes.

"Your daddy's outside," Natalie whispered.

Little Leah shot up from beneath the bedspread, excitement filling her eyes. She couldn't believe that she was about to meet the legend that she had heard so many fond stories about.

"Mommy wants you to wait in the bathroom. I'm going to come and get you when I'm ready. Until then, be quiet, okay? Don't make any noise and don't come out," Natalie coached.

Leah nodded her head in agreement as she was shuffled into the bathroom.

Natalie quickly pulled one of the bedspreads from the bed and grabbed a pillow as she laid Leah in the bathtub and pulled the curtain closed. "Be a good girl for Mommy and don't come out until I tell you to, baby," she said as she put her finger to her lips to indicate silence. Leah nodded and then anxiously watched her mother leave the room.

Natalie welcomed Slim inside, kissing on his neck and unbuttoning his shirt simultaneously as they backed into the room. They were all over each other. Like long lost lovers, they groped and groaned until they flopped down onto the bed. Slim loved sex as much as he loved air, and Natalie was enticing him. He could smell the scent of eager pussy in the air. Her natural essence soaked her silky, neatly trimmed hairs.

"Kiss me, baby," she whispered as she wrapped her hands around his neck while caressing the back of his head gently.

Buchanan Slim frowned as he looked down at Natalie. The more words she spoke, the more his memories of her came rushing back. He recalled exactly who she was. She was the type of woman who tried to make herself a permanent fixture in a man's life. She was pushy and conniving—forceful. She wanted to be wifey. The gold between her legs coaxed him to stay, but he knew he had to put his cards on the table up front with Natalie. She was just a fuck, a casual escapade . . . nothing more or less. Kissing her lips would be too intimate of an act, and he was sure that she would read more into it than what was intended.

"Turn around," he instructed as his hands slid up her dress.

The thought of seducing Slim into submission caused Natalie to obey his command as she spun around and stuck her round behind into the air. She braced herself as he entered her, and bit into her inner jaw as his thickness split her wide open. She tried to control herself, but before she knew it, her agenda became the last thing on her mind. Buchanan Slim put his thing down on her like only he could do.

Leah covered her ears as she sat impatiently in the bathtub. She could hear the moans of a man from the other side of the door, but instinctively she knew that what she was hearing was not meant for the ears of a child. She closed her eyes and began to hum lullabies in her head as she pressed her hands against her ears. She was trying to follow her mother's instructions precisely. She didn't want anything to ruin this chance of a lifetime.

As the minutes ticked away on the clock, Leah became increasingly uncomfortable, but dreams of meeting her father caused her to comply with her mother's request for silence. She squirmed as her tiny bladder filled to its capacity. She held it in with all her might, afraid to make any noise, but eventually she couldn't hold it any longer, and as the urine dripped down her legs, tears melted down her face. Disappointment filled her as the color yellow ruined her pretty dress. Her white stockings were stained with wet spots, and she began to cry silently.

He's not going to want me. Mommy said he only likes the pretty girls, she thought as she began to remove her soiled clothing. She was careful not to make any noise, but when her feet got tangled in her stockings; she fell to the floor; her heart dropped in agony.

The loud crash caused the lovemaking in the other room to cease. Slim stopped mid-stroke.

"What was that? You got somebody else in here?" Thinking the worst, Slim jumped up and scrambled for his slacks as he pulled a switch-blade from his pocket simultaneously. "You trying to set me up, bitch?"

"No, Slim, it's not what you think. Just let me explain before you—"

Natalie couldn't even get the words out of her mouth before her face was met with Slim's right hand. Her head snapped as the sting of his slap burned her cheek. She held her hands up defensively while he charged toward the bathroom.

"Slim! Wait!" Natalie protested as she put herself between him and the bathroom door.

Wrestling with him proved futile. He over-powered her easily, flinging her like a rag doll across the room.

Enraged, Slim reached out with one hand and prepared himself to rush his opponent. He snatched open the door, ready for a fight, but the sight before him caused his brow to fur-row in utter confusion. His mouth hit the floor when he saw Leah standing there with tears in her eyes, stripped down to her panties. Her bare bird chest trembled as she looked up at him in a mixture of awe and uncertainty.

"What the hell is going on, Natalie?" Slim asked as he heaved from the adrenaline that had wrecked his body. He withdrew his switchblade and placed it in his pocket as he looked at her, demanding answers.

"That's what I had to tell you," Natalie shouted emotionally. This was not how she wanted things to unfold. "She's yours," Natalie replied nervously, her voice shaking.

Slim looked at Leah, who was frozen still in the bathroom, and a furnace of anger ignited within him. He wasn't looking for similarities. There was nothing to compare. He knew for a fact that Leah wasn't his kid.

He walked over to Natalie and backed her into the wall until she had nowhere to go. He lowered his voice out of respect for the innocent child in the room and said, "Bitch, you still on the same ol' bullshit? I told you years ago that I wasn't playing daddy to no brat. I gave you the money to take care of that shit!"

Flabbergasted that she was receiving the same reaction that she had gotten years ago, she began to tear up. She could feel herself losing Slim all over again. She wrapped the white sheet tighter around her body as she looked up at him in astonishment. She couldn't understand him. Why didn't he see that she needed him? That she had spent every day of the last eight years of her life thinking about him. Her heart beat deafeningly in her own ear. Why couldn't he hear it breaking?

"Daddy, just listen to me. . . . You were the only one I was with—"

Slim interrupted her before she could get started. "You were on the track, Nat! Fuck you talking about? You talking crazy!"

"I wasn't out there like that, Slim. You were the only one I let go bare. I didn't even go unprotected with my johns," she argued with raw emotion.

"She's not mine," Slim stated harshly between clenched teeth.

"Slim! She is yours," she argued with conviction. Her eyes strained with redness as she heaved, trying to catch her breath. Her love, unrequited, now felt like a curse. It was choking her with grief.

She couldn't believe that Slim hadn't grown up. He was supposed to be eight years older, wiser, but it was clear that he had no intentions of stepping up to the task that she had put in front of him.

But Slim was no fool. There was only one woman who could claim him as her child's biological father. He had one son, Nanzi, and that was the product of a special affair with one of his favorite girls. Shortly after Nanzi was born, Slim had been diagnosed with testicular cancer, and the radiation that he had endured as a younger man had left him sterile. He was sure that his soldiers didn't march. This was one of the reasons why he felt the need to overcompensate to prove his manhood. Having control over his women made him feel like a man, but he had no desire to play daddy to someone else's seed. There wasn't a bitch in the world that could pin a baby on him.

"What, Slim? My baby ain't good enough for you? Huh? You have no problem claiming that bitch Dynasty's baby when it's obvious that she not yours. Nowhere in your black-ass family tree do those green eyes exist," Natalie shot at him, hurt by his rejection.

Slim had to stop himself from flying off the handle. The jabs she was taking at him made him want to snap her neck, but instead he walked away and began to put on the rest of his clothes.

"Everybody knows that ain't your baby, Slim. I don't know what you think is so special about Dynasty. She don't love you the way that I do, baby. She never did," Natalie stated as she ran to his side and began to fiddle with the zipper on his pants.

She had never understood his infatuation with Dynasty. Even after all this time, he still put her on a pedestal. Dynasty was his queen B. "She can't make you feel good like me, baby."

He slapped her hands away, disgusted, as he nodded toward Leah. "Go take care of your daughter."

Now his memory of her was clear as day. She was still needy and clingy. She was one that he had not missed. The money that she used to rake in for him was not worth the headache that she caused.

Completely ignoring Leah, Natalie chased after Slim, following him all the way to his car. "Please! Slim, don't do this again. I love you,

Daddy. Please!" She sobbed as she beat on his car window.

He started the vehicle. The rain that fell drenched her, and her hair stuck to her face. Desperate for affection, she ran through the mud, refusing to let go of his door handle as he picked up speed. It wasn't until he put pressure on the gas that she was thrown to the ground.

She sobbed, her body shuddering from the feeling of emptiness that dwelled inside of her. "Sliiiiiiiiiimmmm!" she screamed as she watched his headlights. "Babyyy!" He had always had a hypnotic effect over her. She was crazy over him.

He heard her animalistic cry and closed his eyes as he hit his brakes.

"Damn it," he mumbled under his breath as he put the car in reverse. He was soft on a bitch. He knew that part of Natalie's infatuation was his own fault. He had sold her one too many dreams in the past to expect her to let go. He had taken her heart without giving his in return. When he began to back up, he knew that he would regret his decision, but he couldn't leave her out in the cold.

"Please, baby. I don't have any money. I spent everything to come find you! I just want you to love me, Slim. Love me, baby . . . the way that you used to," she begged shamelessly. There was no saving face when it came to matters of the heart. It wanted what it wanted, and despite years of being apart, she craved him.

Feeling sympathy for her, Slim rolled down his window. "I love you when you make that money, baby. You go back to bringing Daddy that money and I'll love you to death. You understand?" he said, giving her false hope and provoking her to return to her old profession.

Grateful that he was even willing to keep her around, she nodded her head as she wiped the tears from her cheeks. An invitation back into his stable wasn't what she had intended, but at the moment, it was better than being shut out of his life. If she had to be one of his bitches, she was determined to be the best. She would eventually earn her place at the top; she was sure of it.

"Yeah, Daddy, I understand. I'ma bring you that money, Slim."

"If I even hear about you starting shit or bumping your gums, we're done. I'm not that girl's father, Natalie, so never let the shit slip off your tongue," he threatened.

"I won't, baby. I won't. I'ma be good, Daddy. I promise you," she repeated right before she watched him speed away.

With a combination of fury and hurt battling inside her chest, she stormed into the motel room. "Leah!" she yelled. "I told your ass to be quiet! See what you've done? You've fucked everything up!" She grabbed a wire hanger out of the closet as she cried tears of rejection. "He wasn't ready yet! All you had to do was shut the fuck up, but you had to let everyone know you were hiding in there!"

Leah's eyes widened in fear at her mother's tirade, and she cowered apprehensively as Natalie rushed at her like a madwoman.

Natalie grabbed Leah, and without remorse or hesitation, she brought the hanger down across Leah's naked skin. The thin, pee-soaked panties offered no protection from the whipping, and Leah screamed and twisted her body in agony.

"Your stinky, pissy ass . . . you ruined everything!" Natalie raged, unyielding in the amount of force she used. She swung the hanger with all her might. Each snap of the metal felt as if it set Leah's skin on fire. She was taking out all of her frustrations, and beating all of her own insecurities into her daughter. Slim's rejection had sent her into a blind rage. She was stuck in a place so dark that even she couldn't snap herself out of it. Leah, unfortunately, was the only one there and became Natalie's release.

The beating was so severe that Leah couldn't even cry. The excruciating pain paralyzed her tears, but the slave-like screams could be heard throughout every room of the motel. Welts of flesh arose out of her delicate back. It would undoubtedly scar, leaving her with a constant reminder of the day her mother's heart turned cold.

Natalie didn't stop until she was too tired to continue, and when she looked down at her daughter, all she felt was hate. She needed someone to blame for Slim's departure and his refusal to love her.

"Your stinking ass in here pissing on yourself. You're too damn old for that, Leah! No wonder he didn't want you with your ugly ass!"

Her words were like swords to the heart for young Leah, and as she looked at her broken flesh and welted body, she believed it. Her daddy didn't want her because she wasn't beautiful enough and her mother hated her. Her naïve heart crushed right then and there, as she heaved cries of abandonment on the cruddy bathroom floor.

"Shut up with all that damn crying, Leah!" Natalie screamed. As she looked down at her beaten daughter, Natalie's callous resolve broke. She had groomed Leah from the time she was born, hoping that she could make the perfect child for Slim to love. Now all of her efforts seemed futile, and the little girl, who had been her ace in the hole, had suddenly become a child that she resented.

She had thought of Leah as a valuable pawn in a carefully calculated game of chess. She had never anticipated Slim's rejection—not a second time, not after so many years. She had tried her hardest to become everything that he wanted in a woman, and had instilled countless hours of preparation into Leah. Leah knew how to walk, talk, and charm her way through any situation, but before Natalie even had a chance to put it all on display, Slim shut her down. He didn't want them. Neither Natalie nor her daughter was good enough for Slim, and that realization turned her bitter to the core. He had chosen his HBIC.

From the first day that she met Slim, she knew that Dynasty was his number one, but she had been determined to snatch him away. She wanted nothing more than the loyalty from the very pimp who had introduced her to the streets. Her love knew no limits. She would do anything to attain Slim's heart, and if that meant returning to his stable, then so be it. Nothing was out of bounds. He loved her when she made that money, and that's exactly what she intended to do, even if it meant sacrificing the soul of young Leah.

Chapter Four

"Ooh, baby . . . yes. Give me that dick," Natalie moaned, lying on her back while the white man atop of her had his way with her. It was her first trick in years, and Slim had sent her one of his most docile customers to make it easier for her. As she took dick like a professional, she imagined that it was Slim's hardness drilling inside of her. Her hotbox was soaking wet as the man rode her into ecstasy. He was well endowed and had the stamina of a stallion, so she was enjoying the session just as much as he was.

It didn't matter that her daughter was lying in the bed next to theirs. Natalie had to do what she had to do. The man on top of her hadn't even looked her way. He stared intently at Leah, getting off on the fact that she was so close by. Natalie noticed the look of lust in her john's eyes, and annoyance filled her as she reached up to turn his face away from her daughter.

"What you looking at, baby? I'm right here. I'm all the woman you need. This pussy good to you, baby?" she asked while meeting him thrust for thrust, grinding herself into him.

All he could do was groan as she snapped her muscles around his shaft, but it wasn't long before his head turned toward Leah again. Irritated, she said, "Ain't nothing over there for you." What she didn't know was that he had a fetish for young girls—little girls, in fact.

"There might be," he whispered.

Natalie stopped abruptly and put her hands to his chest to lift him off of her a bit. Staring him straight in the eyes she asked, "What?"

"You heard me. I want her," he stated.

"She's only seven," Natalie said.

"I'll pay double," he negotiated.

Terrified, Leah lay deathly still as she listened to her mother bargain with the man. The sounds that they made had stirred her from her restless sleep, but she had been too afraid to move. She didn't want to receive another beating for doing the wrong thing, so she lay there motionless while she listened to her mother's sexual escapade.

"She's not ready for all that," Natalie protested. "What type of mother do you think I am?"

"The type who fucks a nigga in the bed right next to your kid. I'll pay triple. Just let me lick that. I'll be careful with her. I won't even stick it in. I just want to rub the tip on it," the man said.

Leah's breathing became labored as she waited to hear her mother's reply.

"I'ma make her feel good," the man continued as he reached onto the nightstand for his money clip. He flipped off eight crisp hundred-dollar bills and stuffed them between Natalie's breasts. Too ashamed to hear herself agree to his conditions, but unable to resist the power of the dollar she simply nodded her head. The grin that spread across his face almost made her throw up, but she didn't stop him as he climbed out of her bed.

Leah held her breath when she felt the weight of the man enter her bed, and her heart beat erratically, almost painfully through her chest. Every hair on her neck stood up as the man pulled back the sheet, exposing her to the cool wind of the night. His hands felt foreign on her body, and she trembled violently as he touched her. Every spot he invaded felt dirty.

"Mommy?" she called out. "Mommy!"

Natalie cringed at her daughter's cries, but did nothing to intervene. She simply turned her back to the scene and stared out of the motel window as the man had his way with Leah. She tuned them out with thoughts of Slim. He would be pleased with her profits, and that fact alone was enough for her to allow her daughter to be victimized.

The feeling of his mouth between her legs surprised Leah. A weird sensation overcame her. Physically, it brought her pleasure, but psychologically, she knew it was wrong, and embarrassment filled her. She felt dirty, like something was wrong with her, as a river of tears cascaded down her pillow. "Mommy! Make him stop!" she shouted, but her pleas were in vain.

"Shhh. Be quiet, Leah. Don't fight him. You're doing this for Daddy. Make that money for Daddy, sweetie. Enjoy it. It won't hurt for long," Natalie said without looking her way.

The smell of her youth in his face made him rock hard, and he couldn't contain himself. He grabbed his penis and began to rub it on her opening as she squirmed underneath him. No longer able to speak, Leah choked on her own tears. Sobbing, she prayed for God to save her.

"Hey, you bastard!" Natalie shouted.

Thinking that her prayers had been answered, Leah reached out for her mother.

"If you want to do all of that, it's extra!" Natalie stated. "You said you wouldn't go all the way!"

At that moment, instead of being her savior, her mother became the devil.

Excruciating pain ripped through her, and all she could do was scream as her virginity was snatched away from her, along with her sanity.

"Are you still mad at Mommy?" Natalie asked as she stood behind Leah and combed her long, thick hair.

Leah didn't respond. She was despondent, almost detached from the world as she sat between her mother's legs with tears running down her cheeks. She had washed herself a million times since being raped. She had scrubbed her skin so hard that she had begun to bleed, but still nothing made her feel clean. She felt stained, as if she would forever be branded with the stamp of disgust and shame.

"I know it hurt, baby, but I promise you it starts to feel good after a while. It was your first time. It won't hurt like that the next time. We have to do this. We have to make this money for your daddy so that he will keep us around. Do this for him. Make him love you, Leah. You want a daddy, right?" Natalie asked.

She was manipulating Leah's young mind, confusing her. Of course she wanted a daddy, but if this is what she had to go through to get a father of her own, she wasn't sure it was worth it. Why did she have to work so hard for a man to love her? The tender place between her thighs ached, and instead of being a gift of womanhood, it felt more like a curse.

Natalie stood to her feet and walked over to the vanity table. She pulled out the chair and motioned for Leah to sit down.

"I know what will cheer you up, baby. Let Mommy make you feel pretty again." Mistrust filled Leah's eyes. "Come here."

Leah rose and went to her mother. "It hurt, Mommy," she said.

"I know, baby. It won't hurt ever again. I promise," Natalie replied as she pulled out her makeup brush. "Let me make your face up. This will make you feel better. You'll feel special again."

Leah sat with her hands in her lap, nervously wringing out each finger while her mother applied makeup to her face. As the powder brush tickled her tiny nose, it sent shivers up her spine. She giggled as Natalie pulled out her lipstick tube, and her angry resolve dissolved slightly.

Leah couldn't help but to be excited, feeling like a grown woman as she admired the job her mother was doing in the mirror. Natalie never allowed her to play in her cosmetics, but today she was applying the makeup to Leah's face personally. Leah felt like it was her mother's way of apologizing, and she wanted nothing more than to make things go back to normal. She wanted to be the little girl that her mother used to protect and be proud of.

Ever since they had come to the big city, her mother had changed. What young Leah didn't understand was that around Slim, Natalie wasn't the same. She reverted back to the naïve seventeen-year-old whore, desperate for attention and willing to do anything to get it.

"You can even wear my satin robe tonight," Natalie said as she wrapped the material around Leah's shoulders, making her smile.

A few days had passed since her vicious beating and Leah's molestation, but for the first time, Leah felt pretty again, as if the makeup and silky fabric had revamped her demolished spirit. Leah had watched her mother lay in bed crying for days. She had been unable to bring herself to look at her own daughter, but with this change in attitude, Leah was hopeful that her mother loved her again.

Her smile spread all the way across her face when Natalie finally finished. Leah hopped up from the bed and ran to the mirror.

"I'm pretty now, right, Mommy? You made me look like a princess," Leah said as she jumped up and down while clapping her hands. She couldn't get enough of herself. It was as if she were seeing herself for the first time as she stared intently at her reflection. She was in awe.

A knock at the door caused Leah to turn away from the mirror, but when she looked at her mother, she frowned in confusion. A pool of fresh tears had gathered in Natalie's eyes. The look on her face sent a chill through Leah's body, and her bottom lip began to quiver. It was as if the devil himself had come banging at their door, and an instinctive fear settled into Leah's bones.

"Mommy?" Leah called out uncertainly.

Natalie didn't respond as she walked to the door and opened it. A thin, dark man crept inside. The overwhelming stench of his cheap cologne wrapped its scent around Leah's throat, choking her as her chest heaved up and down in fear. She knew what he was there for. She could tell by the look in her mother's eyes.

"Here, let me take your jacket, baby. Make you more comfortable." Natalie slipped her hands across his broad chest and down the sleeves of his jacket before he could respond. It was one of her first official tricks since returning to the city, and it was just like riding a bike—she could never forget how to do it. With a PhD in seduction, she knew that the slightest grazing of her fingertips against the zipper of his pants made him more eager. The more he anticipated the sex, the more money she could get out of him. The more money she made, the more pleased Slim would be.

"I have a little surprise for you, baby," she whispered. "I hear you like 'em young."

Leah's eyes bucked in fear as she saw the man turn her way. All dolled up, she was every pervert's fantasy, and when she saw the man hand money to Natalie, she knew that she had just been sold—again.

"Where the fuck is he?" Natalie asked as her eyes scanned the digital clock on the nightstand. Slim had called her hours ago, saying that he was coming to pick up his money. She had an entire week's profit waiting for him, $5,500 to be exact, and she was confident that he would be pleased.

After discovering how much more men would pay to sleep with Leah, she sold her daughter's innocence repeatedly. The guilt she felt eventually subsided when the money began to pile up, and whenever her conscience crept up on her, she simply drowned it out with her favorite Five O'Clock gin.

"Not even that bitch Dynasty is bringing in this much dough. He'll see that he needs me," Natalie told herself as she lit a cigarette to calm her nerves.

When day turned to night and the clock struck midnight, Natalie's patience had run out. Slim hadn't shown, and he wasn't responding to her pages. Anticipation turned to anxiety, which turned into anger.

"That mu'fucka promised he would stop by! He knows I have this money here waiting for him. I'm always last on his list of things to fucking do!" Natalie screamed to herself as she paced back and forth. She was a wreck. Slim was the only man who had ever held power over her emotions. He had a strong hold over her; one that she couldn't shake, one that she didn't want to shake, but the unhealthy fixation was causing her to become unstable. She was coming apart at the seams as she nursed her bruised ego with a bottle of cheap gin. Slim's adoration was worth more than gold to her, and she proved it every time she sacrificed her daughter for the sake of making him a quick dollar.

Leah watched, but remained silent as she witnessed her mother grow more and more agitated. She had learned that it was better to be seen and not heard. Exhaustion plagued her as the hours of the night passed them by, but Leah was too afraid to close her eyes. Too many men had visited her bed in the wee hours for her to ever rest peacefully. She was always on guard, always paranoid, and she no longer trusted her mother to keep her safe. So, as Natalie desperately looked out of the blinds for Slim every few minutes, Leah nervously looked at the door, praying that no one came to hurt her.

This routine lasted for hours, until the sun came up and Leah was too tired to keep her eyes open. With her back against the wall, her head drooped down onto her chest as her mother's weary red eyes pooled with emotion. She was chasing a man who didn't want to be caught, and the way he handled her made her feel so unimportant, so dispensable—so unworthy.

"Fuck this," Natalie whispered. "He doesn't want to come to me, then I'ma go find his ass."

She shook Leah out of her sleep. "Get up. We're going to find your daddy!" she shouted. Leah wiped her eyes and slowly got out of bed. Her mother didn't even give her time to put on her shoes before she pulled her out the door.

Natalie raced all the way to Slim's blocks outside of Jimmy's Bar. She knew that night or day, Slim always watched his money. He had women working all shifts. Rain, sleet, or snow, his ladies worked 24/7, 365. There was money to be made around the clock, and Slim didn't want to miss a single dollar.

"There that mu'fucka go right there," Natalie seethed as she parked illegally on the curb and watched Slim walk out of the bar. She was about to call out to him, but when she saw the smile of endearment on his face, she froze. Natalie's eyes connected the dots between Slim and the target of his affection—Dynasty. Her heart fell out of her chest when she saw him wrap his arm around her shoulders and saw their little girl, Disaya, jump into his arms.

"She's not even his real daughter! That fucking bastard!" Natalie shouted as she hit her steering wheel furiously.

Leah peered over the steering wheel, and the sight of Slim hugging the girl proudly made her bottom lip tremble. She was working so hard to get the same attention from him. Natalie had promised her that once Slim realized what a good moneymaker she was, he would love her, but he still hadn't come around. She had done everything that her mother had asked. She had entertained the likes of old dirty men, and still Slim never came. She needed him to look at her the way that he looked at Disaya.

Enviously, she looked on as he kissed the girl's cheek. Everything seemed to move in slow motion as her stomach turned in turmoil. Slim was the only father she knew. Her mother had put it in her head since the day that she was born that the smooth-talking player from New York City was who she belonged to, and seeing him so fond of another child broke Leah in two. Anyone with the sense of sight could see that Slim's adoration for the little girl in his arms was immeasurable, and as Leah's heart filled with sorrow, she looked up at her mother for answers.

"Who is that girl, Mommy?" she asked, her voice breaking from emotion. At such a young age, Leah was experiencing heartbreak for the very first time, and the collapsing feeling of her chest made it hard for her to breathe.

"Is that my sister?" Leah asked, searching for answers.

Natalie gripped the steering wheel so tightly that her knuckles turned white. "No, that's not your sister, baby. That's not even his blood! That bitch Dynasty is up to the same old tricks, and he is just going along with it. He knows that little girl isn't his! He can see that she ain't his!" Natalie yelled. Unable to contain her anger, she grabbed her clutch purse and scrambled out of the car. "Come on, Leah!"

Obediently, Leah climbed across the seat and out of the car. Her mother grabbed her hand roughly before snatching her down the street. Natalie's high heels stabbed the pavement as she waved Slim down, just as he was opening the passenger door for Dynasty.

"Slim! Slim!" she shouted, losing all dignity as Leah ran full speed just to keep up with her. Her voice cut through the air in a high, furious shrill, causing everyone who was out on the block to turn toward the scene she would inevitably cause.

The hair on the back of Slim's neck stood up when he heard her calling his name.

"Who is that lady, Daddy?" Disaya asked as her father put her down on the ground.

"Yeah, who *is* she?" Dynasty repeated with an attitude.

"Nobody. Get in the car," Slim instructed. He tucked Dynasty and Disaya safely inside, then attempted to walk around to the driver's side.

This bitch has lost her damn marbles, Slim thought angrily. *I told her to keep a low profile. Now her crazy ass is parading down the street, putting on a fucking show.*

"Slim! I know you hear me, mu'fucka! Don't you get your ass in that car!"

The disrespectful tone of her voice caused him to cringe in regret. She was asking to be made an example of. Half of the other players in town were out on the block that day, and if he let one ho disrespect him, they would snatch his entire stable as soon as he pulled off. His business was sloppy, and Natalie was trying his patience.

"You better handle that bitch. She's a problem," Dynasty commented slyly as she put on a fresh coat of lipstick, arrogantly looking at herself in the mirror. She tried to appear uninterested, although she was trying her best to ear hustle.

Slim stepped away from the car and approached Natalie aggressively, grabbing her firmly by the elbow.

"Fuck you come here for, Nat? Didn't I tell you I would come to you?" he asked her, whispering harshly as he jerked her, chastising her as if she were a child.

"You said you were coming last night, baby. I waited for you. Why didn't you come by?" she asked sweetly as she reached up to stroke Slim's face. Slim dodged her advances and looked her squarely in the eyes.

"Go back to the motel. I'll be by there later on. Look at you. You're fucked up! You need to leave that liquor alone. You're embarrassing yourself. Don't come around here again," Slim stated, his voice unforgiving, and his clenched teeth giving away his shitty disposition.

Leah clung to her mother's sleeve as she watched the tense interaction between the two.

"What? Don't come around here? Embarrassing myself?" Natalie shouted, loud enough for the entire block to hear. "You son of a bitch!" Natalie removed the money she had earned and threw it at him, causing the bills to rain over him. "What, Slim? I'm not good enough because I'm not that bitch?" Natalie screamed as she pointed toward the car where Dynasty sat.

Dynasty's eyebrows rose in aggravation. "I got your bitch! Keep talking," she said without asserting too much energy. She was arrogant and knew her position. There wasn't another woman in town who could threaten her, but she wasn't above putting a bitch in her place if need be either. She rolled her eyes as she waved her hand in dismissal, leaving it to Slim to handle.

Slim's reaction was instinctive. He wrapped his hand around Natalie's neck and pushed her against the brick wall outside of Jimmy's Bar.

"Me and you, we're done, bitch. That's why I cut you loose all those years ago. You're fucking nuts, and you don't know how to follow my lead," Slim stated, shoving her one last time for good measure before walking away.

Leah looked on in horror as she watched her mother charge Slim, hitting him in the back of the head. Natalie was making a spectacle of him in front of the entire block, and the embarrassment caused him to see red.

"Mommy! Ma! Stop it!" Leah screamed as she ran up to her and tried to pull her away. Her small arms tugged at her mother's body in an attempt to stop the madness.

In a drunken state, Natalie pushed her daughter to the ground with such force that little Leah's knees split wide open. Blood gushed instantly, but the sting of her mother's blatant lack of love burned more than the wound itself.

Slim turned on his heels, and before he could control himself, he punched Natalie with all his might. Her head snapped back so violently that it felt as if her neck had broken, and her legs gave out beneath her.

"Mommy!" Leah screamed as she began to cry hysterically. She scrambled to her feet and ran to her mother's side.

Leah held her mother's bloody face in her hands as she tried to help her up. Natalie shamelessly staggered to her feet, drunk from the knuckle cocktail Slim had just served her.

"You're a dirty mu'fucka, Slim! I'll never be good enough, will I? Fuck you, Slim! Fuck you! This is your daughter!" Natalie yelled as her face began to swell.

"Bitch, I told you she's not my fucking daughter! She's not my kid! She's not mine! Get that through your skull!" he hollered, looking at her in disgust before storming away.

Natalie cried tears from the root of her soul as she watched the love of her life walk away from her. What she didn't know was that love didn't hurt, and what she was experiencing . . . what she was feeling . . . what she was consumed by was control. He had captured her mind so long ago that his hold over her caused her to do unthinkable things. All she wanted was him—his attention, his affection.

Shooing Leah off of her, she called after Slim as she ran behind him. She chased his car all the way down the street, while Leah ran behind her, both in tears, until his tail lights disappeared from their view.

The other working girls on the block laughed at the desperate mess that Natalie had become, but they were all in the same boat. Slim held court over their emotions as well. He had sold them all a dream. It was all a fantasy, a street marriage between a pimp and prostitute that only required one side to remain loyal. Natalie could have easily been any of the young women on the block. They all shared the same circumstance. They were caught up in a man that could never love them back.

Their taunting comments haunted Natalie as she grabbed Leah's wrist tightly and spun around wildly. "What the fuck are you bitches laughing at? What are you looking at?" she yelled as blood dripped from her busted lip.

Leah didn't know what to say or do as she was forced back into the car. Hearing Slim deny her so vehemently was wrenching to her soul. She didn't understand why he didn't want her. Natalie had filled her head with false hope, and now that the truth had come to light, she was crushed beyond comprehension.

As Natalie drove away from the strip, she battled with her own demons. In need of someone to blame, she turned on Leah. "This is all your fault. You see that little girl Slim had? Why would he want a little wench like you when he has her? She's perfect! She's pretty! Why can't you be more like her?"

Natalie selfishly blamed Leah when inside, she knew that the real comparison she was making was between herself and Dynasty. It wasn't Leah who Slim didn't want; it was Natalie. She had never been woman enough for him, but admitting that to herself would be like holding a mirror to her tarnished face.

What she did not know was that she was filling her daughter with insecurity and jealousy. The irrevocable damage she was doing would scar Leah for years to come. For the first time in her life, Leah knew what it felt like to hate another human being. She despised the little girl that she had seen Slim with. The green-eyed monster had his sights set on her. Envy consumed her, and her heart burned so badly that she felt as if she were choking. She couldn't understand what the little girl, Disaya, possessed that she herself did not. Why wasn't she worthy of a father's love?

As her mother belittled her and compared her to the green-eyed beauty queen that Slim claimed as his daughter, Leah hardened herself on the inside. She turned her face toward the window so that her mother would not see the tears that cascaded from her eyes. Her insides were in so much turmoil that her stomach felt hollow.

Why does my daddy love that other little girl more? Why won't he love me? Nothing in the world had ever felt so bad. After everything she had been through in search of his acceptance, she felt scorned. Scorned by life, burnt by the mother who was supposed to love her, and thrown away by the father she never knew. It was on that day that she became a bad seed, and everyone who had ever hurt her became her enemy. She never wanted to be so vulnerable again. She was closing off her heart, and she promised herself that she would never allow anyone to trample on her feelings ever again.

Leah looked down at the puddle of blood that pooled around her bare feet. A sickening calm spread over her as she looked into her mother's eyes. As they stared at one another, hatred filled the space between them. Unspoken apologies were overdue, but unfortunately, it was too late. Whatever needed to be said would be forever lost in translation. Death had silenced Natalie forever as her dead eyes questioned why.

Leah had snapped, and something inside of her felt that her actions were justified. Tired of the nightly abuse that her mother was inflicting upon her, Leah told herself that she had endured enough. Natalie never saw it coming.

After being betrayed by her own mother, Leah felt no remorse for the sinister things she planned in her head. The woman she had loved the most had allowed her to be defiled, had used Leah for her own selfish motives, had brought Leah's world crashing down around her. She was no longer an innocent child. Detached from right and wrong, Leah acted instinctively, defensively.

She was tired of her private parts being touched by different men, and tired of being compared to the little green-eyed girl that had Slim's heart. She would never live up to the unrealistic expectations that Natalie had set for her, and she was constantly terrified of what man may walk through their motel room door next to have his way with her. She did what she had to do. So far detached from what was right and wrong, Leah resorted to her only method of escape—murder.

The many men who had climbed atop of her small body had driven her to her breaking point, and Natalie was the one to blame.

The stench in the room was overwhelming as the summer heat baked her mother's dead body, but still she couldn't move. She was stuck, staring into the lost eyes of the woman who had failed to nurture her. Psychologically, Leah was unstable. Her mental and emotional state had been compromised to the point where she felt nothing. Even the horrid stench of the corpse or the sight of her mother's drying blood didn't disturb her. She was disconnected from all emotion, out of touch with the good little girl that she used to be, unplugged from reality. All she knew was that everything that had happened to her had brought her to this point.

She was so full of hate that it poured out of her eyes, giving her rotten intentions away to anyone who cared to stare into her soul. What could have been a beautiful girl with so much potential had been transformed into a troubled one with too many demons to count.

A knock at the door caused Leah to look up, but she made no effort to move.

"Housekeeping," the voice announced just before she saw a young woman enter. "Oh my God!" the woman shrieked as soon as she laid eyes on the gruesome scene before her. She hesitated, unsure of what to do or what she had just walked in on. She looked around the room in fear, figuring that someone else had committed the crime. When she was sure no one else was in the room, she motioned for Leah.

"Come on, sweetheart. Come to me," she urged.

Leah stood up with a blank stare in her eyes and slowly walked over to the housekeeper. It wasn't until the woman saw the bloody knife in Leah's hand that she realized what had actually occurred.

"Did you do this, honey?" she asked with wide, doubt-filled eyes. No little girl could possibly cause such carnage.

Leah nodded her head as she dropped the knife to the floor. Her bottom lip began to tremble as she stared at the lady who was kneeling before her. The woman grasped her shoulders.

"Why, sweetie? What happened? Why did you do this?" she asked, genuinely concerned.

The tears that rained down her face didn't match the ice-cold look in her gaze. "Because she hurt me," Leah responded, her voice monotone and unflinching, unapologetic.

The woman was taken aback by the satisfied leer that Leah wore, and she stood to her feet as she backed away from the little girl. She could feel the devil in the room, and she instantly knew that something evil lived inside of Leah. She was no ordinary child. She was unremorseful, and had far bypassed the realm of sanity. . . . The blaring shrill of the car horn behind her caused Leah to snap out of her daydream. Thoughts of the past plagued her, and she gripped the steering wheel so tightly that her knuckles turned crimson, the same color of the blood she had spilled over the years. Sticking up her middle finger at the impatient driver behind her, she sped off, running from her troubled past and chasing her own destiny—one that fulfilled her need for acceptance and her obsession for revenge.

Chapter Five

Chase and Khi-P rode through the hood. Black gloves and black masks disguised their identities as they neared their intended destination. No words needed to be exchanged. Everyone had a position to play, and on this cold, black Friday, it was time to put in work. One of their own had been crossed, and the way that they moved, every action had a reaction.

The consequences for snatching baby Sky would be deadly for anyone involved. The gray, overcast skies should have been every indication that it was about to rain, but what Houston had never seen before was the downpour that Indie was about to bring. He wasn't into making it rain dollars. That was for trick niggas. Indie was about to make it rain bullets, and anyone he had ever beefed with was in his crosshairs. The way he felt, the entire fucking city could get it if need be. No one was exempt, and niggas would bleed until he received the answers that he sought, or until his daughter was returned home safely.

He was highly offended by the trespass that had been committed against him. And as he rode in the backseat of Chase's old school '64 Chevelle, anger consumed him. He was silent, stoic, still. He wasn't a rah-rah type of nigga that talked big. He acted big.

These niggas think it's a stage play. I live this. I do this. I don't play gangster. I'ma burn this bitch to the ground if something happens to my baby girl. His brow furrowed deep from a combination of worry and madness. On the outside, one would never know his troubles, but on the inside, there was a bitter and brutal storm brewing. His entire life was flashing before his eyes.

Everything depended on baby Skylar's safe return. He knew that YaYa would never get over her grief if this ended badly, and he would never forgive himself as well.

He was jarred from his thoughts when the car stopped moving. He stared out of his window.

"You sure you want to do this?" Khi-P asked as he peered intently at Indie through his rearview mirror.

Indie didn't even look his way. He simply stared out of the window and nodded his head.

Click-Clack!

The sound of Chase cocking his .380 handgun was the beginning of the end. Indie was the con-

ductor of this street symphony, and he was about
to serenade a couple niggas right to sleep.

Boom!

Chase had just played the first note. Indie
watched as Chase and Khi-P got out of the car
and unloaded their semi-automatic pistols on
the trap house. They wanted to leave a blood
bath behind, sending a message to whoever was
in charge. They didn't know much about the out-
of-towners who had come to Houston, but they
were looking to find the head nigga in charge.

Unwanted beef had caused Indie to murk
one of the Tallahassee boys, and now they were
bringing heat to his front door. He was a man,
so he stood behind everything that he had ever
done, but drawing his family into things had
been a low blow. A deadly line had been crossed.
Like North Korea, he showed no mercy when his
borders were penetrated. YaYa and Skylar were
off limits.

Indie had put word out in the hood that he
was looking for the leader of the out of town
crew, searching high and low for him to no avail.
Finally, Indie decided that if he couldn't find
his enemy, he would make his enemy come find
him. He didn't like war, but sometimes it was
inevitable, and consequently, he was good at it.

The South was too slow for him; they didn't rock the same way as he did. He was ruthless, but at the same time calculating. He moved with intelligence instead of arrogance, and now that he saw how they got down, he was about to teach a lesson that they would be sure to remember.

These niggas don't want to see me, he thought.

Fearless, Chase and Khi-P blazed through the unsuspecting hustlers that ran the trap spot. The two were magnificent when it came to gunplay. Chase had been taught by the best, and was popping off nothing but headshots as he moved through the place. His murder game looked like art as he beat the odds. Two guns in the hands of men like Khi-P and Chase outnumbered the seven ordinary hustlers any day.

It wasn't until they made their way upstairs that they encountered a challenge. Out of nowhere, bullets began to fly in their direction.

"Fuck!" Khi-P yelled as he was grazed by a shot. "This no-aim-having-ass nigga!" he yelled as his nostrils flared in anger. He couldn't believe that he had been hit. In all his time hustling, he had never been shot, and it put a slight bruise on his enormous ego.

Gunshots rang out loudly as the men exchanged fire, and Chase leaned against the living room wall to avoid being hit. Bullets chipped away at the wall around him. They had clipped every hustler in the house, but this last man standing was not going down without a fight. He was reckless, and his gun was spitting hollows nonstop.

Counting the shots in his head, Chase waited patiently. He knew that every shooter would eventually need to reload, and when he heard the pause he was waiting for . . .

Boom!

Chase bent the corner and found his target, hitting him in the leg and dropping him to the ground instantly.

When Indie heard the firing cease, he stepped out of the car and cautiously looked around before proceeding into the house. He walked down an aisle of bodies as he followed the massacre up the stairs to his awaiting crew. Chase and Khi-P stood over the bleeding man, and they both turned to Indie as soon as he entered the room.

"What do you want to do with him?" Khi-P asked.

"I just want to talk to him. Help him up," Indie replied as he grabbed a rickety wooden chair out of the corner and pulled it up to the bed. He waited patiently as they lifted the dude to his feet and then shoved him down on the bed. Not one for disorder and chaos, Indie sat down across from the guy. Emotionless and unreadable, he gave away no sense of his inner instability. Visibly shaken and trembling from the wound to the leg, the guy watched as Indie studied him.

"I'm not here for you, but you know how to get in contact with who I'm looking for. Who do you work for?" Indie asked.

"Fuck you, ol' pussy-ass nigga," the hustler responded with bravado.

With no time for games, Indie was unimpressed by the show of loyalty. He sighed with deep distress. "This can go two ways, my man. The easy way . . ." Indie paused for emphasis as he stared the young thug in the eye, penetrating his hard shell.

Out of nowhere, Indie hauled off and smacked fire from the dude. The butt of Indie's snub nose pistol broke the bones in his jaw.

"Or my way," Indie finished as he sat back and watched the man before him writhe in pain.

"Fuck, man! Fuck type of shit you on? I don't know nothing," the hustler stammered as blood spewed from his mouth.

Indie didn't hesitate to put a hollow tip through his uninjured leg.

"Aghh!"

"You don't got no more legs left. The next one going through your head," Indie warned as he wrapped his finger around the trigger and put the barrel of the gun directly against the temple of the man's head.

Fear captivated the man as urine ran down his leg. "W–w–wait," the guy stammered nervously.

Indie removed the gun and waited for the man to speak.

"I'll talk, man. What do you want to know?" he asked.

"My daughter . . . a baby girl. What do you know about a kidnapping?" Indie asked.

"I don't know nothing about no kidnapping. We ain't even on no shit like that. I swear, man," the guy pleaded.

Indie jabbed the gun hard into his temple, an unspoken threat that the hustler was trying his patience.

"I swear! I swear! Minnie ain't ordered no kidnappings. We were here to settle the beef with you for killing Duke. I don't know shit about snatching no kids!"

The desperation in his voice revealed the truth in the words he spoke, and Indie withdrew his pistol. He had gotten a name. Minnie was who he needed to see, and by leaving the hustler alive, he knew that Minnie would come looking for him.

"Tell Minnie that Indie is looking for him and that it would be in his best interest to holla at me immediately," Indie stated.

Indie and his crew retreated, leaving the bleeding young man to act as the messenger.

With red-rimmed eyes, Disaya waited by the living room bay window all night for Indie to return home. It had been an entire day, and the weight of the world was heavy on her shoulders. Everything in her wanted to call for help. Her maternal instincts were steering her to reach out to someone. Under these circumstances, she embraced authority. She welcomed the idea of handing this burden off to them, but at Indie's request, she refrained from calling the cops. Against her better judgment, she was allowing him to handle this.

Helplessness made every minute seem like two, and the only thing that she could do was send her prayers up to God. She needed Him to send her a resolution. She was on the brink of insanity, and it wouldn't take much for her to lose her mind. Knowing that she had done so many grimy things to so many people made her feel like this was her karma, but she hoped that God wasn't that cruel. Punishing baby Sky for her mistakes would be unjust.

Please just bring my daughter home. Keep her safe, YaYa begged as she fell to her knees to show humility. Speaking with God had not been a ritual that she frequently partook in, but desperate times called for desperate measures.

She couldn't continue doing the same things, solving her problems with deceit and manipulation. She concluded that insanity was repetitive, doing the same thing and receiving the same results. It was time to try something new, and for her, that meant putting her faith in something greater, something bigger than herself, something holy.

This had broken her all the way down. There was no ego, no diva, no bitch left in her. She was at her purest and most raw state. Disaya Morgan was in rare form, as open and susceptible to pain as the day she was born. She was feeling the greatest worry possible, which was that of a mother, and her vulnerability was getting the best of her. Every fleeting thought revolved around baby Sky. Nothing else mattered at this point.

When the headlights from Indie's vehicle shone through her window, she rushed to the door. Frantic yet hopeful, she rushed outside shoeless, her eyes roaming the backseat of his car, desperately searching for Sky.

"Where is she? She's not here, Indie!" she sobbed. "Where is our baby?" she asked as she turned to him.

Defeated by the look of despair on his lady's face, he shook his head and pulled her into his chest. "I don't know, ma. I'm doing all I can. I put word out in the streets, but nobody's talking," he admitted. He hid the disappointment and his own fear in an attempt to keep her calm. He had a responsibility to his family. He was accountable for them, and if this played out badly, he would only have himself to blame.

He could see the turmoil in her gaze.

"She's out there somewhere . . . without me. What if they're hurting her?" YaYa asked. A million and one possibilities ran through her mind, and her entire body shuddered.

"Stop doing that to yourself. Let's go inside and try to rest. I need you strong, ma. We have to hold each other up and get through this together. I'ma take care of this. I promise you that," he said. He didn't know who he was trying to convince more, YaYa or himself.

Lying in bed beside Indie, YaYa's chest caved in slightly from anxiety. Not a single fiber of her body was at ease. She was restless. Calm was a state of mind that she couldn't attain.

"Indie?" she called out. The only response she got was the light sound of him snoring. She couldn't understand how Indie could sleep. There was too much at stake. Images of her innocent baby flashed before her eyes, and she felt for a moment as if this were all a bad dream.

This can't be real. No one is cruel enough to do something like this, she told herself. She pushed the covers off and hopped out of bed as she made her way to Skylar's room. *This is all a bad dream. This can't be happening. My baby is going to be safe and sound in her room.*

"She's all right," she said aloud, trying her hardest to speak it into existence. Pulling open the door in desperation, she rushed over to the crib, only to be hit with reality. The bare crib caused her knees to buckle, and she grabbed onto the wooden rails for support.

What am I doing? My daughter needs me. I'm all she has, she thought.

Although Indie was in their lives now, she thought back to how he had abandoned her before in her time of need. Feeling like a traitor, she reached for the cordless phone. She knew that the call she was about to make would jeopardize everything between her and Indie. It was risky, and would shine the spotlight directly on top of them, but her back was against the wall. There was no other solution. She had seen it in Indie's eyes the moment he had returned home. Even he didn't know if he would be able to bring their baby home. She took a deep breath and dialed the numbers.

"Nine-one-one. What is your emergency?"

"Someone took my baby. My daughter has been kidnapped," YaYa whispered with a stifled cry as she covered her mouth to contain her fear.

She turned around and saw Indie standing in the doorway. She jumped and released the phone as if it had suddenly grown hot in her hand.

"What did you do, ma?" he asked as he shook his head from side to side. He knew the magnitude of her actions. Within the hour, their home would be swarming with cops, every part of their lives monitored and picked apart. They were about to be under a federal microscope, and to a hustler of Indie's stature, that was worse than death. "What did you do?"

YaYa looked him directly in the eyes and wiped her tears as she replied, "I did what I had to do . . . for my daughter."

Chapter Six

The red, white, and blue flashing lights lit up the streets like it was the Fourth of July. While Disaya felt a sense of relief from the presence of authority, Indie's chest tightened uncomfortably. He was cut from a completely different cloth than Disaya. Under no circumstances did he trust the police; even something as daunting as Skylar's disappearance didn't spark an urge for him to request their help.

Tension thickened the air as YaYa looked at Indie from across the room. She could see his anger in his pulsing temples as he spoke with the lead federal agent in charge of Skylar's case. She herself had been questioned a million times in a million different ways. They asked the same questions repetitively in an attempt to find a loophole in her story, but YaYa had nothing to hide. She was as honest as she could be, but as she watched Indie's demeanor she knew that things were not going as smoothly for him.

YaYa could see that Indie needed her by his side. She was his regulator and could calm him down just by standing beside him. Her presence was therapeutic for him. She made her way to him and interrupted the line of questioning that the agent was taking him through.

"Hi. I'm Disaya Morgan, Skylar's mother," she said as she extended one hand and rubbed Indie's back gently with the other. She could feel his shoulders relaxing from her touch.

"Federal Agent Norris," he replied as he shook her hand. His tone of voice was tight and unfriendly, his eyes accusatory and stern. YaYa could tell that the man would not extend them the benefit of the doubt. He cleared his throat and continued with his interrogation.

"Where were the two of you when your daughter was taken?" he asked.

"Asleep in the master bedroom," Indie replied.

"There was no sign of forced entry? Neither of you heard anything? An infant usually cries when their rest is disturbed. You must be a pretty heavy sleeper, huh?"

YaYa could hear the sarcasm in his voice, and she frowned slightly, but kept her cool. Now was not the time for theatrics. She didn't care how much of a jerk the guy was, as long as he did his job and recovered baby Sky.

"We don't know how they got in, and we didn't hear anything," Indie said.

"Hmm, convenient," the agent scoffed. "Excuse me?" YaYa asked.

Norris shook his head and replied, "Why did you wait an entire day before reporting her disappearance? You wake up in the middle of the night and your baby is missing. Why hesitate to call?"

YaYa was at a loss for words. She didn't know how to respond. The innuendo of guilt that Agent Norris expressed was enough to let YaYa know that she had no ally in him.

Before they could even answer him, he continued, "Do you see how this looks from where I'm sitting? So, tell me what really happened. Ms. Morgan, did you accidentally bring harm to your baby? And did Dad help you cover your tracks?"

"I would never—" YaYa began to defend herself, but Agent Norris held up a hand to stop her midsentence.

"That's what they all say. I've been doing this for a long time, and nine times out of ten, the parents are the guilty party," he stated firmly. "That's enough," Indie finally spoke up and said. "I thought this was an interview, not an interrogation. You can contact my attorney if these are the types of questions you're going to ask.

Somebody has my daughter, and it would be in your best interest to start doing your job instead of insulting my family."

Norris smirked, unimpressed and unthreatened by Indie's show of manhood. "We're going to set up in the living room for forty-eight hours. This could be a ransom kidnapping. All we can do is sit back and wait for the perpetrator to make contact." He began to walk away. His cocky attitude displayed dominance, as if he owned the place.

He stopped when he was halfway across the room and snapped his fingers. "Oh, yeah, Mr. Perkins. What line of business did you say you were in?" he asked.

"I didn't," Indie replied.

Agent Norris looked around the plush townhome while nodding his head in approval. "Whatever it is, must be lucrative," he commented sarcastically as he took in the luxury around him.

Indie's jaw tightened as he watched local and federal cops take over his home. "This is just the beginning," he said loud enough for only YaYa to hear him. "Be careful what you say to them, YaYa. If it's not about Sky, they don't need to know," he warned as he kissed her cheek before making his way out of the room.

"Indie," YaYa called to him, but he ignored her calls as he stormed out of the room. Indie made his way into their master bath and locked the door behind him. There was only so much one man could take. All control had been shifted out of his hands, and the possibility of Skylar's safe return was fading. The realization that he may never see her again tore his heart out of his chest. His resolve broke, and as he stared at himself in the mirror, he sobbed silently. It was a moment that he would never share with another soul, tears that were only meant for God to see.

YaYa stared out of her bedroom window in awe at all of the media outlets that were parked outside of her house. News stations all over Houston had come out at the chance to jump on the big story of a kidnapped infant. A part of YaYa was relieved. The more people who knew about Skylar's disappearance, the more eyes there would be to look for her, but she knew that the attention would put a lot of strangers in their business. Indie's empire would be at a standstill as long as the spotlight was shining so brightly upon them.

She felt his presence behind her and closed her eyes as he wrapped his toned arms around her waist. He kissed the top of her head and she sighed.

"I didn't know that all of this would come about when I called the police," she said.

"I know you didn't, ma. Don't worry about that. That's one thing that you don't need to let stress you out. Everybody will just have to be careful, watch what they say, and be aware of how they move while this is going on. I'll let Khi, Chase, and the girls know to be low key.

"I've got a feeling that Agent Norris has a hard-on for a nigga like me. He would love nothing more than to see me in jail, so I have to play the cut and act accordingly," he replied.

YaYa could hear the anxiety in his tone, and she looked at him apologetically. "I'm sorry, Indie," she said.

"Don't be. As long as this brings our daughter home, there is nothing to be sorry about. She's worth more than a little inconvenience," he said. "Now, get ready for the cameras. They are going to want a statement."

YaYa watched nervously as every national news station in the country littered her front lawn. Skylar's case miraculously made the headlines all over. Out of all the little missing black girls out there, somehow Skylar was interesting enough to make the cut. Her face was amongst all the white news stories. Nancy Grace, MSNBC, Fox, and every local station were all waiting anxiously to witness the reaction of her parents. They were all waiting to either support or persecute Disaya Morgan.

YaYa stood on the podium in front of her home as she looked out on the flashing lights in front of her. There were so many microphones shoved in her face and cameras aimed directly at her that they made her shake nervously. Her eyes watered as the intense pressure of the moment stifled her. The statement that she was about to make would be broadcast live all over the state of Texas.

She looked over to Indie for support, and he nodded his head confidently. The subtle wink that he gave her sent a wave a reassurance over her, and finally she found her voice to speak.

"My name is Disaya Morgan. Two days ago, my daughter Skylar was taken from my home in the middle of the night. She's not even a year old. She needs to be with her family . . . with me. Please do not hurt my baby girl. I will do anything for her safe return. She is all I have. This is a mother's plea. To the person responsible for taking her . . . I beg of you, please just return her to me unharmed."

The look of worry on her face could not be faked by the best of actresses. YaYa was distraught, and as the media and the police watched her step down from the podium, they all felt a little bit of her pain. It was as if she had chipped off a tiny piece of it and placed it in their hands.

It was then that Agent Norris concluded that she was not a part of this escapade, but as he looked at Indie, he wasn't so sure. He could smell a drug dealer from a mile away, and Indie fit the bill. The arrogance and shrewd authority that Indie possessed was a dead giveaway. He was a hustler, and his swagger was too great to conceal. He was too large, and despite the fact that his operation ran with efficiency, he still drew attention.

As YaYa stepped off of the platform, she walked directly into Indie's warm embrace. Although there were people all around him, when her head hit his chest, everyone else disappeared. She closed her eyes and exhaled as he rocked her gently from side to side.

"You did good, ma. Everything will be okay," he said.

The more he said it, the better it made her feel, but inside, he was well aware that this thing could end badly.

She looked up at him and frowned. Her heartbeat quickened, but everything else seemed to move in slow motion as she noticed the red dot appear in the middle of his chest. She stepped back from him instinctively and fixed her mouth to warn him, but before the words could even leave her mouth, the red dot was replaced with a red hole.

Muffled by a silencer, the gunshot gave off no sound. Indie gripped his chest as his mouth fell open in an O of horror. The hot lead spread through his chest like a wildfire, burning his insides and tearing apart his organs as he collapsed forward into YaYa's arms.

Everything happened so fast and discreet that it wasn't until YaYa screamed that the crowd realized something had gone horribly wrong.

"Somebody help me!" she shouted as she caught the weight of his body. "Oh my God, Indie!" she screamed.

The heat ricocheting inside of his body was unbearable. He couldn't speak. All he could do was gasp for air as he grasped at his chest while staring YaYa in the eyes with desperation. His mouth hung open in agony as he groaned. He gulped as he tried to suck in oxygen, but he was choking on his own blood as it overflowed from his mouth.

"Indie, talk to me! Say something, baby. Wake up!" he heard Disaya scream. Her voice seemed so far away, so muffled, as he slipped in and out of consciousness.

Agent Norris rushed over to Indie and YaYa, immediately calling for assistance as he looked around simultaneously for the shooter. He was already suspicious of Indie's profession, but this confirmed things. Legit businessmen didn't take bullets in broad daylight. Indie ran Houston, and although he hid his thuggish nature extremely well, the streets had given him away. Beef was left stinking at his front door, and Norris was about to come sniffing.

Leah lay in bed in agony. The bleeding between her legs had gotten worse. She was sure that she had an infection from the miscarriage she had suffered. She was fighting the inevitable. Eventually she would have to go to the hospital. The pain was growing too great to self-treat, and the fever she was running indicated just how serious it was. A layer of sweat glistened on her body as she watched YaYa's press conference on the motel television. She could see that YaYa was falling apart at the seams, and she smiled in satisfaction.

You deserve everything that's coming to you, bitch. Shit ain't so sweet for you now, is it?

Leah couldn't help but laugh hysterically at YaYa. It was funny how things had changed. Leah felt overdue triumph, because YaYa finally knew what it felt like to be on the bottom, and this was only the beginning. Shit was about to get real for YaYa.

I'm about to tear that fairytale life of hers apart.

Waaa! Waaa!

Leah's antics of insanity were broken up by the shrill wails inside her head. She covered her ears and closed her eyes.

"Shut the fuck up!" she screamed. For days, the sounds of infant cries had tormented her, reminding her of the atrocity she had committed. A few tears of regret slipped out of her eyes, but she quickly swiped them off of her ashen cheeks. The cries were so loud and daunting that she was almost certain they could be heard through the walls. She wasn't prepared for this. Although she was pressing the buttons and calling the shots in this entire thing, the crying was throwing her off, distracting her, making it difficult to decipher through the pain of her past and present.

The crying was reminding her of all the tears she had shed in her lifetime. It forced her to relive all of the bad she had done. The crying wouldn't stop. It was the one factor in this entire thing that she could not control. No matter what she did, it was a reoccurrence that was unavoidable.

Acting as her conscience, the wails caused her to think of the shallow grave she had dug and the innocence she had shattered. Leah put her hands over her ears and closed her eyes as she sat Indian-style on the bed.

"Please, just stop!" she hollered in frustration, but it continued. She leapt angrily to her feet and grabbed the keys to her car. The only way to get away from the screams was to run from it, but she knew that her relief was only temporary. She had to finish this. She had no time to waste. The sooner she got her revenge, the better.

Sticking around to see Disaya crack under pressure would be so sweet, but she knew that she needed money to get away. She wasn't the type of chick to punch anyone's time clock. She had gotten by off her looks and sexuality for so long that she should have been rich, but the old saying "easy come, easy go" was true. She never stacked the cash that she accumulated from selling ass. Instead, she spent dough and replenished it as she needed it. It was nothing for her to find a new trick or gain a new hustle. She didn't have to label her game; she was about getting paper. But with her insides feeling as if they would fall out at any moment, she knew that lying on her back would no longer work. Besides, she didn't have time to sit back and let money stack.

She had to get rich quick so that after her plans for YaYa were fulfilled, she could skip town.

Thoughts of dead babies caused her to shiver as she gripped her steering wheel tightly. *Get it together, Leah. It don't matter what you did. You can't take it back now. Just make this situation work for you. Fuck everybody else.*

She threw her car in park and rushed back into the motel room, and as sinister thoughts filled her, the crying in her ear returned. A smile spread across her face, and she tuned it out as she grabbed a piece of paper from the desk. The ransom note she was about to write was a sure way to get her paid.

They're never going to see their baby again regardless, but they don't know that. They'll come up off that cash to try to get her back. I'm selling their ass a $250,000 dream.

She placed the letter in a red envelope and rushed out. With YaYa preoccupied at the hospital with Indie, Leah had just enough time to slip into their home unnoticed to deliver her note.

Chapter Seven

The foreboding vibe that spread through the hospital room was daunting as YaYa, Chase, Khi-P, Trina and the girls sat nervously around Indie's bed. Forty-eight hours had passed, and Indie still hadn't come to. Suffering a gunshot wound to the chest, he was in a critical state. He was teetering on the edge of life and death, and no one knew which path God intended for him.

YaYa refused to leave his side, and she gripped his hand while she closed her eyes to pray. Her world was crashing down around her, and the redundant hums and beeps of the machines supporting Indie caused her to shake slightly. Just the possibility of losing him was earth-shattering. Her very existence was compromised. When Indie bled, she bled with him. Symbolically, she felt his pain, and as he fought for his life, she was right beside him fighting for it too.

She wanted to be strong for him, but her reserve was failing her. He was her backbone, and now that he needed her, she was crumpling at the knees. She didn't have it in her to stand tall at the moment. Everything in her wanted to give up.

"Do you need anything?" Trina asked. The room was so deathly silent that her words sounded odd as they echoed off of the walls.

YaYa was so stuck in emotion that she couldn't respond. She simply shook her head without even looking up.

"You need to go home and at least get a few hours of rest. Take a shower, get a good meal in you, ma," Mekhi said as he stared at her sympathetically.

"I can't leave him here," she said, her eyes never leaving Indie. "I can't drive right now or eat or sleep. I just want to be here with him."

"The girls will drive you," Chase said. "Indie would want you to go, YaYa. Take a moment for yourself. You've been through a lot."

"Somebody shot him. They tried to kill him. What if they come back to finish the job?" she asked.

"No offense, shorty, but what are you going to do if they do? You being here ain't stopping nobody from popping off," Khi-P stated. He nodded toward Chase. "We'll take care of this, so don't worry about anything. Just go take care of yourself. You've still got his blood on you, ma. He wouldn't want you here stressing like this."

YaYa looked down at her blood-stained hands. The burgundy had dried underneath her fingernails, and just seeing her love's spilled blood brought tears to her eyes.

She nodded her head, knowing that she was in desperate need of a shower. "Okay. I'll go home, but only for a few minutes. I want to be here when he wakes up."

YaYa stood and followed Trina, Miesha, and Sydney to the car. As she stared out of her window blankly, the darkened city passed her by in one big blur. She had thought New York City was cold, but the South was just as callous. Her escape to a new life had turned into a nightmare.

When they arrived at her house, yellow police tape blocked off the crime scene, and flashes of Indie falling into her arms flooded her brain. She closed her eyes and shook her head from side to side to clear her mind as she inhaled sharply and exited the car. Miesha hurried ahead of YaYa and ripped down the tape, knowing that it was hard for YaYa to see.

"Was it really necessary to leave all this bright shit all over the place?" she cussed as she balled it up in her hands.

"Thanks, Mimi," YaYa said with a weak smile as she proceeded into the house.

Trina grabbed YaYa's keys out of her handbag and unlocked the door as Sydney ushered YaYa inside.

"You ladies don't have to stay. I'll be okay," YaYa said. She really just wanted to be alone.

She was grateful for the solace that her home provided. As she looked around, she noticed that all of the feds' equipment was still scattered about her living room, but Indie's shooting had distracted their efforts and gave them new suspicions. It didn't matter to her at that point, as long as they had gone. She needed privacy for the cries that she wanted to release.

They would be back tomorrow, but today she needed solitude so she could allow the sorrow to spill from her heart. The way she was feeling was too personal to share with anyone. Her wails were ones that only the walls could hear. Anyone else's ears would be intrusive. Her pain was too personal, too intimate for another to witness.

"I don't think you should be by yourself, YaYa. You need people around you right now. How about we give you some time to get cleaned up, and we'll come back for you in a couple hours. You're in no shape to drive yourself back to the hospital anyway. We'll go to a diner, grab some food, and then come back for you in a few," Trina offered.

YaYa shook her head and then hugged Trina. She was such a good friend to be such a young girl. "I'm a big girl, Trina. I just need some time to myself to clear my head. I'll see you guys back at the hospital," she said.

Reluctantly, Trina agreed as YaYa ushered them out of her house and then headed up the stairs after the girls exited. Turning her shower on full blast, YaYa stepped beneath the hot water and for a brief moment, her worries washed away. Closing her eyes, she tilted her head back, but the minute she opened them and saw Indie's blood swirling down the drain, her heart sank.

"Aghh!" she screamed in an attempt to let go of some of the sadness that was pent up inside of her. Bullshit always seemed to find her. She attracted misery as if it were a long lost boyfriend.

She was emotionally drained, and her chest heaved from the weight of it all as tears mixed with water and trickled down her face. She stepped out of the shower and wrapped herself in a plush towel. Exhaustion plagued her, but she couldn't stop herself from rushing to get back to Indie. Sleep was the cousin to death, and she didn't want any association with the Grim Reaper while Indie was fighting just to live.

She walked into Skylar's room, and the scent of her precious baby filled her nose. She sighed and turned on the light. The blood red envelope that sat inside Skylar's crib stood out like a sore thumb. She gasped as she looked around, feeling invaded. Someone had been in her house, and now she wondered if she was being watched. She ran over to the crib, grabbed the letter, and ripped it open with urgency.

Drop $250,000 at Memorial Park Friday at noon. Come alone or she dies. No cops! When we get our money, your daughter will be returned.

Mixed emotions filled her. YaYa was relieved because Sky's abductors had finally put it on the table what they wanted, but fear paralyzed her because now it was game time. The ransom made the kidnapping real. Friday was only a few days away. She didn't even know if Indie had that type of money lying around, and in the shape he was in, they had no hope of getting it.

She covered her mouth with her hand as her heart raced from uncertainty. She would have to go alone, handle the drop by herself. It was up to her to bring her daughter home.

YaYa's sixth sense caused the hairs on the back of her fragile neck to stand up, and she froze. Suddenly every sound in her house was amplified, and she listened closely. The sounds of weight shifting against her hardwood floors sent warning bells off in her head.

Someone is still in here, she thought. She remembered plugging her phone up on the charger downstairs, and she began to creep slowly, cautiously out of Sky's room. She had no idea who was in her home, and her first instincts were to run, but when she thought of her baby, she was filled with blind courage. She went into Skylar's closet and pulled out a chrome .45.

Indie had a loaded gun stashed in every room of the house, just in case, and she pulled back the chamber just like he'd taught her as she walked timidly out of the room. Her aim was so shaky that the gun was more for show than an actual threat, but she kept creeping through the house, waiting for someone to jump out of the shadows. Every sound was amplified, including her own shallow breaths, as anxiety pulsed through her.

"Trina? Is that y'all down there?" she called out. She already knew the answer to her question. Her gut told her that something was wrong.

The sound of a dining chair scraping across the floor caused her to jump as her neck whipped toward the direction of her kitchen. Undoubtedly, she was not alone, but running away was not an option—not when her child's life was at stake.

Whoever delivered this note is still in here, she thought as she swallowed the nervous lump in her throat. There were two people in the house, but as YaYa made her way to confront the intruder, she knew that only one of them would be walking out of there alive.

"Fuck!" Leah mouthed as she bumped into the chair. She knew that YaYa had heard the noise. The still house seemed to vibrate from the loud sound. She heard YaYa drawing near, and she knew that she couldn't make it out of the back door without being seen. She wasn't ready for her presence to be known.

Leah looked around frantically, knowing that she didn't have time to make an exit. She cursed beneath her breath as she slid into the full-size kitchen pantry. She adjusted the wooden slats on the door so that she couldn't be seen, and she held her breath as she watched YaYa enter the room.

Seeing YaYa in person after all this time brought out feelings of rage inside Leah, but at the same time, she was mesmerized, intrigued. The infatuation that she had for YaYa reignited instantly from the close proximity. Like a voyeur, she watched . . . stalked . . . observed from the shadows of the pantry.

YaYa could hear her own pounding fear as she looked around her kitchen, gun ready, heart uneasy. She had turned on every single light in her home as she moved from room to room. She looked at her dining room set. It was as she had left it—precise, clean, all chairs in the correct position.

I know what I heard, she thought as she lowered the gun while turning around in a full circle, confused. *There's nobody here?* she thought skeptically. Breathing a sigh of uncertain relief, she put her hand on her forehead, sweeping her messy hair off of her face. She was paranoid and on edge. The entire situation had her discombobulated.

Just as she put her guard down completely, she heard someone walk up behind her. Before she even had time to think logically, she turned around and fired a wild shot.

"Whoa! Ma, it's me, Mekhi!" he shouted as he raised his hands defensively and looked at her like she was insane. He looked over his shoulder at the hole she had blown through the wall, knowing that she had barely missed him.

"Oh my God. I'm so sorry. I thought—" Flustered, she tried to explain. "I don't know what I thought. I heard someone in the house and—" She couldn't even get the words out of her mouth before the floodgates let up and tears overflowed.

"It's a'ight, ma. There's nobody here but me. It's okay. Everything is going to be a'ight," he said as he stepped to her, giving her a shoulder to cry on. "Let it out."

Mekhi wrapped his arms around her shoulders, and she poured her all into him. She was so vulnerable that she would accept strength from anyone at that point. His strong arms around her were exactly what she needed in her time of weakness, and for a moment, they became intimate on a level that neither of them would ever share or admit to.

There was no tension with him. Since Skylar had disappeared, a small wedge sat between Indie and YaYa. They both felt that Indie's lifestyle was the motive for Sky's disappearance, and although they had never spoken about it, that fact was the elephant in the room between them. The presence of the feds was straining for them, but with Khi-P's arms around her, she felt nothing but support.

They both knew that they should let go. Mekhi felt the line he had crossed and tried to withdraw his embrace, but YaYa tightened her arms around his waist and buried her head deeper into his chest as she cried. She was overwhelmed with grief, and this felt too secure, too safe, too right to let go.

Their loyalty to Indie was pushed to the back of their minds as they held each other. Her delicate hands moved up and down his toned back, sending thrills to his manhood and causing it to harden. Even her natural scent was enough to drive a man toward disloyalty. His hands had a mind of their own as they moved south, until they palmed her rear side.

Pulling her into him, he waited for her to stop him, but she never did. At that moment, she wanted it just as badly as he did. Raw desire pushed them both forward without thinking of the consequences. That, coupled with intoxication, gave YaYa the green light. For this one moment, he felt what it was like to step into Indie's shoes.

Lust filled the room and spilled over into the pantry where Leah hid. Throbbing with the idea of revenge and desire, her clit hardened. Her hands wanted to fulfill the urge that was growing between her thighs. She was wet and horny, but as her hands slipped toward her private parts, she remembered what she was there for—to ruin Disaya's life.

She thought she had done that before, back in New York, when Indie left her for dead, but somehow the golden girl had resurrected herself. This time Leah would make sure that there would be no way for YaYa to piece her life back together.

This bitch makes this shit too easy, Leah thought as she controlled her sexual urges and grabbed her Black-Berry off of her hip. She focused her camera phone on YaYa and snapped a picture of the sexual tryst.

If Indie didn't stop messing with her before, he will now, she thought maliciously, knowing that the picture would eventually be of good use to her.

YaYa pulled away from Khi-P suddenly as her conscience hit her like a ton of bricks. "Stop. I can't . . . we can't do this," she said. "What the fuck am I thinking?" she asked rhetorically while shaking her head from side to side in disappointment. "He's laid up in the hospital and I'm here with you. This shouldn't be happening. What are you even doing here?" she asked.

"The girls came back without you, so I came to check on you. I apologize, YaYa. This was disrespectful. I didn't mean to push up on you. Shit just got out of hand. I'm a man, and you was looking like this . . . I fucked up. This ain't even your fault, ma. You're in a vulnerable state, and I shouldn't have stepped to you, period."

YaYa's guilt caused her to completely forget the ransom note she had discovered.

"This is between us," Mekhi stated trustingly.

She nodded gratefully as he squeezed her shoulder.

"Go get dressed, ma. We need to be getting back," he said.

YaYa and Mekhi rushed back to the hospital. With no sleep, she was running on E, and she sluggishly forced herself to keep going. An eerie feeling passed over her, causing her heart to gallop in anticipation. Something in her bones felt wrong, and she wanted nothing more than to get back to Indie's bedside.

I shouldn't have left, she thought.

"Khi, please hurry," she said.

Fifteen minutes later, they were pulling up to the hospital and YaYa hopped out before the car even stopped moving. Anxious to get back to Indie, she almost ran through the halls, but when she got to his room, she stopped abruptly, noticing Agent Norris waiting outside the door.

"What are you doing here? Did you find my baby?" she asked, experiencing a brief glimmer of hope.

Norris stepped toward YaYa and shook his head. "Ugh, no. I umm . . ."

"Then why are you here?" she asked as she looked at him in suspicion and folded her arms across her chest defensively.

Agent Norris cleared his throat and stepped toward her as he looked around nervously. "Listen, Ms. Morgan. Your daughter is missing, and it's your job to protect her. Do you love your daughter?"

YaYa frowned, insulted by the question. "Of course I do. What kind of question is that?"

"If you love her, then you will do the right thing here and help me."

"Help you what?" YaYa asked.

"I know the type of business that your boyfriend in there is into. His dealings got him shot. They almost got you shot and I believe your daughter was taken because of his connection to the streets as well," Norris said.

"I don't know what you're talking about," YaYa replied sharply as she proceeded past him.

Agent Norris grabbed her elbow and pulled her close. "You can either help me get Indie, or you can go down with him as his accomplice. RICO laws can get me a conviction on anyone involved, even if you are only indirectly connected. You better think of what's best for your daughter right now," he warned, "because sooner or later he'll get sloppy, and when that happens, I'm going to be there waiting with the silver bracelets."

A part of her wanted to tell the federal agent about the ransom note she had received, but he obviously had a different agenda than she did. He was focused on the wrong person. He had deemed guilt on the wrong individual, and his mind was already set.

YaYa held the red ransom envelope in her hands, tightly gripping it as her words caught in her throat. She put it in her purse and shook her head, knowing that Norris couldn't help her. He wasn't the resolution to her problem. The only person that she could count on was herself. She had to ensure Skylar's safety, which meant going alone.

At that moment, Mekhi came walking up. "Is everything okay?" he asked as she looked menacingly at Agent Norris.

YaYa snatched her arm back and replied, "Everything's fine." She turned to Norris. "If you would put as much energy into Skylar's case as you are putting into Indie, she would be home by now. I'm not going to sit by and watch you piece together some bullshit case. I want you and all your fucking pig-ass friends out of my home." She stormed past him with Mekhi on her heels as she resumed her place at the head of the bed.

"You guys can go now," she said. "I'll sit with him." She wanted more than anything to be alone with him, to whisper in his ear that she would be there for him forever.

Mekhi and Chase stood to their feet. "No offense, but we not leaving until he wakes up. We'll give you some privacy. We'll be down the hall in the waiting room if you need us," Chase said.

YaYa nodded her head as they left the room.

Hours of worry lulled YaYa to sleep, her head resting on the hospital bed while she held onto Indie's hand. The lightest squeeze of her fingers aroused her from her sleep, and as she focused on Indie, she noticed that his eyelids were fluttering wildly.

"Indie, baby, it's me. I'm here," she whispered.

Indie's heart rate increased at the sound of Disaya's sweet nothings in his ear. She was bringing him back to life, making him want to ignore the shining light he had been ready to walk into.

"Open your eyes, Indie. Wake up. I need you more than ever right now," she urged as grateful emotions made her voice crack. The place in his chest where he had been hit would have killed most men, but the love of a woman was keeping him breathing, was making living worth more than dying and retiring to grace.

Indie heard her, and the sweet melody of her voice was distracting him from the beautiful bright light that was beckoning him, enticing him to walk into it. He could decipher her voice clearly, and despite the fact that he wanted to, his body would not allow him to open his eyes. He was too weak, but he kept her sweet tone in his memory and used it as a guide to stay coherent. Unconscious he could handle, but dead he refused to be. There was no way he was leaving YaYa in the world alone—not yet, at least. He planned on being old and gray when it was his time to go. By then she would be able to handle it.

Chapter Eight

YaYa talked to Indie the entire night, and when his eyes finally opened the next morning, all she could do was smile. It took a while for clarity to return to his sight, but when it did, YaYa's face was refreshing. Like a cold drink on a scalding summer day, she was what he needed.

He weakly cleared his throat as he attempted to speak. "Hey, beautiful," he said.

YaYa laughed as she shook her head and touched his cheek gently. Even after being shot, his swagger was still out of this world.

"Hey yourself," she responded, elated.

Indie's hands searched his body until they found his bandaged chest. He grimaced in excruciating pain as his hands probed.

"Stop it, Indie. You'll be okay," YaYa soothed.

"Where's Khi and Chase?" he asked. He was losing his strength as the pain medicine in his IV made him groggy. She wanted to tell him about the ransom note, but she knew that now was not the time. It was a burden that she would have to carry on her own for now.

"I'll go get them," she said with a weak smile as she hopped up and rushed to the waiting room. "He's up. He's awake!" she shouted. "He's asking for the two of you."

Chase and Mekhi rushed to the room as Trina and the girls engulfed YaYa in a supportive group hug. "We'll stay out here. We don't want to crowd him. Tell him we said we're glad he's up," Miesha said.

YaYa nodded and then went back into Indie's room. When she entered, all conversation stopped. Indie's creased brow let her know that he was angry about something, but she didn't ask, in fear that she may overstep her boundaries.

"YaYa, can you go grab the nurse for me? I'm in a lot of pain. See if they can give me something for it," he instructed.

YaYa nodded her head, all the while knowing she was being sent on a dummy mission. Indie didn't want her to hear the conversation he was indulged in. The less she knew, the better. She couldn't tell what she did not know. It was his way of keeping her nose clean. She was simply the wife to a hustler, but she knew no details, so at the end of the day, she would always be deemed innocent.

Indie waited until he heard the hospital door click closed, and then he looked at Chase and Khi-P. "I want to be out of here as soon as possible. The sooner the doctors sign off on my release, the sooner I can get at that nigga Minnie. He brought heat to my home. YaYa could have been hurt. I'm done playing tit for tat with this mu'fucka," Indie said. His voice was weak, but his tone lethal.

"You want me to just handle that for you? The nigga can disappear like a magic act. Poof!" Chase said, throwing his hands up as if he were really performing a trick. "You're hit. You need your rest. You don't got to put in your own work. That's what you got soldiers for."

Indie's chest was on fire, and he knew that he was overexerting himself. He inhaled deeply as a sharp pain filled him. "I don't need soldiers for this one, fam. You just bring him to me. The day that I'm out of here, I want to see this nigga in front of me. I'm not doing no more talking. I'm tired of yapping. These slow Southern-ass niggas ain't hearing me. I'ma let my cannons bark until my baby girl is back home."

Against the advice of his physicians, Indie checked himself out of the hospital the very next day. His legs barely worked, and he was forced to submit to a wheelchair, but he was determined to leave. Too much time had passed and there was too much to do. His daughter was still missing, and that was more important than his own injuries. The police had made no progress, and although the media was keeping the case alive, it did little to help. Everyone was starting to give up—everyone except YaYa and Indie.

When YaYa wasn't at Indie's bedside, she was out canvassing the neighborhoods, searching for Skylar, and passing out flyers. Calling in the authorities had been useless. Their presence only complicated things, and as she walked beside Indie, holding his hand as the nurse wheeled him outside, she felt hopeful that he would fix everything. Somebody had to, before she went insane.

When they emerged from the hospital, Chase was waiting in front of a black Lex coupe. The girls were parked behind him in a matching silver vehicle. He walked up to Indie and helped him to his feet as the two slowly embraced.

"Good to see you standing, fam," Chase greeted.

Indie nodded his head and replied, "Feels good, man. Feels real good. Did you and Khi set that up for me?"

Chase nodded.

Indie turned to YaYa and kissed her forehead. "The girls are going to take you home. I'll be there shortly. I have something to handle real quick," Indie said.

"Indie . . ." she whispered as her eyes grew sad.

"I'm coming home, ma. Don't worry yourself. Have dinner waiting for me when I get there." He gave her a playful tap on her derriere, causing her to smile.

She folded her arms and watched him enter the car, and then Chase pulled away from the curb.

Indie sat back as Chase wheeled him into the warehouse. The single bulb that illuminated the space shone down on the man who was re-strained in the middle of the room. He was un-touched. He had no injuries, yet fear still burned in his gaze. He was alarmed. With his legs tied to a wooden chair and his hands bound tightly in front of him, he knew that the worst was yet to come.

When Indie had given the order to snatch him, it had been executed efficiently. The slip of a pillowcase over the head and a .45 to the neck was all it took to get him to oblige. Minnie had been sitting in the pitch black warehouse for the past two days, anticipating death. Khi-P had shown no mercy on the nigga either. Under no circumstances was he untied.

"Shit on yourself," was the response when Minnie requested a bathroom.

"Eat a dick, you bitch-ass nigga," Mekhi had told him when Minnie asked for food.

Like a newborn baby, Minnie's life was in their hands, and until Indie was released from the hospital, he sat in limbo, wondering what would become of him.

Chase wheeled an injured Indie directly up to Minnie until the two men were sitting face to face.

When Minnie saw Indie's face, he chuckled slightly as he shook his head from side to side. "Ol' fuck nigga. I should've known. This is how you East Coast bitches do it, huh? Had to hire a pit bull from the South just to catch a nigga slipping?" he asked, referring to Mekhi doing his dirty work.

Indie looked at Chase and nodded his head. Chase walked over to Minnie and forcefully grabbed his wrists. He squeezed so tightly that Minnie opened his balled fists, giving Indie access to his fingers. Without second-guessing, Indie pulled out a box cutter and sliced off one of the digits. He wasn't playing any games. The time for bullshit was about to come to an end. He didn't have anything to prove. He wasn't beefing for control of the streets or to floss for the hood.

His every action at that point was on behalf of his daughter. He was done with the shoot-'em-out, bang-bang shit. He was ready to take it to the next level. Either Minnie told him where his daughter was, or it was lights out. He was fully prepared to execute the man in front of him if the answers he spoke weren't to Indie's liking.

"Aghh!" Minnie screamed in agony as blood spurted everywhere. His blood pressure dropped from the loss of blood, and he could feel the spot where his finger used to be as it throbbed. Slobber dripped from his mouth as he grimaced uncontrollably.

"That's for the bullet you put in me," Indie said calmly. He saw Minnie's eyes closing as his body attempted to fall into unconsciousness. Indie slapped his cheeks to revive him. "Yo, my man, wake the fuck up. We are far from finished, playboy." "You came at me first, my dude. You started the shit. I was just retal—"

Before Minnie could get the excuse out of his mouth, Indie had relieved him of another finger. "Aghhh! Man, stop! Please!" Minnie hollered, his voice echoing off the walls as blood spurted everywhere. His shits was leaking like a bad engine.

Mekhi grimaced as he watched Indie mercilessly torture the dude, and he shot Chase a knowing glance. *This nigga ain't bullshitting,* he thought as he shook his head at the gruesome sight.

"You lost that finger for pulling triggers at my family. Now you got eight left and ten toes. We can do this all night, or you can tell me what I want to know," Indie threatened. He was so weak from being shot that he remained seated in his wheelchair. He didn't need to loom over Minnie in order to intimidate him. Indie was an imminent threat; he didn't have to do anything extra. He didn't talk the life, he lived it, and Minnie was about to be the first example he set for all of Houston to see.

"You can have it all, man. All the ki's, the money . . . I got two hundred thou in my safe. Take it. It's yours. Just let me go," he pleaded.

Indie shook his head in contempt. "You bitch up real fast. You the type who'll sing like a canary if your back is ever against the wall. Pressure burst pipes," Indie said.

"Please, man! You can have it all!" Indie chuckled arrogantly. "Nigga, I don't want your little chump change and that bullshit-ass coca you selling. Shit been stepped on more than hardwood floors."

"What do you want then?" Minnie asked desperately.

Indie motioned for the next finger, and Minnie broke down, crying like a baby.

Indie smirked because he had instilled enough fear. He had beaten his opponent mentally. Now it was information time.

"Where is my daughter?" he asked.

"W—what?" Minnie questioned, genuinely confused. That was the last question he had expected to come out of Indie's mouth.

Indie's patience was running thin, and he immediately clipped another finger.

"Aghh!"

"I didn't fucking stutter, my nigga," Indie said through clenched teeth. "Where is she?"

"I don't know what you talking about! I swear on my mama, man. I don't know," Minnie groveled.

"You been gunning for me since we deaded young at the car show. All of a sudden my daughter comes up missing, and you saying you had nothing to do with it? I'm a logical man, my nigga, and your shit ain't making sense to me. You made the wrong move. My family is off limits," Indie stated as he cut off another finger.

"Aghh! Man, stop! Stop! I can't take no more. I swear to God, man, I don't got your daughter. I don't know anything about it," Minnie pleaded.

Chase and Khi-P looked at each other uncomfortably because it was painfully obvious that Minnie was telling the truth. With the torture that Indie was taking him through, he would have talked two fingers ago if he had any information to tell. Chase stepped up to Indie and bent down to whisper in his ear.

"Indie, if he knew anything, he would have told you by now. Maybe he's not behind this," Chase said logically.

Indie looked at the panting, bleeding man in front of him. He was falling in and out of consciousness. "If not him, then who?" Indie asked rhetorically, but his gut instinct told him that Chase was right.

He pulled a 9 mm handgun from his waistline and without flinching, he popped one into Minnie's head. On impact, his dome exploded like a watermelon, sending brain matter flying onto Indie's shirt.

"Fuck was that for?" Mekhi asked as he jumped from the unexpected blast.

"Had to put the nigga out of his misery. If I didn't, he would have eventually come for me. I don't let my beef cook for too long," Indie replied.

He turned to Chase. "Take care of this for me?"

Chase nodded, knowing that by the time he was done, there would be no trace of a murder, and barely a trace that Minnie ever existed.

Agent Norris sat back smugly as the digital camera flashed repeatedly in his hand. He smiled, knowing that he had Indie exactly where he wanted him. He knew that a man with an ego as large as Indie's would have to retaliate, and he was positive that the gunshot he had heard was connected to a murder. He had a hard-on for Indie.

Being assigned to Skylar's kidnapping was the best thing that could have happened to him. Taking down a big city New York player like Indie would surely earn Agent Norris a promotion and national recognition. The kiddie crimes division didn't hold enough prestige. If he couldn't be a gangster, he wanted to catch them, and he would stop at nothing until Indie was under the jail.

Chapter Nine

When Indie finally made it home, he was covered in blood and exhausted as Chase wheeled him through the front door. YaYa had fallen asleep at her kitchen table. He was so defeated that he didn't want to wake her. His murder session had gotten them no closer to finding Sky, and inside he felt as if he were failing his family.

"We'll get her back, fam, or the entire city gonna feel it until we do," Chase said encouragingly. Even he didn't believe the words he spoke, but he knew that it was his duty to stand tall. He slapped hands with Indie and then left, knowing that there was nothing left that he could do.

Indie grimaced as he wheeled himself over to YaYa. Her arms were crossed on the table and her head rested atop them. She clasped the red envelope tightly in her hand.

Indie moved her hair out of her face gently with his finger.

"Wake up, YaYa," he whispered, then squeezed her hand.

Hearing his voice, she stirred from her unpleasant slumber. Her red eyes revealed her aching heart. "Indie . . ." she whispered.

"I have to tell you something, ma," Indie said. He knew that it was time to tell her that he was at a dead end and there was a big possibility that baby Sky would never be returned. He was at a loss. His street tactics hadn't gotten him anywhere.

"Me too," she said. Indie put his finger to her lips to silence her. "Let me get this out, YaYa. I've done everything I can to find my baby girl. I don't think—"

"Indie, listen to me," YaYa said, interrupting him. "There's a ransom note."

She handed him the red envelope and watched as his eyes turned dark while reading the demands.

"Someone came into the house the day that you were shot and left it in Sky's room, in her crib. Whoever took her was here, Indie, and they have my baby," YaYa cried.

"Why didn't you tell me about this?" Indie asked quietly, feeling as if YaYa had lost hope in him.

"When was I supposed to tell you, Indie? When the doctors were removing bullets from your chest?" YaYa asked sincerely. "I didn't want to put anything else on you. You couldn't take the stress. You barely survived, babe. I knew that if I had told you this, it might have killed you. I was going to tell you when the time was right. Do we have half a million, Indie?"

The look on his face gave her the answer before he even opened his lips to speak. Five hundred thousand dollars in liquid cash was hard to come by. He had real estate, cars, jewelry, and had recently made some investments in the campaigns of key political figures in Houston, so his liquid assets were low at the moment. He only had $250,000 but knew that he had access to the finest coke connect in the world.

"Indie, just tell me the truth. Do you have the money?" YaYa asked.

"I'll get it," he assured.

"Friday is only three days away," YaYa stated.

"I said I'll get it," he said as he pushed away from the table. He had no time to recuperate or rest. He would have to move a lot of bricks to come up with the other half of the ransom money, and the time frame under which he was attempting to do it was almost impossible.

He went into the family room and put in a call. It was time to contact Zya, his coke connection, one of the largest female suppliers in the world and a member of the Supreme Clientele round table.

Zya got off of the international flight and raised her Gucci sunglasses off of her tanned face as she stepped into the airport. Her cream-colored Prada pantsuit and matching shoes gave her an aura of sex appeal, yet the mystery of her persona was hidden by the large shades and silk headscarf that she wore. Heads turned as her stilettos echoed off of the tiled floor and she wheeled her designer luggage through the terminal. Zya was much more than a bad bitch; she was a boss. Taught by the best, she knew all of the ins and outs of the dope game. From corner hustling to private jet setting, she had seen it all. Under any other circumstances, she wouldn't be caught dead in the States, let alone "lynch a nigga" Texas, but one of her most valued customers had called in a favor.

As she exited the airport, she saw a black Lincoln Town Car waiting curbside for her. She walked over to it and nodded to the driver as he opened the back door for her. Indie sat inside. They had come up in the game together. Back when she was hustling small time for her ex-boyfriend Jules, Indie was buying work from them. He had graduated from ounces to kilos, and she had been upgraded from wifey to HBIC. They both had come a long way since their days of Harlem dreamin'. They were both major now, and in the game so deep that they knew they would die playing it. They couldn't leave their coke hustles alone. Just like they needed the paper, the game needed them. There were very few players left who understood the rules, and Zya and Indie were veterans.

"Hello, Indie Perkins," Zya said, her voice like a sweet melody. Her creamy brown skin and Coke-bottle figure were the most beautiful features Indie had ever seen on a woman. She was stunning, the last person anyone would ever suspect of drug trafficking, but looks could be deceiving. Zya moved more bricks than a cement mason.

"What's good, Zya Miller?" he replied with a friendly smile. There had never been anything between them but good vibes and chemistry, and they never acted on it. The only thing they did well together was make money. Two hustlers with such fervent love for getting paid had no time for one another. They both understood what it took to be great in the game, and they respected one another enough to not be each other's downfall. On top of that, Zya's husband, Snow, was a good friend of Indie's, and messing with Zya would be going against the code completely. He was a man, however, and her pretty face was always nice to look at.

"Since when do you get hit?" Zya asked. She knew everything about everyone she dealt with, and was surprised to hear the news of Indie's shooting. "In all the years that you've been at this, now you want to get caught slipping?" Her tone was playful, but the worry could be seen in her gaze. She was concerned.

"I'm fine," he replied. "Indie, you're not fine," she shot back. "You wanna tell me what's going on?"

Indie wasn't one to throw a pity party for himself. He needed Zya to hit him with the bricks, but he wanted her to extend her services based on her trust in him, not out of sympathy.

"I'm not really gonna get into that right now. I need you to front me some work. A lot of work, actually. I've got some buyers lined up, but I'm not in a position to put up the money right now," Indie stated.

"You flew me back to the States to discuss a consignment deal?" Zya asked, surprised. "You know I don't fuck with consignment, Indie. It's cash and carry."

"You know I wouldn't come at you unless it would be beneficial for you. I'm willing to put a twenty percent tax on your repayment," Indie proposed.

Knowing that Indie was good money, she nodded her head. This wasn't a favor she would extend to just anyone, but Indie had been one of her best buyers for years, and she knew that although he didn't want to disclose what was going on, if he was even asking this favor, then he really needed it.

"I can have the bricks delivered to you tonight," she said. "You know if you need shooters, I got them for days," Zya said, offering her soldiers for whatever war Indie was wrapped up in.

"I appreciate it, ma, but I'm good. The bricks are more than enough," Indie said.

Zya nodded and then clapped her hands together.

"Well, I flew all the way here for you. Now I think you owe me lunch," she said with a dazzling smile.

Indie put his hand over his heart and said, "I owe you more than that, but lunch will do."

Knowing that Zya was top notch and used to the best things life had to offer, Indie escorted her to the best restaurant in town. They dined like old friends, but couldn't entertain one another for long. Zya was wanted in the States and never visited often. So, like a ghost, she had to disappear before she came up on anyone's radar.

"Be careful, Indie. I see the way that this business is beginning to change for you. You don't want to end up like me, ostracized and lonely. I can't go back home to Harlem. I can't even be here with you without looking over my shoulder every minute. But it's either this or spend the rest of my life in prison, and I refuse to do that.

"Don't end up like me. Sometimes the money and the power are not worth the sacrifice. Get out while you're on top, not when you're about to fall," Zya said.

"I will, ma. I just have to take care of a couple things for my family. After that I'm out for good," he said.

Zya stood from her seat and walked over to where Indie was seated. She bent over and kissed both of his cheeks. "I have to be going. You know I can't stay for too long. YaYa is a very lucky woman. You remind me a lot of my own husband. I hope that baby Skylar is returned back to you," she whispered. She grabbed his hand and patted it gently before she walked out of the room.

Indie turned and looked at her backside as she strutted out of the restaurant with a model's precision. He had no idea how she knew about his situation with Sky. He had never even told her about his relationship with YaYa, but she had subtly let him know that she was well versed in his affairs. All he could do was shake his head as he thought, *That's a bad bitch.*

Ding! Dong!

YaYa opened the door and was greeted by two deliverymen.

"Disaya Morgan?" one of the men asked.

Confused, she replied, "Uh . . . yeah, I'm Disaya."

"We have a furniture delivery for you," the guy said as he handed her a clipboard. YaYa frowned, but gave him her John Hancock and then watched as they carried a $10,000 Italian leather group into her home. She smiled slightly, thinking that it was a gift from Indie that would lift her spirits, but she was too low to truly appreciate the thoughtfulness.

Indie came into the room, and without speaking, he walked over to the furniture.

"Can you hand me the box cutter from the kitchen drawer?" he asked.

YaYa did as she was told and winced when she saw him cut into the leather furniture.

"Indie! What are you doing?" she asked, but when she saw the plastic-wrapped kilos that he pulled out of the couch she fully understood.

"I have to make this money for Sky," he said.

Anxious about the cash drop, YaYa remained silent as she watched an injured Indie put the bricks in several duffle bags. The feds had pulled out of their home. Their attention had been turned elsewhere, and although the case was still open, they had little help that it would ever be solved. With them gone, Indie was able to move freely. The last thing he needed was a watchful eye over him while he was trying to move weight.

Zya had made good on her promise and had Indie's package delivered to him. Now he had to make good on his promise and find their daughter.

The night was too still. Everything seemed so peaceful as YaYa looked out her second story bedroom window, but a storm was brewing. She could feel it. The red numbers on her alarm clock were a horrible reminder the lack of sleep she was suffering from. She had only taken catnaps here and there, but true peace of mind had been evasive. She couldn't rest with her life in shambles and her daughter lost to the streets; so, she stayed up day and night as her body begged for a break.

She turned toward the bed where Indie lay. The bandages on his chest were soaked in blood, and she knew that he needed to be in a hospital, but he refused. He insisted that he remain at home with her. Attempting to be her rock was slowly killing him. His snore was a result of the pain medication rather than true dreams. She tightened her short silk robe and walked over to his bedside.

"I love you," she whispered as she bent over him and kissed his forehead. The night was so still that the sound of feet against her walkway erupted in her ears like a bomb. She didn't know if it was her nerves that put her on edge, but she rushed to the window as a bad omen swept over her.

Her hand flew to her mouth in disbelief as her eyes widened. "Indie . . . Indie!" she called out in alarm. Twenty FBI agents swarmed her home in full SWAT gear and automatic weapons in their hands. Instinctively, the little ghetto girl in her came out as her mind went to the bricks of cocaine that Indie had in the closet. He had not gotten a chance to get them off yet. A meeting had been set up and Indie was supposed to make a large sale the very next day. If only the Feds had held off for a few more hours, there would be no bricks to find, but they were coming, and it looked as if tomorrow would never come. YaYa knew that if the cops found them, both she and Indie could kiss their freedom good-bye.

"Indie!" she called out as she sprinted to the walk-in closet. There was no way she was dumping the bricks. It was too much money to lose, and she had too little time to get rid of them all anyway. She grabbed the duffle bags and pulled up the trap door to the bottom of the closet.

Boom!

She heard the front door crash to the ground as the feds knocked it off the hinges and came flooding into her home. Her hands shook violently as she put the combination into the safe, her fingers turning the dial right, then left, then right again. She closed her eyes as she visualized Indie opening the safe. He didn't even think she knew it was there, but YaYa knew everything that went on underneath her roof. It was a woman's job to snoop, and now she was glad that she had.

Bingo! she thought as it came open. She stuffed the bag inside and quickly secured the safe. Just as she kicked a pile of clothes over the trap door, federal agents came flooding into her room.

"Get on the ground! Put your hands up and get on the floor now!" they hollered as they pointed guns her way.

"Wait! He's medicated and recovering from a gunshot wound! He can't get on the ground!" she screamed as she fought to make her way toward Indie's side.

"On the ground, ma'am, now! I won't say it again!" one of the agents said as he pointed his gun at her. YaYa put her hands up near her head and reluctantly got on her knees as she watched the agents manhandle Indie.

He was under such heavy medication that he couldn't shake the haze that had fallen over him. He could hear what was going on, but his eyes felt too heavy to open.

"Stop it! You're hurting him," she screamed as they pulled him forcefully from the bed.

Agent Norris finally made his way into the room and he locked eyes with YaYa.

"Please. Tell them to take it easy with him," YaYa pleaded as they cuffed her.

Norris turned to the officers and said, "Bring it down a couple notches, fellas, and remove her cuffs. We are not here for her."

The men did as they were told, and YaYa rushed behind them as they took Indie into custody. They had come out of nowhere like thieves in the night, and YaYa demanded to know why.

"What is going on? What did he do?" she asked, frantically running behind him as he was being read his rights. "Don't try that bullshit. He is in no condition to even understand you right now. He isn't even coherent enough to be read his rights!"

YaYa watched helplessly as they stuffed Indie into the back of a black unmarked vehicle.

"Where are you taking him?" she asked.

Her questions were ignored, and just as mysteriously as they appeared, they disappeared from sight, leaving YaYa standing in the middle of the street.

Chapter Ten

Doing ninety miles per hour, YaYa sped down the freeway, headed downtown to the federal holding facility. She had already called Mekhi and informed him of what was going on, but she couldn't wait for him to come and solve this problem. She had to act immediately. She had to solve it herself, and as she raced with determination, she grew angrier by the second. She pulled up to her destination and slammed her car door as she stalked inside.

"I'm here for Indie Perkins," she announced as soon as she walked up to the agent sitting behind the front desk.

He looked at her in disinterest as he typed the name into his database.

"Don't got an Indie Perkins here, miss," he said without even looking her way.

"Oh, he's here. I want to see him now!" she said sternly with one eyebrow raised as if daring him to challenge her. Today was not the day to fuck with YaYa. With a daughter missing and her man in federal custody, she had nothing to lose. "I know he's here! Where is he?" She spazzed as her fist pounded down on the wooden desk.

"Ma'am, I'm going to have to ask you to leave the building," the agent said as he stood.

"I'm not going anywhere until you answer my question. Where is Indie Perkins?" she said insistently, so loud that her voice echoed through the building.

All of a sudden, she felt someone grab her arm and pull her backward out of the building as she continued her demands for answers.

"Fuck is you thinking, ma?" Khi-P scolded sternly once he had her in front of the building, out of earshot of the officers inside.

"I'm thinking that they're holding Indie in there unjustly, Khi-P! He isn't even in the right state of mind. They could be getting him to sign anything. I'm getting him out of there even if I have to blow the fucking building up," YaYa argued.

"Take it easy, gangsta," he said with a smirk. "All that grandstanding you doing is just going to make things more difficult. They definitely ain't gonna tell you what you want to know now."

He shook his head as he pulled out his cell phone and called his attorney. He had legal counsel on speed dial. Chauncey Stanzler, Esq., was one of the top criminal defense lawyers in the state, and Khi-P kept a good working relationship with him because he was well aware that the cops had a target on his back.

One phone call and a $15,000 retainer fee later, the charges were laid out in front of them. Indie was facing murder one. They didn't know much more than that. Not even the lawyer could get much out of the feds.

"Oh my God . . . oh my God. They have him for murder? What am I going to do?" YaYa asked as she thought of the ransom drop.

"He'll be arraigned Monday morning and go before the judge so that a trial date can be set," Stanzler informed. "It's late. It's the middle of the night, so it's hard to pump information out of them right now. I'll know much more top of the week. There isn't much that can be done before then."

Khi-P shook hands with his lawyer and then put his hand on the small of YaYa's back as he walked her to her car.

"Go home. I'll pick you up Monday morning for the arraignment," Mekhi said.

"Mekhi, we got a ransom note. I'm supposed to deliver five hundred thousand the day after tomorrow. They said if we pay up then they'll return Skylar. Only problem is Indie doesn't have the cash. There are two hundred bricks of cocaine sitting at home in his safe, but what can I do with that? I don't know how to come up with that money, and now he can't," YaYa whispered. "I can get two hundred fifty thousand from his safe deposit box, but I need you, Khi-P. You have to get the rest of those bricks off so that I can make the drop."

"The feds don't know about the ransom note?" Mekhi asked as he looked around to make sure no one was around.

"Nobody knows. Just Indie and I . . . and now you," YaYa responded.

"Where is the drop?" Khi-P asked.

"Day after tomorrow at noon. Memorial Park," she replied.

Khi-P knew that the bricks in Indie's possession were worth way more than the $250,000 YaYa needed. He could smell his come-up, and he began to scheme. There was nothing that YaYa could do with the bricks. She wasn't on her hustle. She was simply used to reaping the rewards of the good life by being wifey. She had no idea of the gold mine that she was sitting on. Indie was going away; there was no doubt about it. A jailed man couldn't do shit with that much coke. The only logical thing to do would be to purchase the ki's from YaYa so that she would have enough dough to pay the ransom.

"Indie must have had buyers already lined up for the bricks," Khi-P stated. "But I don't know anybody that's ready to buy at that quantity, and I definitely don't know enough get money cats to get off two hundred under such short notice."

"I need this money, Khi. You have to get these sold for me," she said, the desperation so evident in her tone.

"Look, ma, I have a quarter mill for you. I don't know why Indie didn't just come to me for it to begin with. I can take the bricks off your hands in exchange for the other half of the ransom," Khi-P said.

The way that he broke it down to her, she felt as if he were her knight in shining armor. Her worries began to dissipate and she sighed in relief. What she didn't know was that he was getting her ass. Bricks of cocaine were going for $21,500 around the South, and that was at a good rate. She had well over four million dollars worth of product in her possession and didn't even realize it.

Khi-P did, however, which was why he was willing to put up other half of the ransom as payment for all of the drugs. He was profiting big time and upping his status to kingpin. No one other than Indie even had access to that type of quantity. Everybody else was small balling, but now Khi-P had the birds on deck, and he was ready to let them fly. He was the birdman.

"When can you give me the money?" she asked.

"I don't know. I mean, I got the paper all day, YaYa, but Indie's my man. Niggas is real sensitive about their position in the street. If he know I'm the one buying 'em he might not be too sweet on that. I don't want no static," Khi-P said.

"Indie doesn't have to know you bought them. I'll tell him I was robbed. That somebody ran in the house and took them. What he doesn't know can't hurt him. Right?" she asked.

YaYa played right into Mekhi's hand. When the dust settled, he would emerge unscathed. He didn't want Indie to think that he was trying to snake him. Although Indie was locked up, he had not yet been convicted. Khi-P wasn't ready to beef with Indie. He wasn't stupid by far. Neither Mekhi's paper nor his reach was long enough to touch Indie, and until it was, he planned to use a weakened YaYa to his advantage. These bricks were about to become his put-on.

"Yeah, I guess you right," Mekhi finally replied. "We can go get it now, and I can pick up the bricks when I drop you off. You with that?"

he asked her. He didn't want her to feel as if she were being taken advantage of, despite the fact that he was being grimy. When the truth came to the surface, he wanted to be the martyr, so he had to make sure Disaya was on board. He couldn't have her looking like the victim. He had seen firsthand Indie's wrath, and he didn't want to spark a beef with the man. He simply wanted to come up.

He kept his excitement under wraps as he ushered her to her car. "Go home. I'll be by shortly with the dough," Khi-P said. He hit the top of her car gently as she pulled off.

YaYa flew home feeling relieved. She didn't know that she was practically giving Indie's product away for free. The flip wasn't even large enough to pay back the debt that Indie owed to Zya. She was solving one problem, but unknowingly creating ten new ones.

When she arrived home, she pulled the bricks out of the safe and waited impatiently for Khi-P to arrive. As promised, he showed up with the money for Sky's ransom. He wasn't even decent enough to throw her dough to get by on. He knew that without Indie, YaYa was dead broke.

She wouldn't be able to survive long on her own, and just like so many other beautiful girls, she would be looking for the next get-money cat to finance her lifestyle. She would run straight to him, and Khi-P wouldn't turn her away. Disaya was one of the most beautiful women that he had ever seen. Her style was new to the South, and he definitely wouldn't have a problem helping to keep her afloat. Although she was loyal to Indie, Khi-P knew that if he got convicted, that jailbird love song would play out quickly. The promises to be there forever always grew stale after the guilty verdict. That was just the way street love went. It could fizzle out just as quickly as it began. Chicks were drawn to the money, not the man, and once Indie wasn't bringing in the bread anymore, it would be on to the next one. Niggas flipped birds, bitches flipped niggas; it was the game, and Khi-P knew it.

"Thank you," she said. She wrung her hands nervously. "Now all I have to do is get her back."

"I can come with you. As a matter of fact, I'll handle it for you if you want me to," he said.

She shook her head in dissent. "No. They told me to come alone. I don't want to even take the chance of doing something wrong. If I do, they'll kill her," YaYa said.

"I can't let you go to that park by yourself. You keep me on speed dial, YaYa. I'll be parked a block up the street so if you ever feel threatened or shit don't seem right, you call," he said.

She nodded as she showed him to the door. She was so close to her daughter, yet she was so far away.

Sleep was evasive that night, but as she lay in bed, she sent a prayer up to God. She was going to need a whole lot of strength to make it through this ordeal—more than she could ever muster on her own. God was her only hope.

Chapter Eleven

Nervous energy filled YaYa so much that she felt like she was drowning in it. She went deaf as she looked around the crowded park, realizing that there was a parade and carnival that day. There were more than fifty thousand people there, and she quickly became overwhelmed in the sea of faces. As she looked around, everyone looked suspicious. She thought everyone was involved in the kidnapping. She had no idea what or who she was looking for.

As she made her way through the masses, her heart quickened. Every person who bumped her, she mugged. Every child's cry that passed through her ear caused her to whip her head eagerly. As she looked around and spun 360 degrees, she surveyed her surroundings.

The tiny Swiss Mini Gun she carried was tucked in the large bun in her hair. There was no way she was walking into that situation unarmed. She had no clue what she was going up against, but it felt like it was her against the world, so she definitely needed the strap.

Her instruction had been to bring the money to the park at noon. She was there. She had fulfilled her end of things. Now where were the culprits at large?

Leah watched YaYa like a hawk as she carried the money-filled tote bag around the park. She smirked as she noticed the look of terror on YaYa's face. The large sun hat she wore shaded the features of her face. YaYa would never spot her out of the crowd.

Leah was grateful to be away from the screams. They clouded her judgment and made it hard for her to concentrate. The wails were so loud that she was sure that others heard them. She looked back at her car to make sure that it was undisturbed. It was her getaway car. The last thing she needed was some nosy bystander getting in her business and messing things up.

YaYa went into the restrooms, and Leah followed behind her. It was going to be a piece of cake getting that cash from her. YaYa was weak in Leah's eyes. The pampered princess always had been, from Leah's vantage point.

Leah hadn't stuck around long enough to see YaYa's struggle. When Slim was alive, she was the Snow White of her neighborhood, but her world fell apart after her mother was killed. Leah had no clue that Disaya and she shared the same history of sexual abuse. Maybe if she did, her envy wouldn't be so concentrated. If she knew that YaYa had struggled on her own for years, her own jealousy may have been diluted.

When Leah entered the bathroom, YaYa was bent over the sink. The pressure from the situation was obviously more than she could handle because she was vomiting uncontrollably. Leah swiftly walked up behind her, and before YaYa could even look up, Leah grabbed her bun and smashed her head against the sink.

YaYa crumbled like a house of cards as she grabbed her face and sank to the floor. Disoriented and stunned, she tried to get to her feet, but gravity pushed her right back down. She couldn't see through the blood in her eyes. The room began to spin as she tried to focus. The last thing she saw was the clouded figure of a woman's back as she exited the bathroom. Suddenly, everything went black.

Leah fired a gunshot into the air and immediately, like roaches in light, the people in the park began to scatter. It was the perfect distraction.

Leah blended into the mass pandemonium with the tote bag tucked securely under her arms. If YaYa did have anyone at the park watching her back, they would surely be thrown off now. Leah made it to her car half a million dollars richer with a big smile on her face. She was ready to get out of Dodge.

Waaa! Waaa!

The sharp cries turned Leah's smile into a frown, reminding her of all the things she had done and the things she still had to do. The first thing on the agenda was to blow town. Things were too hot, and now she had the financial resources to disappear.

Chapter Twelve

"Bitch, your kid is dead!"

YaYa kept replaying the words in her head. She had received the anonymous call as soon as she walked in her door. The voice was disguised, and before she even got the chance to beg on Skylar's behalf, she heard the dial tone. The drop had gone awry in the worst way. In the end, YaYa had no money, no Skylar, and had left Indie owing a debt to his connect with no way to repay it. Their entire plan had gone to shit, and she felt it in her bones that Skylar had paid the ultimate price.

Somebody was playing mind games with her, and the cruel joke was slowly tormenting her. There was no hope left to be had. Skylar was gone forever. The feeling of loss that she had was immeasurable. She felt like she was suffocating. The greatest joy she had ever felt had resulted in the greatest pain. Skylar had been her dearest love, but also her darkest hour.

Everyone was silent. The only sound that could be heard were YaYa's wrenching sobs as they waited for the phone to ring. Indie was the only person that didn't know, and YaYa had to be the one to tell him that their daughter was no more.

The phone rang loudly, cutting through the overwhelming sadness in the room. YaYa held the cordless phone in her hand, but as the tears fell from her cheeks, she couldn't bring herself to answer it. She just let it ring as she shook her head.

"I can't," she whispered as she lowered her head and closed her eyes in agony. She knew how damaging the news would be for Indie. It was a blow that she wasn't ready to deliver. She knew him, and the fact that he couldn't do anything but sit behind a jail cell would crush him.

"Somebody has to answer the phone for him, YaYa. His mind is gon' spin like crazy if you don't. Don't let his imagination fill in the blanks. It'll just drive him crazy," Chase said.

The phone began to ring again, and YaYa held it out for Chase. "You tell him, because I can't."

Chase looked around the room at Trina and the girls, then toward Khi-P. Nobody else was willing to do it. The task at hand was too hard, but Chase felt as if he owed Indie. He couldn't just ignore the call. He answered the phone.

The operator's voice announced, "You have a prepaid debit call from—"

Before Indie could even say his name, Chase accepted the call.

"YaYa, tell me my daughter is safe," he said.

"It's me. Chase."

"Chase?" Indie stated. His heart sank into his stomach when he registered the tone of his li'l man's voice. He already knew what to expect.

"The drop . . ." Chase stopped to clear his throat of the emotion that threatened to spill out. "It went bad. We didn't get her back."

Indie gripped the phone tightly and couldn't stop the sob that was building in his throat. He wanted to break down, but knew that the other inmates were watching him. He had to remain tough, to keep his gangster intact. If not, the days he spent awaiting trial would be hellacious. Niggas would think he was soft and try him, so Indie gathered himself and restored his composure before responding.

"Where is YaYa?" he asked. "Let me speak to her."

Chase knew that the moment of silence Indie took meant that he was trying to hold it together. "I'ma put her on the jack, but you keep your head up in there, big homie. I love you, baby. Ring me if you need anything," Chase stated.

He turned to YaYa and held out the phone. She exhaled and took it before she left the room to get some privacy.

"Indie," she whispered as she sniffled and wiped her tears. "Indie, she's gone, baby. They took her away from me, Indie. What am I going to do without her?"

"I'm so sorry, ma. I let you down. I was supposed to make this right. I should have never asked you to move down here with me if I couldn't take care of you," Indie said in a low tone.

"I feel like I'm dying, Indie. I really do. Thinking about what they might have done to her . . ." YaYa was so broken up that she couldn't even finish her sentence.

"Don't think about that, ma. You just think about the good times. Think about how much you loved her. This isn't your fault, Disaya. I want you to be strong. Skylar wouldn't want you to hurt. You have to send our baby girl off. She deserves to be with the angels. She was too good for this world," he said. He was trying to say all of the right things, but he knew that no words could undo this tragedy. It hurt worse than the bullets he had taken in the chest.

"Okay, I will. I wish you were here, Indie. It's too hard doing this without you," she replied.

"I know, ma, and I'm so sorry," Indie said. Indie was apologizing for all of his shortcomings as a man, as a father, as a partner, and as a friend.

His time for conversing came to a close and he reluctantly told YaYa good-bye. As soon as he hung up the phone, his rage overtook him. He slammed the pay phone repeatedly on its base.

"Fuck!" he shouted as he finally tossed it and then stormed back to his cell block. Suddenly, the murder charge he was facing was pushed to the back of his mind. That night, he grieved the loss of his child. He knew that from that moment forward, he would have to keep those close to him safe.

His thoughts inadvertently drifted to Leah and the child she was carrying for him. He had put her on the back burner when YaYa had come to town, but now more than ever he felt the need to be close to her. She was about to become the mother of his seed, and although he would never put her over YaYa, he still felt the need to take care of her. The loss of Skylar made him want to be better for his other child. He vowed to be a better father on Skylar's behalf. What he didn't know was that Leah was the one behind it all, and by dealing with her he was helping to destroy YaYa. He had reignited the one-sided feud that had been going on for years, and the only thing that could possibly end it was death.

YaYa planned the most beautiful memorial service that money could buy. Indie made sure that every expense was covered. He had a lot of connections and had looked out for a lot of people when he was free, so money for the funeral was not an option. She filled her days with choosing flower arrangements and framing poster-sized baby pictures of Skylar for the event.

She never wanted to bury her child, and she couldn't understand how God could take such an innocent life. *If this is what he had planned for Sky, what is in store for me?*

Khi-P and Chase became her personal escorts. Whatever she needed was always a phone call away. Her days were filled with lonely thoughts. Eyes covered with diva shades, she felt detached from the world. She was on auto pilot, walking through life in a fog. To avoid feeling devastated, she turned off her emotions so that she didn't feel anything at all. She was tired. Her expectations were low. Life had taught her a valuable lesson—if she didn't expect anything at all, then she could never be disappointed.

She had been stripped of everyone that she had ever loved, and she was defeated. The closer she got to saying good-bye, the more she withdrew. Going through an entire day was starting to become impossible for Disaya, and soon she stopped trying altogether. Days before Sky's memorial, her heart had turned completely cold. The only thing that warmed her up was the bottle of Patrón that sat near her bedside. Drowning her sorrows in the tequila felt so good. Her liquid high was her only relief. It gave her the courage to even consider reuniting with her daughter.

With the alcohol as her only sustenance, she began to feel sick. Vomit tickled the back of her throat, and she was so weak that she let it erupt on the side of her bed.

"Aghhhh!" she hurled as she staggered to her feet.

She smelled like death as liquor and vomit covered her. The full-length mirror revealed her true self. The bags under her eyes gave away her exhaustion. Disgusted with the reflection she saw, YaYa threw the bottle of Patrón at the mirror, shattering both. Fed up and ready to give in, she stormed into her closet to retrieve the nickel-plated pistol that Indie hid inside.

It would be so easy to just end all of this, she thought.

A picture of Skylar sat on her dresser and pulled her near almost magnetically. She picked it up and held it in one hand as she gripped the gun in the other.

I miss you, baby doll. Mama's coming, she thought.

She took the picture with her to her bed and lay down. She held the picture against her heart and put the gun to her head, then closed her eyes. Before she could even find the strength to pull the trigger, the liquor-induced fog took her away to her dreams, the only place where Skylar lived.

Chapter Thirteen

Ding! Ding!

Disaya lay deathly still as her doorbell went off, sending an earth-shattering headache vibrating through her brain. She couldn't move. A broken heart paralyzed her as she stared at the picture of her baby girl that sat on the nightstand beside the bed. Although her hand gripped Indie's 9 mm pistol, she didn't have enough energy to lift it to her head and end the misery.

She had been in that same position for days and had already held her own personal vigil for Skylar. Night after night, she had prayed for her daughter's soul, but she felt as if God had rejected her. He had taken away the one good thing she had ever done. Her ashen face was swollen with grief as she lay unflinching, her red eyes burning with sorrow. There was no way to fill the void that had come plunging into her life. She was completely hollow, and it hurt more than anything she had ever experienced before.

It was an incomparable pain, a dull ache that would last a lifetime.

Her daughter was dead. There would be no homecoming for baby Sky, no celebration of birthdays or good night kisses. She was lost forever to a cruel world. Baby Skylar had disappeared from her life almost as if she had never existed to begin with, and that thought alone was enough to bring her to her knees.

She heard the footsteps ascend the hardwood staircase, but still she didn't move. Today was not a day that she was looking forward to. She could not bring herself to embrace Skylar's departure. She refused to.

"YaYa?" Trina called out as she peeked into the darkened room. The smell of Disaya's body odor immediately hit her, and tears came to her eyes when she saw the state that Disaya was in. She was usually so composed. Trina had never seen YaYa less than perfect. From her hair and nails to the designer threads that always graced her Coke-bottle figure, YaYa was always put together with precision. Looking at her defeated demeanor, it appeared as if she had come apart at the seams. Her world had been devastated, and her weakness was on display for all to see.

"YaYa, it's me, Trina," she said gently. When she received no response, she turned around toward Miesha and Sydney to stop them from following her inside the room. "Can y'all wait downstairs? Everybody don't need to see her like this."

They nodded in understanding and retreated to the living room as Trina walked into the bedroom. A wine bottle was shattered in pieces, and the sticky liquid had left a red stain running down the white walls. The room was a mess.

Trina stepped over broken glass and crumpled piles of clothes. She knelt beside YaYa's bedside to look her in the eyes and gasped at what she saw. The glamorous woman that she looked up to had disappeared. Only a fragment of her former self survived, and as Trina stared into her empty gaze, sympathy filled her.

"YaYa, you have to get up. Sky's memorial is today," she said.

YaYa didn't respond. She didn't even lift her eyes in acknowledgment. A black fog smothered her as death loomed over her.

"I know you're hurting, YaYa, but you want to be there to say your good-byes," Trina said.

Click! Clack!

Trina heard the sound of the hammer of a gun being pulled back and her eyes widened as she realized YaYa was gripping a pistol.

"I can't . . . I can't tell my daughter good-bye. This can't be real. . . . She was supposed to bury me. It wasn't supposed to happen like this," YaYa said, her voice a hoarse whisper and her face a river of regret as tears fell freely. She gripped the trigger so tightly that Trina feared it might go off.

"It hurts," YaYa whispered as she put the gun to her head.

"Don't do this, YaYa. You have too many people who still love you. Think about what this would do to Indie. You still have him," Trina said as she tried desperately to convince YaYa to live.

"Indie isn't here," YaYa shot back. "He's never around when I need him. Where is he?" she cried. She knew that Indie's arrest was not his fault, but she couldn't help but to point fingers. It seemed as if she was always facing the unbeatable alone. He was never by her side, and this time she felt completely helpless. She wanted to be strong, but she had nothing left inside. There was no confidence, no determination, no strength left in reserve. She was on E. Drained of everything but sorrow, she just wanted all the pain to end.

"You know he wants to be here with you right now. He loves you. Give me the gun, YaYa. Please. I don't want to be the one to tell Indie that he has to bury the woman he loves right next to his daughter," Trina pleaded.

Her words were like a shot of hard liquor for YaYa, and she became sick to her stomach. An emotional hangover caused her head to pound as she closed her bloodshot eyes in agony.

Trina reached for the gun and wrapped her hand around YaYa's. She removed each finger, one by one, until she had removed it completely from YaYa's grasp. As if she had been holding her breath in fear, Trina sighed deeply in relief.

"I don't even have a body to bury today. This just doesn't feel right. I can't do this. What if she's still out there, waiting on me to come and save her?" YaYa asked.

"She's gone, and it's time for you to let her go," Trina said soothingly. She leaned over and helped YaYa out of bed. She was so weak that Trina had to wrap YaYa's arm around her shoulders just to keep her on her feet.

"I got you," Trina assured. "You still have family, YaYa, and we are going to help you get through this."

Makeup flawless and dressed in an all-black Marc Jacobs pencil skirt set, YaYa stepped out of the limo like old money. Her fragile state was hidden behind the sheer silk scarf and oversized Chanel sunglasses that covered her. Trina, Miesha, and Sydney had put her together as if she were a Barbie doll. From her hair to the Prada heels on her feet, they had chosen everything as YaYa sat in a zombie-like state.

Her life had become so surreal, and all eyes were on her as she silently urged her shaky limbs to keep her upright. She was amongst a community of strangers. Besides Indie's immediate crew, there wasn't a familiar face in sight.

As the ladies approached Chase and Khi-P, they embraced each other with open arms, each of them giving their condolences to YaYa.

"Who are all of these people?" she managed to find her voice to ask.

"This is Houston, baby girl. This is Indie's city. They're just coming out to show their respect," Khi-P answered as he held out his hand for her to walk in front of him. "Indie's mother is waiting inside for you."

YaYa couldn't believe how large of an empire Indie had built in Houston. Although she didn't know the masses of people who had come out on baby Sky's behalf, she appreciated the love, and at that moment, she embraced Houston as home.

Beautiful on the outside but hollow on the inside, YaYa was an empty shell. She was simply going through the motions. Elaine's maternal presence eased her weary soul a bit as she made her way inside. YaYa couldn't help but think how lucky Indie was to have a mother like her. Once a lady of the night, Elaine had seen her share of tragedies, but nothing had ever felt like this. To have to bury her own grandbaby's memory was a daunting task that was proving to be too difficult for everyone in attendance.

When the two women saw one another, they embraced tightly. Elaine was so motherly and supportive as YaYa cried heavily on her shoulder, releasing it all through her muffled cries.

"Thank you for being here," YaYa whispered.

"Where else would I be?" Elaine asked. "I loved that baby, and I love you too. Someone should have called me sooner. I—" She stopped speaking to wipe away a few stray tears as she willed herself to stay strong. She was well aware that YaYa needed a rock to lean on, and breaking down wouldn't do either of them any good.

She regained her composure and cleared her throat as she continued, "Bill is meeting with Indie's lawyers to find out what we can do to get him out of there."

Overwhelmed by the family support, YaYa hugged Elaine with all of her might as she swayed from side to side. "I'm so glad you're here."

Leah sat in the back of the church practically hysterical as she observed Skylar's funeral proceedings. She had to admit that YaYa had gone all out to send Skylar home. Leah hid her identity behind dark shades and a large black Dior hat. She knew that it was risky, but she had to see firsthand how she had affected YaYa.

Weakened by the infection that was destroying her womb, she almost didn't make it to the services, but nothing could stop her from having her moment of victory. She knew that by not being treated after her miscarriage, she was doing harm to herself, but none of it mattered to her. In a way, she enjoyed the pain, indulging in it.

Leah was beyond bitter. Her obsession with Disaya and her fixation on revenge was psychotic. Her mental was broken, and not even her life mattered. She had no regard for humanity or morality, and as she looked on eagerly, she gripped the church pew in front of her to keep her from keeling over in excruciating pain.

Hiding the smile that graced her face was hard. Amongst a sea of somber faces, her delight would have given her away, so she contained it to avoid suspicion. The crying had stopped momentarily, but there was not a doubt in her mind that it would return.

Disaya was at her breaking point. She held Elaine's hand while listening to the pastor deliver a sermon on pure souls. A huge picture of Skylar was on display at the front of the church, and there was no doubt in YaYa's mind that her daughter was one of the souls that the lesson was referring to. This was her daughter's homegoing ceremony, but something inside of YaYa couldn't let go. She felt her daughter in her spirit and sobs wrecked her as she thought of how she had failed as a mother.

I let her down. It was my job to protect her, she thought solemnly.

She tuned the pastor out as her body went completely numb. She had never lost someone so dear to her. The last funeral she had attended had been her mother's, and the feeling of loss was just as great now as it had been back then.

As the service came to an end, YaYa rose from her seat. Elaine looped her arm through YaYa's as they made their exit from the church.

As soon as she stepped foot outside, she saw Indie and his father emerging from the back of an unmarked police car. She froze mid-step in disbelief as she watched him dust himself off. He was still dressed in the city-issued jail suit, but to YaYa, he looked as if he had just stepped off of the cover of *GQ*. Although he was in his most submissive state, handcuffed and labeled state property, he still emanated power. Everything about him gave off the aura of authority.

She ran to him at full speed, and despite the protests of his police escorts, she jumped into his arms.

"Oh my God! Indie! I'm so sorry. I should have listened to you. I should have never gotten the police involved," she said as she poured out her every regret.

"Shh. It's okay, ma. I know you were just doing what you felt was right. I don't blame you for anything," Indie replied.

"I didn't think you would be able to come. How did you get them to let you out?" she asked hysterically.

"Those bars can't hold me, ma. I wouldn't have missed this for anyone. I had to be here for her." He paused as he lifted his handcuffed hands to grace her cheek. "For you." Feeling as though his movements were restricted, he turned to his police escort and leaned into his ear. "My man, there is a lot of money to be made by removing these handcuffs."

Although tempted, the officer appeared unsure.

"I'm not going to run. I just want to hold my wife," Indie stated sincerely.

The officer nodded and removed the handcuffs, allowing Indie to wrap his arms around YaYa, lifting her from her feet. "I love you, ma.

I love you more than life. Walk with me inside. I need to talk to you about something important."

As they walked past his friends and family, he embraced his mother and exchanged hugs with his crew before following Disaya inside. The church's sanctuary had cleared out, leaving them alone, but the heavy sadness still lingered in the air.

"My baby girl," Indie whispered as he looked up at the poster-sized picture. "How did this happen, ma? All I ever wanted to do was love you and take care of my family."

"I can't do this, Indie. It feels like I'm dying inside," Disaya admitted, wrapping her arms around herself as she shook her head in defeat.

"I need you to be strong, YaYa. This is only the beginning of the storm. I might be going away for a little while, and I need to know that you are okay out here," Indie said as he lifted her chin, forcing her to look him in the eyes.

"I just don't know if I can get through this by myself, Indie. I can't lose you too, not after everything we've been through," YaYa replied. "You just came back into my life. You were just getting to know our daughter! Why us? What happened to our fairytale ending?"

"That's not real life," he whispered as his strong composure gave out. He closed his eyes as he tipped his forehead to hers. His bottom lip quivered with grief at the thought of his fragile family. Their most innocent member had been taken away, and now he was being forced to leave YaYa to pick up the pieces.

She reached up and kissed her man's lips . . . his eyes . . . his cheeks . . . the tip of his nose. Their love had never been everlasting. All God ever gave them were fleeting moments, glimpses of happiness. The forces surrounding them were all plotting against them. When things were right between them, they were so right, but misery always found them, and it seemed as though their separation was inevitable. So, she kissed him as if it would be the last one that they shared, taking his full lips into her mouth while pouring her torn soul into him. She caressed his face, inhaled his scent, and allowed her hands to feel his broad chest as if she would never see him again.

Indie's fingers became tangled in her long hair as tears finally fell from his eyes. Not only had he come to say good-bye to baby Sky; he had come to set Disaya free. He knew that things didn't look good. The odds were stacked against him, and he had already put YaYa through enough pain. He loved her enough to allow her to walk away. He knew that he could never love her fully from behind prison walls. He wanted to give her all of him. She deserved one hundred percent of a man, and being enslaved to the system made him only half of one. He was a liability to her, rather than an asset.

He had never loved a woman the way that he loved YaYa. She was his rib, and he would do anything for her. He knew that she wouldn't understand his logic right away. In the days to come, her heart would be broken by his decision, but in the long run, her life would be much grander without the stress of sticking by an inmate.

As the soul mates' lips intertwined, they felt each other's strife. They were burying their child's memory, and with it a piece of the love they had for each other.

Their intimate kiss was interrupted by the sound of the church doors opening as Indie's police escort entered the room. He cleared his throat and said, "I'm sorry. It's time to go."

"No," YaYa uttered. She gripped Indie's hand desperately as her eyes pleaded with him to stay.

"I've got to go, ma. I love you, Disaya . . . YaYa . . . I've never loved anyone like I love you," Indie stated seriously, unashamed of his candid display of emotion. "Don't come visit me. You move on. Do something great . . . be someone better. Let go of all the pain and fulfill your life, ma. Don't get stuck in the grief. That's my job. I'll hurt over everything that we lost. Every day I'll feel that pain. Let that be my burden. All I want for you is happiness."

Her tears overwhelmed her to the point where she couldn't speak. Sobs were her only reply.

"Live, YaYa. Don't let this break you. Don't let me stop you. Sky would want you to be happy," he whispered in her ear.

The officer cleared his throat. It was time. Indie kissed her wet cheek before allowing the officer to do his job.

Watching him walk away evoked tyranny within her. Misery might as well have been her name. Indie had a way of giving her the extremes of love. Nothing had ever felt so good than life with him, but the flip side was the intense feeling of loneliness when he was away. Living without him and without their daughter was an ache that couldn't be dulled.

Leah was disgusted at the connection she witnessed between Indie and YaYa. As she sat in the pews on the second floor balcony, she fumed at the sight of them. No matter what she did to wound YaYa, someone always came to her rescue. She had tried to snatch Indie away from her before and had failed, but as she looked at the picture on her cell phone, she knew that the ball was in her court. YaYa had played herself when she kissed Khi-P. Leah had known Indie long enough to know that this would send him over the edge.

Leah pulled out the burnout that she had purchased and forwarded the picture to the untraceable phone before finally sending it to Indie. She knew that a man of Indie's caliber would have pull in jail, and he would receive the picture of his beloved YaYa sooner or later. It was the law of the pecking order. Big-timers like Indie ran the prisons, and a cell phone was necessary to ensure they kept in constant communication with the outside.

As she smirked devilishly, Leah felt a wave of twisted satisfaction. She was pulling all the strings from behind the scenes. Indie and YaYa were simply her puppets. She was the rule maker in a cruel game called life, and she was playing them both.

Chapter Fourteen

Indie walked out of the church without looking back because he knew if he did, it would only break him down. He couldn't think of YaYa where he was going. It was about survival. He had yet to stand before a judge, but he was almost sure that they would put him away for the crime that he had committed. His incarceration was inevitable.

He watched as Chase slid one of his escorts a cell phone and a handsome knot full of dead presidents as compensation. Indie nodded his head in appreciation as he passed. At least now he would be able to make calls at his leisure. He needed to be able to reach YaYa and his lawyer at will. The BlackBerry also provided him with internet access to communicate.

He powered on his phone and sifted through the messages that he had missed. Déjà vu hit him when he opened the text message from a number he didn't recognize. The picture of YaYa and Khi-

P intimately kissing set a blaze in him, reminding him of her previous indiscretions involving his brother.

Fuck is this? he thought as he peered closer at the image. They were in the process of removing each other's clothing, and the sight was like a bullet to the heart. It hurt much worse than any gunshot ever could.

He hid his emotions well. The only thing that gave him away was the rise and fall of his heaving chest. To say he was astounded would be an understatement, and pain didn't do justice to the emotions he felt. It wasn't the fact that she had cheated that hurt him. It was the betrayal that stung.

And with my nigga, he thought as he shook his head. *They both looked me in my face today like the shit never happened.*

Indie forwarded the photo to YaYa. He wanted her to know that he knew. Before she could respond, he powered off his phone and leaned his head against the backseat. He didn't want to hear from her. He wanted to give her time to think, time to get her words together before she came out of her mouth with a lie. After all that he had done for YaYa, he felt like a fool. Reckless murder wasn't even in Indie's character. He had gone all out for YaYa, for his family. He had risked his freedom trying to protect her, and this was how she repaid him.

YaYa's phone vibrated in her purse, and she removed it as she stepped into the limo. She smiled when she saw Indie's name pop up on her screen, but when she opened the text, her heart sank. As if the oxygen was sucked out of the room, she gasped as her hand flew to her mouth in disbelief.

How did he . . .? Where did this . . .?

So many questions ran through her mind that she couldn't think straight. As she thought about that night, she shivered.

Someone was still in the house, she concluded. *Who*ever took Sky was still there. That had to be who took *this picture!* She dialed Indie's number with urgency. *I have to explain this to him. I have to make this right.*

Her call went directly to voice mail, causing YaYa to burst into tears. She knew at that moment that her world was over. Losing Indie was the last straw. There was only so much that one person could take, and she had reached her breaking point.

"Mr. Perkins, you were supposed to appear in this courtroom over a week ago to be arraigned," Judge Lawson said as he peered down at Indie sternly.

Einstein stood up on Indie's behalf. "Your Honor, his daughter was the little girl that has been on the news. Skylar Perkins . . . her memorial is what held up the arraignment proceedings."

Judge Lawson softened his tone a bit as he replied, "I see. My condolences to you, Mr. Perkins. How does the defendant plead?"

"Not guilty," Einstein replied. "We wish to request a speedy trial. We would like to deliver opening statements as soon as possible."

"This courtroom does not run on Mr. Perkins' schedule. Trial will be set for December third at 9:00 A.M.," the judge ordered.

The trial date was six months away, but Indie was indifferent as he sat stone-faced. He was there physically, but his mind was a million miles away. He could feel YaYa sitting behind him, urging him to turn her way, but he refused. He couldn't look at her. He was afraid of how he might feel when he did finally look her in her deceitful eyes. He couldn't help but wonder how she was holding up. They both had lost the greatest child in the world. He hoped that she was well, but he would never let her know that.

Once bail was denied and the court date was set, the bailiff came to escort him back to the prison van. Not once did he acknowledge Disaya.

He walked out of the courtroom in handcuffs, and his head low as he ignored her voice calling his name.

YaYa stood and gripped the wooden pew in front of her as she watched Indie leave the room. "Indie," she called helplessly, but he just kept walking. Every step he took felt like a punch to the gut. He was literally walking out of her life. She had waited by the phone day and night, hoping that he would call. All she wanted to do was explain the picture to him. She needed him to know that they had stopped before things had gone too far. She would take any form of communication from him at this point. He could yell at her, scream on her, he could call her a bitch, as long as he was talking to her. She would take anything she could get, but he gave her nothing, and the silence was deafening.

With Indie gone, YaYa's dream quickly transformed into a nightmare. Her life was no picnic. The fairytale was over and reality was cold. Without the security of her man to hold her down, things became extremely tight. Bills were piling up, and the responsibility of taking care of herself weighed heavily upon her.

Houston wasn't New York. She wasn't home. She couldn't just pick up a quick hustle to get by. She didn't know a damn thing about the South.

The little bit that she had experienced had put a bitter taste in her mouth. Niggas got down differently in Houston. They were treacherous, and nothing was off limits. A stranger to the big Southern city, she was left on stuck.

The love she had relocated for was non-existent at this point. When Indie had gotten arrested, her love had been locked down. Whatever time Indie got, she knew that her soul would do the time with him. Even if she moved on with her life, her ability to love a man would forever be stuck with Indie. The ying to her yang, he had all of her. Indie was her other half, the greatest man she had ever known, but now things were just fucked up. They had created the most magnificent form of beauty that had ever existed when they made their daughter. The guilt of her demise was enough to rip them apart. Add the stress of a jail sentence to the equation, and the end of their relationship became inevitable. The entire setup was just all bad. No matter what either of them did, there were too many roadblocks hindering them from furthering their relationship.

YaYa knew that all good things would eventually end. Indie had made things too easy for her. He had given her everything and made her earn nothing. He had made her his queen, but the feds had dethroned her, and she had fallen from grace back into the realm of the regular.

As she sat at her dining room table gripping a glass of vodka, tears fell from her eyes. *Things weren't supposed to be like this,* she thought as she glanced out of the window and watched the tow truck pull her vehicle away. She couldn't afford to pay her note, and frankly, she didn't have the energy to try. They could have that shit. Everything from the furs to the luxury vehicles could go. She would give it all up to regain her family. No cost was too high to have her daughter back and to wake up to Indie every morning. It wasn't the lifestyle that she was infatuated with; it was the man. She would have lived out of a cardboard box with Indie.

Other cats from her past had to impress her with the finer things, but Indie was the exception. He was her reckless love, her unconditional love, but now it felt like none of it had ever really happened. It felt like a good/bad dream—good because she got to feel what it was like to love so greatly, but bad because she had lost him and the product of his seed.

Life in general overwhelmed her. She was already emotionally devastated, but now her finances were at an all-time low. She knew eventually they would come for her house. There was no way she could keep up her mortgage or even afford to maintain the utilities, and when they did, she would be out on her ass. She had nothing and no one.

In the wake of the storm, she was left with nothing but a broken heart, so to rid herself of the pain, she drank like a fish. YaYa consumed hard, liver-rotting liquor. It was the only thing that helped her get by. Pain was an understatement. She felt responsible for Skylar's and Indie's fate. It hurt so bad that it numbed her.

Thinking about it drove her to madness, yet at the same time, she couldn't stop. It was all she could think of. She tried to recall from memory the beat of Skylar's heart and the feel of Indie's embrace, but with each day that passed, she could recall less. She knew that with time her pain would fade and her wounds would heal, but when they did, she would forget. A little bit every day would leave her, and she never wanted to leave Indie or Sky behind.

She stood from the table and walked around the home, admiring everything that Indie had purchased her. Her glass was glued to her hand as she took it all in. She couldn't help but ask herself if it was really worth it. She would rather not have been acquainted with love at all than to have it disappear from her life. In the blink of an eye, everything had changed for the worse. She was still standing, but who wanted to survive alone? Being the sole survivor was lonely. With all of her loved ones gone, she felt as if she would be better off dead.

YaYa realized that she was wallowing in her sorrow, but she felt as if she were entitled to her moment. So, she finished off the bottle that she was working on and walked over to the liquor cabinet. She pulled out a bottle of Patrón, not even caring that she was mixing all different types of liquor. Her mission was to get fucked up to provide her with a temporary escape.

She went up to her bedroom and over to her closet. She had an entire department store inside: clothes, cash, cars, even jewels. She had it all. Indie had deprived her of nothing, but losing it all felt so bad that she wished she had never attained it in the first place.

As she sipped her liquor, she went through her jewels, packing them all away in her suitcase. She took only her most expensive pieces. With no real cash to her name, she knew that the jewels would prove valuable one day.

It was so ironic how quickly things could fall apart. Usually she could easily rebound when the game knocked her down, but this time she had no one around her to pick her back up. No

Mona, no Indie, and no Sky. This time the only one she had was herself, but she was too weak to stand up alone. So instead, she gave up, and as she whisked the strong liquor down her throat, it numbed the aching pain she felt and filled the void inside of her—with misery.

Life was too hard. Everything about it hurt. It had never been easy, but now with the death of her daughter and the loss of her only love weighing her down, she had nothing left to fight for. Disaya was on stuck. In the past, her fly girl antics had always gotten her by. Everything had been about a dollar. She was always chasing cashmere dreams, trying to climb from the bottom to the top. From the ground up, the throne looked so appealing, but now that she was on top, she realized it was all an illusion. Being queen was lonely. Being the woman to a man like Indie was stressful. Expectations of beauty were impossible to meet, and although the position came with hood prestige, it also carried a risk of inherent danger. Being wifey to a hustler was overrated because at the end of the day, the man she depended on more than anyone was always pulled away from her.

A crippling pain corrupted her soul as she lay sulking in her own sadness. She knew that she had power over her own emotions, and that it was up to her to piece her life back together, but she didn't want to. She didn't want to go on without her family. She had been through too much. The death of her mother, the rape she endured as a child, the hard-knock hustle she had used to survive on the streets, the death of Mona—it was all overwhelming, and losing Sky and Indie was the straw that broke the camel's back. No one could survive so many hard times. Life had beaten her to the point where she could no longer conceal the bruises it left behind.

Scarred, she knew what she had to do. She ran a hot bubble bath in her porcelain claw foot tub and immersed her body. It was so hot that she could barely stand it, and steam rose into the air, but once she adjusted to the temperature, the warmth was like tiny hands rubbing her tense body, melting her worries away. It was inviting, convincing, and soothing. The feeling of euphoria it brought over her was enough to take her fears away. Suddenly, her future seemed perfectly clear—her destiny, inevitable.

She reached to the side of the tub and grabbed Indie's old school barber's razor. She was in a daze, as if someone else were pushing the buttons and causing her to move. She didn't even feel the sting of the blade as she ran it vertically down her wrists, slicing her flesh in half. She submerged her entire body in the water. Only her nose and eyes peeked above the bath as her blood spilled out, tinting the water rose red.

Memories of her life flashed before her eyes. The blood flowing from her wrists felt serene, and a peaceful calm took over her. The throbbing of her wrist was an indication of redemption for her. All of the wrong she had done in her life and all of the trespasses that had been committed against her no longer mattered. This was her moment of clarity, and as she slipped away, she could feel God's embrace. She was going to meet her maker and to be with the loved ones she had lost. She had made the choice. This world no longer had anything here for her.

As her eyelids grew heavy, she saw her mother's smiling face and Mona's inviting grin, and she heard Skylar's innocent coos. She no longer feared death; she welcomed it. It was her only escape, an ugly end to a beautiful life. Too many things had led to the destruction of YaYa. She was tired of losing and having no control over her own life. Committing suicide, in an odd way, was self-empowering. If she was going to be taken out of the game, it was going to be on her own terms, in her own way.

Mekhi pulled up to YaYa's townhome and noticed that it was pitch black inside. Khi-P had been attracted to YaYa from the first day she set foot on Southern soil, and with Indie away, he knew that she needed a shoulder to cry on. He checked in with YaYa once a week, making sure she was straight and offering money if she needed it. She always declined. There wasn't another man in the world that could take care of her the way Indie had. Mekhi could sense her loyalty to Indie. Even now that he was locked up, she still carried herself as his lady, unyielding and unapologetic about her emotions toward him.

Mekhi could sense that YaYa was a thorough and loyal woman, so he respected her as such. He didn't mind checking in on her from time to time. It only gave him an excuse to visit the beautiful woman, and surprisingly, they had established somewhat of a friendship, or rather an understanding. She was swimming in the deep end right now, just trying to stay afloat, and he was her life jacket. He was trying to stand in for Indie as best he could, but YaYa's heart didn't want a substitute. She craved the real thing, the original, the authenticity of Indie Perkins.

Activating the alarm on his Cadillac Escalade ESV, he hopped out and proceeded to YaYa's door. He felt bad for YaYa. A chick like her deserved to be taken care of, protected. Somewhere along the line Indie had dropped the ball and allowed his lady to be accessible. She had been touched by the cruel hand of the streets, something that she should have never been exposed to in the first place. Now she was forced live without him. With Indie in prison, she had been demoted. YaYa was just another girlfriend to another hustler who had gotten penned up in the streets. With him, she was royalty; without him, she was typical.

As Mekhi rang her doorbell, he waited patiently for her to let him in. He frowned when he didn't get an answer. Her car was parked out front, so he knew that she was home. He peered up at the townhome and saw a small light flickering on the top floor. He reached for the door handle, and to his surprise, turned it with ease.

"Yo! YaYa! It's Khi-P. You home, ma?" he called as he walked slowly through the front door.

Receiving no response, he made his way toward the staircase, only to find that the hardwood floors were covered in water. It trickled down the stairs like a mini waterfall.

"YaYa!" he called with urgency, frowning while ascending the steps. He followed the wet path into her bedroom, knocking respectfully be-

The Prada Plan 2: Leah's Story 195

fore he entered. "Yo!" he shouted. "Yo, ma, your shit is all fucked up downstairs. There's water every—" He finally rounded the corner into the master bathroom and his words caught in his throat.

"YaYa!" he yelled as he rushed over to her and pulled her from the bloody, overflowing water. He turned off the faucet as he picked her up and carried her into the bedroom.

"YaYa! Ma, wake up for me. Wake up!" he shouted as he inspected her shredded wrists while simultaneously pulling out his cell phone. There was blood everywhere. It was oozing out of her freely and soaking into her crisp white bed linens. She wasn't breathing. He had no idea how long she had been bleeding.

Sympathy took over him as he shook his head from side to side. "What did you do, baby?" he asked her with his Southern drawl.

Dialing 911, he hoped that they could save her. Her body was so limp in his arms that he feared it may be too late. As he gave the address to the operator, he tried his hardest to dress her wounds. He didn't want to have to tell Indie that his girl had died right before his eyes.

As Khi-P fought for her life, he called her name repeatedly, hoping that she could hear his voice and would come to. They had taken enough L's from their camp. They couldn't afford to lose her too. She didn't deserve the hand that she had been dealt.

"You should have never come down South, ma. This ain't for you," he said, knowing that it was too late for her to hear him.

Little did he know her troubles started way before she came to Houston. Leah Richards was her predator, and she was lurking in the shadows, waiting, watching, enjoying every moment of chaos she was stirring up in Disaya's life.

When YaYa came to, the first face that she saw was Mekhi's, and tears came to her eyes. *What the fuck happened? Why am I still here? Where's my baby girl?*

I should be with her right now, she thought as she attempted to sit up in the hospital bed.

"Relax, YaYa. Lay back," Mekhi stated as he adjusted the covers around her body to make her more comfortable.

"You brought me here?" she asked, her voice raspy.

Mekhi nodded as he looked at her in concern. "I came by to check on you. Nobody's heard from you. I just wanted to make sure everything was all right. I see that things aren't," he said.

"I can't do this anymore, Khi. I don't have anything left. All I feel is pain . . . so much pain it's almost indescribable," YaYa whispered as she closed her eyes. "You should've just left me where you found me."

Her wrists felt like they had been put into a shredder, and her head throbbed from the stress of it all. Awaking from a suicide attempt was worse than dying from one. Now she had to face everyone she had tried to leave behind and hear the whispers while facing the inquisitions of why.

"Nah, ma, don't say that. Stop letting life beat you. You can get through this. You just need some time to get your head together," Mekhi said as he reached for her hand.

Her hospital door opened, and an Indian woman in a white doctor's coat entered the room. Behind her stood two male nurses.

"She's finally awake?" the doctor observed.

Khi-P nodded his head as he avoided YaYa's gaze.

"I've made room for her on our eleventh floor psych ward. We'll commit her there until we are sure she is fit to go home without risk."

"Khi-P, what is she talking about?" YaYa asked as she sat up. She attempted to get out of bed, but her body felt as if she had been hit by a Mack truck. The pain medication that she had been given had her drowsy, and she felt as if she weighed a thousand pounds.

The doctor never looked her way as she continued to speak. "This is not a long-term stay. Her release is fully dependent on herself. She is in control of her own freedom. When she proves that she will not bring harm to herself, then we will release her."

"Bitch, why are you talking to him? I'm right here. Speak to me!" YaYa yelled angrily.

She looked toward Khi-P for answers, but he couldn't bring himself to look her in the eyes. Having her institutionalized was not his decision, but the hospital could not simply ignore what she had done to herself. Her attempt to end her life was blatant. Unlike so many others who simply crave attention, YaYa had gone all out. She had cut her veins in half. If Mekhi hadn't shown up when he did, she would already be a distant memory.

Seeing no ally in Khi-P, she focused her rage and confusion back on the doctor. "You're not committing me! I'm not crazy!" she shouted.

The doctor simply turned toward the male nurses and nodded her head.

As she watched them approach her, she pleaded with Mekhi. "Khi! No! Don't let them do this to me!" she shouted as the two men rolled her hospital bed out of the room.

Mekhi lowered his face into his hands and closed his eyes while YaYa's screams of protest rang in his ears.

Chapter Fifteen

The padded walls closed in on YaYa as she thought about how her life had come to this. The cramped space of the eight-by-seven room was enough to send her over the edge.

She knew that one day the past would catch up to her. Her Prada Plan had backfired. Yes, it got her paid and even earned her the position of wifey, but it never gained her happiness. The one thing she was seeking was forever elusive.

Nothing about Disaya was insane. Grief-stricken, yes. Angry, yes. Tired, yes. But there was nothing crazy about her. No one understood her actions. Her therapist couldn't fathom the love she had for her daughter. Killing herself was an easy feat in order to be reunited with baby Sky. Her love as a mother ran that deep, but they punished her for it, keeping her locked away as if her mind had abandoned her. They pumped her with narcotics for depression and to put her to sleep, but all it did was numb the pain. Nothing short of the grave could take it away.

YaYa heard the locks being opened on her door and she looked up blankly. Her therapist walked in.

"You have a visitor today, Ms. Morgan. You told me that you have no living family, but your sister is here for you," the white man announced as he jotted notes in his notepad to record her reaction.

"I don't have a sister," she replied dryly. "There must be a mistake. She must be here for someone else."

"Well, why don't you go and see for yourself? This will be good for you."

Frowning, YaYa arose. The laceless slippers on her feet slapped the tiled floor as she walked down the hall. She figured that Mekhi had sent Trina or one of the other girls to check in on her. Nothing could have prepared her for the face that waited at her table.

She stopped mid-step when she saw Leah sitting smugly, legs crossed as if she were truly there with good intentions. She instantly flashed back to the hell that Leah had caused in New York. Images of Indie's beating appeared in her head, and her breath caught in her throat as she remembered how Leah had ruined her life. She had come through like a hurricane and blown YaYa's spot all the way up, leaving nothing but destruction in her wake.

What is she doing here? How did she—

All of the rage that YaYa had bubbled to the surface all at once, and YaYa charged at Leah.

"You fuckin' bitch!" YaYa yelled. Her outburst caused the guards to rush her as they restrained her arms. She bucked wildly against them. "Let me go! I just want to talk to her! I'm not going to do anything!"

"Calm down! You have to calm down!" one of the guards ordered.

"I'm fucking calm!" YaYa shouted back as she snatched away from them. She put her hands up and flipped her hair out of her face. "I'm calm."

YaYa walked over to the table slowly in an effort to look composed, but on the inside, she was boiling as she examined Leah's appearance. She had always been beautiful, but something about her was different, sickly. Her skin was an ashen green color, and a light sweat covered her face, making her skin appear waxy.

The baby bump that she sported couldn't be missed. The sight of her made YaYa yearn for her daughter. Jealousy filled her because Leah didn't deserve a baby, not after all of the horrible things that she had done. YaYa knew that she was a far cry from the glamorous hot girl she once was. Insecurity filled her as she began to fidget with her hospital clothes.

She knew that Leah was there for a reason. YaYa knew how the bitch ticked. Every move Leah made was a prelude to a future set-up.

She didn't come all this way for nothing, YaYa thought, but what she didn't know was that Leah had been there all along.

Leah sat with her arms folded as YaYa took the seat across from her. The arrogant smirk on Leah's face infuriated YaYa. She was so smug, so confident, as if she held a secret that no one else knew.

"How did you find me?" YaYa asked.

"Ha!" Leah scoffed. "You are giving me too much credit, YaYa. I didn't find you, honey. You found me. I've been in Houston for quite some time now." Leah pulled a manila folder out of her Hermès bag and slid them across the table for YaYa to see.

She continued to talk as YaYa began to flip through the contents. "You see, I told you I was going to take everything you ever loved, and that includes the men in your life, YaYa."

"Bitch, Indie is locked up. You can't get your claws into him now. He's not getting out anytime soon, so your little plan is all fucked up," YaYa spat.

"What makes you think I'm talking about Indie?" Leah asked.

YaYa frowned. "I don't have time for mind games."

"Besides, Indie was easy. I already got to him," Leah said as she touched her bulging stomach. The fake belly bump that she sported served its purpose well. It was convincing, and the look on YaYa's face was priceless.

"I'm about to have his baby. What happened to your daughter is a shame, YaYa. Our kids would have been siblings." Her every word was crushing YaYa syllable by syllable. "When I said I would take everything from you, nothing was off limits . . . nothing or no one."

As if a light bulb had gone off in her head, YaYa's eyes grew wide. *This bitch has been down here all along. She's behind it all. She took my baby. She hurt my baby!*

"You bitch!" she shouted as she completely spazzed, standing up and tossing her chair directly at Leah. "What did you do to my daughter?" she screamed hysterically as she reached across the table for Leah. The guards were already on alert and restrained her before she could attack Leah.

Leah smiled deviously as she stood to her feet. "Checkmate," she said, waving at YaYa as the guards pulled her from the room.

"I'm going to kill you! What did you do to my baby? What did you do? Leah, please! Aghh! You dirty bitch!" Her shrill cries bounced off the walls as they pulled YaYa down the hall and out of sight.

As YaYa's shrink came rushing into the room, Leah's glare was replaced by an innocent look of concern.

"What happened? Your visit was supposed to help. What did you say to her?" the therapist asked.

"Nothing at all. She just erupted. My sister is sick. This is exactly where she needs to be," Leah said. She turned and walked out of the hospital, satisfied.

As soon as she made it to her car, the contents of her stomach came up. She was growing more and more ill by the day. The pain in her womb was so unbearable that even walking hurt, but she was determined to finish this, even if it meant self-destruction as well.

She removed the strap-on belly as soon as she got into the car, but it wasn't long before the crying resumed.

Waaa! Waaa!

Leah covered her ears and tried to breathe, but the sounds wouldn't go away. She pulled away from the mental hospital and turned up her radio, but her efforts were futile. Nothing could silence the screams of the innocent. Every cry caused her pain to multiply, and she gripped her stomach in agony.

The cry turned into nerve-shattering wails, causing her to lose it. She pulled over on the side of the road and stumbled out of the car. She couldn't take it anymore. What had started out as a planned kidnapping had quickly gotten out of hand. It was becoming too much for her to handle, and Leah couldn't take it anymore. She walked to the back of her car and popped the trunk. There sat baby Skylar, crying her heart out. "Shut up! Shut . . . the fuck . . . up!" Leah shouted, causing the cries to grow louder.

Leah started to just slam the trunk closed, but something stopped her. As she looked down at Skylar, she wished that she really had gotten rid of her. Killing her own baby had been a selfish mistake, an accident. It was her body's reaction to uncontrollable and irresponsible cocaine use. When it came time to get rid of Sky, she couldn't bring herself to do it. Murdering a child who had already been born into the world took more malice than even Leah possessed. She was waiting to build the moxie to do it, to harm the infant, but the longer she kept her and the more she cried, Leah began to realize that she didn't have it in her. If she wasn't going to kill her, there was only one other alternative. She had absolutely no intentions of giving YaYa her daughter back.

For the first time since taking her, Leah looked at her, she really looked at her, and saw what a beautiful little girl Skylar actually was. The crying pierced through her cold exterior and resonated with the neglected and abused child that still lived inside.

Leah picked Skylar up out of the trunk and held her up in front of her face. Tears began to flood involuntarily from her eyes as she felt her insides warming. The cold layer of ice that surrounded her heart was slowing melting away as she fell in love with baby Sky. As she looked at the infant, she connected with her. She realized that the baby needed her. She couldn't eat unless Leah fed her; she couldn't survive unless Leah allowed her. Everything in Skylar's world depended on Leah. It was the purest relationship that Leah had ever had, and she loved it—loved the control.

Her face transformed from one of irritation to one of satisfaction. The only reason she even wanted Skylar was because YaYa did too. She always wanted what didn't belong to her, and baby Sky was no exception. Leah was nuts in every sense of the word. If she couldn't be with YaYa, then she wanted to be just like her. She was determined to strip YaYa of everything.

Skylar's cries diminished as Leah rocked her back and forth. She had been hiding the baby in hotel rooms, closets, and the trunk of her car, but now she felt like she had approached things all wrong. Skylar was innocent, like Leah used to be. They belonged together.

"It's okay. Shh . . . it's okay. I'm not going to ever let anyone hurt you. They won't hurt you the way that they hurt me, and they'll never tear us apart. You're such a pretty girl, Skylar. Daddy only likes the pretty girls. He would have liked you. He would have wanted you."

On the outside, Leah looked like a gorgeous, fully functioning young woman, but on the inside, she was unstable. Her mental state had many shortcomings as a direct result of her childhood.

"Daddy only likes the pretty girls," she repeated, mimicking the teachings of her own mother.

Her eyes held a far-away gaze as she rocked Skylar in her arms. It was then that she concluded that Skylar belonged with her. YaYa had always been selfish and didn't deserve to be a mother.

"I'm going to take good care of you, Skylar. You have a new mommy now."

When YaYa came to, she was drowsy from the sleep-inducing narcotic that the nurses had forced into her arm.

"Hmm," she moaned as she turned her head to the side. When she tried to move, she realized that one of her hands was restrained on the bed railing. They thought she was crazy. Everyone thought she had lost it, but she knew the truth.

When she turned her head, she noticed the manila envelope sitting on the nightstand beside her bed. It was just out of her reach, and she stretched her free arm with all her might until she grabbed it. Her stomach sank when she flipped through the contents. Inside were pictures of Leah with Indie. *My Indie . . . my man,* she thought as jealousy, rage, and resentment filled her. There were photos of them living the good life together. Indie had indeed wifed her when he moved to Houston. He had unknowingly kept time with the same woman who had torn him and YaYa apart.

When YaYa got to the sonogram photo, she dropped the folder as if it were hot to the touch. A vacuum had sucked all of the air out of her lungs. She knew that Indie had gotten involved with someone else after he deserted her in New

York, but for it to be Leah was a slap in the face. Logic told her that he didn't know who he had gotten involved with, but emotion told her that she didn't care.

Resentment and animosity consumed her as she thought of the intimate moments that Leah and Indie had shared. Leah now knew things about her man that YaYa felt only she should know. She knew how Indie liked to whisper sweet nothings in a woman's ear while they fucked; she knew how thick he was, how long he was; she knew that the first thing Indie ate in the morning was always his woman. Quiet as it was kept, Leah just knew too fucking much, and YaYa hated her for it.

YaYa was crushed because these secrets were supposed to be hers, and now Indie had shared them with someone else—with Leah. She didn't know why Leah had such a personal vendetta against her, but YaYa was tired of being the victim. Everywhere YaYa was, Leah wanted to be. Everyone she loved, Leah wanted for herself.

The bitch is in love with me or something, she thought. Their relationship had turned hostile long ago, and YaYa was tired of running. She was sick of being the one waving white surrender flags. Last time they had beefed over sex, money, and men, Leah had won that battle, but this time, YaYa was fighting over her daughter, her flesh and blood. It was a war that she intended to win. She refused to concede defeat this time.

There were no limits when it came to what a mother would do on behalf of her child, and murder was on YaYa's mind. An eye for an eye seemed like the only justice. There was no more forgiveness in YaYa's heart. Leah would pay for the things she had done.

The head nurse came into the room wheeling the medicine cart. Usually YaYa looked forward to the prescription sleeping pill and the dose of Valium, but tonight she was on some brand new shit. That depressed look didn't fit her. Now that she thought about it, she was upset with herself for becoming that girl—that woe-is-me drama queen. Yeah, her life was fucked five ways from Sunday, but she was in control of her own destiny. Leah had played the notes, but that didn't mean that YaYa had to dance to her tune.

"Open up," the nurse said.

YaYa opened her mouth and the nurse placed the two pills on her tongue and then handed YaYa a small paper cup filled with water. "Let's see it," the nurse instructed. YaYa opened her mouth and held out her tongue to prove that the pills were gone, and then watched as the old woman wheeled the cart to the next room. When the coast was clear, she spit the pills out of her mouth. Her gag reflex was too good to ever swallow anything she didn't want to. She rolled the pills up in a piece of toilet tissue and stored them beneath her mattress. YaYa had given up when she had lost her daughter. She had let the misery take her mind and spirit away, but now that she knew who was responsible for her daughter's misfortunes, she was motivated by revenge.

The bitch thinks this shit is a wrap. She got me all the way fucked up, YaYa thought.

"It's far from over." It was a threat that had been made once before, but this time she meant it. There was nothing that could stop her from following through. It wasn't over until YaYa ended it, and for her, the beef was just beginning to simmer.

Chapter Sixteen

YaYa was on her best behavior from that moment forward. Instead of slipping into a deeper depression, she was rebounding from it. She opened up to her therapist and told the woman everything she wanted to hear. She was antsy, and would have said anything to get out of the hospital.

Her mind was no longer clouded with pain. It was fueled by anger. She was about to get back at those who had ruined her life, and even though she loved him, it was time for Indie to be cut out of her heart. She couldn't get past the dealings he had with Leah. She couldn't fault him because she had never disclosed Leah's identity to him, but she couldn't erase the images of them together. It was unforgettable.

The late night therapy sessions with her doctor were her way out. The dedicated woman always made sure to be accessible to her patients twenty-four hours a day, and YaYa knew that this routine would work to her advantage. It was the only time when the security staff wasn't on guard, and only one nurse monitored the floor. All YaYa needed was the doctor's ID badge to unlock the secured doors and she would be home free.

She waited for days until the right moment presented itself for her to make her escape. As she sat in front of the therapist, all she could think of was riding off into the night and never looking back.

"Disaya, I see you've been doing your journal writing," the doctor said. "Does that outlet help you to deal with your daughter's death?"

YaYa looked at Dr. Samuels and responded, "Yes, it helps a lot. I have somewhere to put my emotions now. I can let them be free in my journal without anyone judging me." She was giving the good doctor a whole bowl of nothing. Her generic, cookie-cutter answers were right up the doctor's alley. YaYa only wrote in the journal to show that she was making progress. The sooner that she could convince the hospital that she was no longer a danger to herself, the sooner they would release her. She had no intentions of killing herself anymore. There was only one person who she posed a threat to.

YaYa talked about everything that she could think of, and Dr. Samuels was amazed at her sudden willingness to talk about her life. YaYa was candid in her descriptions of her childhood, leaving out nothing. Her story was one for the street fiction books, and the little old black lady could not fathom it. She was enthralled in it all as she jotted down notes, scribbling her thoughts and anecdotes for YaYa.

YaYa ran her mouth until the 11 P.M. shift change occurred. It was then that she knew she could slip out unnoticed.

"I wish I had opened up to you sooner, Dr. Samuels. I feel like I'm ten pounds lighter, getting all of this off my chest. I have so much more to say," she said. "I don't want you to get tired of me, though."

"As long as you'd like to talk, I'd like to listen, Disaya," the doctor replied.

"Can I have some coffee first?" YaYa asked innocently.

Dr. Samuels was so thrilled with her patient's new forthcoming attitude that she stood up to retrieve the coffee herself. When she returned, she set a cup in front of YaYa and one in front of herself.

YaYa smiled as she held the tissue square that had twelve Valium pills crushed inside. She had crushed them up so fine that it resembled blow. All she had to do was slip it into the doctor's drink. All it took was a phone call to distract the old woman.

"I'm going to step outside and take this call. I will be back shortly, Disaya," Dr. Samuels said.

As soon as the door clicked shut, YaYa emptied the contents into the Styrofoam cup. She quickly mixed it with her finger and sat back in her seat.

After the doctor came back, YaYa anxiously watched the minutes tick by. Time moved excruciatingly slow, almost as if it were standing still.

They should be working by now, she thought as she tapped her foot impatiently. *I'm running out of stories to tell.*

As the clock struck eleven, YaYa began to notice the drowsy side effects of the drug. In mid-sentence, Dr. Samuels dozed off and leaned into her desk as a drug-induced sleep took over.

YaYa stood and sprang into action, first grabbing her ID badge and then searching for her car keys. "Got 'em," she whispered when she saw the Lexus keychain.

She peered cautiously out of the office door and saw the nurse manning her station. She walked over to the nurse and smiled. "Hi. Dr. Samuels told me to ask if you could brew us a fresh pot of coffee. Our session is running kind of long, but we are making good progress," YaYa said, selling the lie with expertise.

The nurse sighed and mumbled complaints beneath her breath as she got up and walked down the hall to complete the task. YaYa walked as quickly as possible toward the exit. Everything in her wanted to run, but she knew that she had to keep a low profile.

She used the doctor's hospital barcode to unlock the security door and then took the elevator to the lobby of the hospital. It was Saturday night, so the hospital was more crowded than usual. All of the gunshot victims from the local clubs were in the ER, and YaYa blended in as she made her way outside.

The fresh air felt so good on her skin. She inhaled deeply, loving the smell of anything other than the sanitary scent inside the hospital. YaYa didn't know which car belonged to Dr. Samuels. There were too many foreign cars in the lot to pick one out of the crowd. She ran around the employee lot hitting the alarm button.

"Come on . . . come on. I don't have time for this shit," she muttered as she kept hitting the unlock button on Dr. Samuels' alarm. Finally she heard the noise she wanted to hear.

Beep! Beep!

The headlights to the doctor's navy Lex flashed on and off. YaYa quickly hopped inside and sped out of the lot. By the time anyone noticed she was gone, the car would be ditched and she would be on the other side of town.

YaYa drove twenty miles away from the hospital before ditching it on the side of a dark road. She walked to a gas station on the corner and collect-called Khi-P, but received no answer. She knew that he would help her. She didn't have any money or anywhere else to go.

Her nerves were shot as she stood in front of the station. She knew she looked hot. She was still wearing the hospital gown and paper shoes that were issued to her. She had to get out of sight before someone called the police on her.

She wanted to catch a cab, but she knew that none would stop for her with the way that she looked, so she began the long hike to Mekhi's side of town.

Hours later, she sat in the rain. The Southern heat mixed with the crying sky made it feel as if she were sitting inside a sauna. Khi-P wasn't home, and she had waited for hours on his front porch, hoping that he would arrive soon.

She wrapped her arms around her body as the thin fabric of the wet gown clung to her. As the time crept slowly by, she grew impatient. She went to the street and looked both ways as she silently urged Khi-P to come home. When she didn't see his car, she decided enough was enough.

She walked around to the back of his house, determined to get out of the rain. YaYa looked to make sure no nosy neighbors were watching, and she broke the glass to his back door with her elbow. She reached in and unlocked the door before stepping inside.

It was two o'clock in the morning. Making herself comfortable in his living room, she dozed off as her impatience turned to exhaustion.

It wasn't until YaYa heard the moans of passion coming from upstairs that she awoke from her slumber. She looked around and noticed that Mekhi's keys were strewn across the dining table. She didn't want to interrupt his fuck fest. She was sure that he was smashing one of his many groupie broads, and YaYa wasn't trying to block.

The sounds drew her toward his bedroom like a magnet as she crept down the hall, the plush carpet sinking under the weight of her body. His bedroom door was open, and YaYa froze in amazement when she saw him. His naked body was beautiful, and her breath caught in her throat as she admired his toned back. His muscular buttocks contracted as he dipped in and out of the set of legs that were wrapped about his waist. He was putting his thing down, and as he grinded in and out, slowly working over his prey, the special box between her legs grew wet with jealousy. Her clit throbbed as she spied on the sex scene. Her mind told her to give them privacy, but her treasure chest overflowed with wetness and urged her to stay.

The satisfied moans of the girl beneath him only proved what she suspected—Khi-P's fuck game was out of this world. It had been so long. She had been wrapped up in all of the chaos that corrupted her life. She needed to release. An orgasm was just what was needed, and as her hands developed a mind of their own, she didn't protest. She rolled her nipple in one hand and found her clit with the other.

She was so slick that her fingers slid effortlessly as she fondled herself. Her love button grew more stiff with each stroke she gave it, mashing it as she clenched her thighs together, rubbing it gently, twisting it slightly. She closed her eyes and imagined that it was Indie working her over that way, and when she opened her eyes, she noticed that they were about to change positions.

She was almost ready to explode, but if she stood there a minute longer, Khi-P would surely bust her. She ducked to the side of the door frame before she was caught, and breathed deeply as she pulled her hand from her panties. She was slightly annoyed that she didn't get hers, and decided that they wouldn't get theirs either.

She boldly knocked on the bedroom door, startling Mekhi and his guest.

"Shit!" Khi-P shouted as he withdrew from the young lady. "YaYa? What the fuck are you doing here?" he asked in confusion as he scrambled out of the bed.

YaYa's eyes dropped to his manhood, surprised by its size. Chocolate, thick, and long, he looked good enough to eat—like her favorite candy bar. The freak in his bed was on all fours and didn't even make an effort to move. She lifted her head, rolled her eyes at YaYa, and moaned, "Put it back in, Daddy."

YaYa crossed her arms and cocked a hip. "Get rid of the bitch, Khi . . . like yesterday."

"Bitch? I got your—"

Khi-P shook his head and threw the girl's clothes at her face to shut her up. "Nah, baby girl. You don't want to do that," he said, referring to disrespecting YaYa. "You barking up the wrong tree. Get your shit. I'll put you in a cab."

"A cab?" The young lady frowned.

"Yeah, bitch, a cab," YaYa shot back, sounding a little bit too pissed considering that the dick in the room didn't belong to her.

The girl looked at Khi-P, but he already had the cab fare held out for her.

"Fuck you. Dick wasn't all that anyway!" she shouted as she threw on her clothes and stormed out.

Liar, YaYa thought. She couldn't help but to crack a smile.

"You foul, ma. You could have let a nigga get his shit off first," Khi-P said as he smiled back. He took his time wrapping a towel around his waist. "What are you even doing here anyway? How you get out?" Before she could even answer, he held up his hand and said, "Let me get this bitch's stink off of me."

Mekhi was still brick, and his dick imprint was showing through the fabric of the towel. YaYa forced herself to look away as he walked into his adjoining master bath. She heard him turn on the shower.

"Now, how did you get out?" he yelled.

YaYa walked to the bed and sat on the edge then responded, "I put Valium in my doctor's coffee and bounced as soon as her head hit the desk."

Mekhi let out a hearty laugh as he washed his body. YaYa walked toward the bathroom door and peered inside. His shower door was made of crushed glass, so she didn't have a clear view of him, but she watched his blurry form as he scrubbed his back and arms, then washed his long pole. She held her breath as he began to stroke his penis, trying to relieve himself of his hard-on. His rhythm was slow but powerful. She watched his head fall back on his shoulders. She heard a low grunt, and she creamed in her panties right there on the spot. She tiptoed back to his bed just as he turned off his shower.

"What happened, ma? You wouldn't be here unless something was up," Mekhi said.

Remembering why she had come, she said, "I know who killed Sky."

"What? Who?" he asked.

"There's this bitch named Leah—"

Khi-P sighed when he heard the name. He knew of Indie's relationship with Leah and assumed that YaYa was bugging from jealousy. "It's his baby's ma, YaYa. No more, no less. She don't mean what you mean to him," he tried to explain.

"I know what you're thinking, Mekhi, but just listen to me, please. I'm not crazy. Leah isn't who you think she is. We were into some foul shit together back in New York. She followed Indie here. The only reason she even fucked with Indie was to get to me," she explained.

"You're not making sense, YaYa. Why would she take Skylar? I've met the bitch. She don't seem crazy, just a regular broad," Khi-P reasoned.

"The same reason she had for killing Indie's brother, and the same reason she had for coming to visit me in the hospital," YaYa said. "She lives to fuck up my world, but I'm tired of it. I'm tired of running, and I'm tired of her winning."

"She came to see you?" he asked.

YaYa nodded. "And the bitch was talking real slick, too, about my daughter. She took her, Mekhi. She took her away from me."

"Have you spoken to Indie about it?" Khi-P asked.

"I don't even want to speak to him. He should have never gotten any girl pregnant down here. But just the fact that it's her makes me hate him," she whispered. "I need your help, Khi. Everybody else thinks I'm crazy."

Khi-P looked at her sincerely. "What you need from me, ma? Just tell me what you want to do."

"I want to dead this bitch," she answered.

His eyebrows rose in concern. He knew what it took to take a life. "Are you sure you wanna handle it this way?"

YaYa nodded as she thought of her little girl. "She's taken too much from me for it to be handled any other way."

Shocked that YaYa could even be so ruthless, Khi-P didn't respond. If that was what she wanted, he was more than capable of making it happen. Now that Indie was locked up, Khi-P was the next in line to be crowned king. He had a crazy good squad behind him.

"Let's discuss this tomorrow. Maybe some sleep will get your mind right. If you're still on this rah-rah shit in the morning, then we'll talk," Khi-P said. "Take a fresh bath and relax. Things have been rough for you. Just rest your mental, ma. You're welcome to whatever is in my home."

"I don't have anything or anywhere to go. I went for broke trying to get Sky back, and now I have nothing," she whispered as she shook her head.

"You're a hustler's wife, YaYa. Indie looked out for enough people for his peoples to look out for you now that he's down. I got you, ma. We'll go grab you some clothes tomorrow, and you can stay here until you get on your feet."

Chapter Seventeen

The next morning when YaYa awoke, she sat up in complete shock. She was lying in Mekhi's guestroom in a plush king bed, surrounded by hundred dollar bills. She had seen money before and had been showered with it before, but this over the top display of wealth was too much even for her.

She got out of bed, and her mouth fell in an O of surprise when she felt the bills beneath her feet. It was all over the floor as well, and a trail of bills was littered out into the hallway. She followed the money all the way down into the kitchen, where breakfast was waiting.

"Khi-P!" she shouted in confusion. When she got no response, she went looking for him, searching high and low through the plush home. She didn't know what all of this was about, but it was flattering nonetheless. She finally found her way back to the kitchen and sat down to eat when the phone rang. She hesitated when she reached for the phone. YaYa wasn't trying to blow up Khi-P's spot, but the caller ID said unknown, and she figured it could be him calling.

"Hello?" she answered. "YaYa?" As soon as he heard her voice, the picture of Khi-P and Disaya flashed before Indie's eyes. A sudden rage filled him as he gripped the phone tightly. "YaYa!" he called out again, this time with more authority. He didn't know all of the details of what had occurred between the two of them, and he didn't want to know. All he knew was that if it happened again, he was going to see Khi-P. He had chalked the first indiscretion up to YaYa's vulnerability, but the next time he wouldn't be as passive.

YaYa's hands began to tremble and she almost dropped the phone when she heard his voice. The familiarity of Indie's tone softened her for a brief second. She closed her eyes and exhaled deeply, not knowing what to say to him. Everything in her wanted to confront him, but she couldn't. Instead, she hung up the phone without responding.

Why did I even answer the phone? she thought, cursing herself. She knew that Indie had recognized her voice when the phone rang right back. Indie had a personal cell phone in jail, so he didn't have to go through the jail operators. He had heard her loud and clear, and she couldn't help but to feel guilty, as if she had to explain.

Khi-P walked through the front door and stopped when he saw her holding his cordless phone. The worried look on her face gave her away.

"Indie called?" he asked.

YaYa nodded as tears came to her eyes. When the phone blared loudly in her hand, she was so nervous that she dropped it. Mekhi bent down calmly and retrieved the phone.

"Please don't answer it. I don't want to talk to him," YaYa pleaded.

Khi-P could tell that Indie had a hold over YaYa. She was already trained for a hustler.

"He heard my voice. What is he going to think?"

Mekhi put his finger to his lips to signal for her to be silent, and then he answered. "Indie, my nigga," he stated.

"Put YaYa on the phone," he said, slightly vexed. Mekhi could hear the anger through the phone.

"She's real upset, fam. She not really up to talking right now," Khi-P responded as YaYa looked on with wide eyes, biting her nails anxiously.

"What? You speaking for my bitch now?" Indie asked. "Fuck is she doing at your crib anyway? I heard you been real involved with what's mine." Indie was slightly out of character as he raised his voice, something he rarely ever did.

"Family, calm down. It's not like that. She ran away from the hospital this morning," Khi-P said, changing up the facts a little bit. "She didn't have no paper, no clothes, no nothing, fam. She out here on E."

Hearing that YaYa was down bad filled Indie with guilt. He hadn't set her up for the inevitable. He had known that eventually he would have to leave her. It was every hustler's fate, and he should have put some cash up for her just in case. Everything from the cars to the roof that she slept under had been in his name. The temper that had threatened to explode instantly went away once he realized she had nowhere else to go.

"You right, fam. You take care of my baby girl. You know I'm good for it, baby. Just make sure she don't want for anything," Indie stated. "Put her on the phone. I can't believe she don't want to talk to me. What's wrong with her, fam? A nigga need to hear her voice in here, nah mean? I thought I could do this bid without her, but I can't, fam."

Mekhi didn't even offer YaYa the line before he responded, "She's exhausted, duke. She walked damn near across town to get here, and she's out of it from all of the drugs and bullshit they pumped into her system. The next time you call she'll feel better. She's not really talking to anybody. She's just here . . . kind of a blank canvas."

What Mekhi was saying was partially true, but he was laying it on extra thick.

"Take care of her for me. Put her up in a nice spot. I'll figure out how to get some paper to you," Indie said.

"Don't worry about it, fam. The money is nothing," he replied. "I'll handle it."

Indie wanted to take Khi-P's words as truth, but the picture that he had seen with his own eyes contradicted what his ears were hearing. He was in a tough position. Khi-P was the only person he could ask to watch over YaYa in Houston. He would never put the burden on Chase because he knew of his family situation. Chase was taking care of a drug-addicted mother and keeping a watchful eye over Trina and the girls. Adding YaYa to his plate would be unfair, and it wasn't his responsibility. Mekhi was the only other option. Indie only hoped that YaYa would hold him down.

"Mekhi . . ." Indie stated, his tone serious. "Respect me, duke. You slipped up once before. I know everything, my nigga. Don't let it happen again."

Mekhi knew a friendly threat when he heard one. He had no response for Indie, partly because he didn't know what to say.

Indie didn't need Khi-P to speak to know that he heard him. He left Mekhi with a dial tone in his ear.

Indie's jaw tightened when he hung up the phone on Khi-P. Hearing YaYa answer Khi-P's phone had him vexed. His imagination ran wild as he thought of his lady being with another man. Although he had told himself that he was done with her, he was still possessive of her. She would always be his. Even when he hated her, he couldn't help but love her.

He wanted to tell himself that his team would remain loyal while he was locked down. He kept telling himself, *not YaYa*. She wouldn't do that to him, not his lady, but the reality of the situation was that it could happen. It happened every day. Time stood still for no one, and a prison sentence made the inmate irrelevant.

Indie was far from stupid. There wasn't a nigga in the world that could give him the okeydoke. Something was going on underneath his nose. Just because he was locked down didn't mean he was out of the loop.

Just as quickly as he hung up the phone, he picked it back up to dial Chase. He didn't need to be on the outside to see what was going on. He had eyes everywhere, and his intuition told him that the situation with Khi-P needed looking into.

When Mekhi hung up the phone, he turned to see YaYa waiting for answers. He could practically smell her loyalty to Indie. A slight twinge of envy filled him. YaYa was the perfect specimen of a woman. He had his work cut out for him if he wanted to snatch her.

"What did he say?" she asked, her voice shaky.

"Don't worry about it, YaYa. His head ain't right in there. He's on some other shit. Give him time to cool down," he said as he walked into the kitchen.

"What did he say, Mekhi? Tell me!" she said as she followed behind him, desperate for answers.

"He didn't really say shit about you, ma," Mekhi said, knowing that his indirect answers were killing YaYa.

"Mekhi!"

"He said he didn't give a fuck about you. He was just calling to ask me to go check on Leah and to make sure that she and his baby are well taken care of," Mekhi stated.

YaYa's face fell, and her stomach dropped into her knees. She didn't have a response for that. It was official. She was done. If she hadn't been sure about it before, she most definitely was now. In an attempt to save face, she turned away from Khi-P so that he wouldn't see the fresh emotion in her eyes.

He hated to see her hurting, but he had to break her down in order to build her back up. She was molded for Indie, and he wanted her molded for him. This was what it would take, and although he never wanted to see her cry, it was necessary.

He stepped up behind her and wrapped his arms around her body playfully as he lifted her from the floor.

"Stop, Khi!" she shouted, but then laughed hesitantly.

"Stop crying then. We don't have time for all that. We've got some shopping to do, ma. You ain't see all the paper I left for you? I don't just do this for anybody. I went all out, ma," he said with a smirk and a charming wink.

"What is all of this about?" she asked as she motioned to the money she had awoken to.

"I don't do the rose petal thing, so I did money, scattered it everywhere, and it's all for you. There's fifty stacks for you to get fresh with. Buy yourself a new wardrobe," he offered.

She shook her head. "Mekhi, clothes are the last of my worries right now. I need a house and a car. I have to find the bitch that killed my baby. I have to—"

"Relax," Khi-P interrupted. "That's all you have to do. You can put everything else in my hands. I'm not Indie. I won't drop the ball."

YaYa looked skeptically at Mekhi.

"Trust me."

YaYa nodded, feeling as if she had no choice but to put her life in his hands. Houston was his neck of the woods. Without Indie, there was no one better to trust than Khi-P. He was the next best thing.

Khi-P escorted YaYa to the suburbs to shop, and it was like a relapse for her. She far exceeded the $50,000 that he had originally given her. As she passed through the designer shops, she blocked out everything and purchased all that was in sight, until her heart was content.

Khi-P spared no expense either. He went all out. He had something to prove. When he was done with YaYa, he wanted Indie to be a distant memory, a regret of the past, so he overcompensated just to please her. He enjoyed the attention that she got as her 7 For All Mankind jeans mesmerized both female and males alike. She was almost regal, ripping through the mall as if it were a runway. The Prada glasses she wore covered her sad, red eyes, and the Chanel bag made every girl in the shopping center green with envy.

On the outside, she looked so well put together, but on the inside, she was in turmoil.

As the day wrapped up and they were headed to the car, YaYa had spent well into the six figures. What she didn't know was that she was spending Indie's money. She had practically given Khi-P Indie's bricks. She had put him on, so the shopping spree was nothing to him. He held open her door for her, and she sat down in his brand new Lamborghini. When he entered the car, he looked over at her.

"So, how about it, ma?" he asked.

She knew what he was asking of her. He wanted to be her man. What he was doing was nothing new. She couldn't be bought. YaYa wasn't for sale.

"I'm too empty to start anything with anyone, Khi. My situation with Indie is still too sloppy. The only thing I can offer you right now is my friendship. Wherever it goes from there is up to fate," she said.

Chapter Eighteen

Club Aura was packed to its 2500-person capacity as YaYa tried to squeeze through the crowd. There was no denying that Khi-P was the man. He was Houston's king, and flashy was an understatement. The world was his for the taking. He wanted everyone to know that he was sitting on top of the throne. The kingdom had been overthrown, and there was new management in town. No one knew exactly how Khi-P had gotten so large, but the boy was grand, and he was shitting on everyone with his status.

He had practically bought out the entire city. Young hustlers who were hesitant about switching teams were enticed with diamond tokens of Khi-P's appreciation. Once he showed that there was money to be made, greed overrode loyalty. Khi-P had every get-money cat in Houston dealing with him, and every hoodrat in town trying to be down, but he had his sights set on one chick and one chick only—YaYa.

It wasn't just her stunning looks that attracted him. It was YaYa's previous association that was alluring to him. Everybody knew her as Indie's. Khi-P wanted to take her. He wanted to give her a new title.

YaYa turned heads as she walked through the crowd. With the jewels that adorned her wrists, neck, and ears, she was blinding. Everything about her shined.

She was a queen. Whether she had a king or not, her crown couldn't be taken away. Every man in the room wanted a piece of her.

She walked up to VIP and saw Khi-P sitting back amongst his peers as they popped bottles. Chase, always on point, enjoyed his glass of cognac, but didn't indulge in the theatrics. He sat back calmly in the booth, palming his drink with one hand while his other rested on his hip. He was never separated from his strap, and YaYa had to smile because she saw Indie's demeanor all up and through the young boy. It was so obvious that Chase was Indie's protégé. He had him down to a science.

She walked up to Khi-P, who stood and grabbed her hand as he made room for her in the booth. They weren't officially "together," but they were definitely more than friendly. Khi-P was taking claims, and no other hustler dared step to her.

He was doing a lot of flirting and showing a lot of public displays of affection.

It didn't go unnoticed by Chase, either. Two months had passed since Indie had asked him to gauge the situation, and he was beginning to see things he did not like. He knew that YaYa was staying with Khi-P and that things between her and Indie were rocky, but Khi was supposed to be loyal. He was supposed to hold Indie down.

Look like Duke is getting too comfortable with Indie's bitch, Chase thought as he took a sip from his drink.

Although Chase was getting mad money with Khi-P, he had a bad feeling that it was dirty money. Khi-P had come into a lot of product lately, and unbeknownst to Chase, it was Indie's. He was suspicious of Khi-P's sudden rise to power, and even more irritated by his overzealous affections toward his homie's girl.

Chase wondered if YaYa was just naïve, or if she was simply foul. Their relationship crossed a line, and if things progressed, Chase would have no choice but to pull Indie's coat tails.

Shits is just disrespectful, Chase thought as he shook his head.

Khi-P was the new captain, but Chase couldn't be his lieutenant if he thought that there was foul play. If Mekhi was a bad seed, he would contaminate the game, and Chase wasn't having it. Dishonor was a trait that he despised, and any nigga that was around him had to be thorough. Things had run too smoothly under Indie's watch, and Indie had been too good to him for Chase to let something like this go unnoticed.

Before Indie had taken him under his wing, Chase had been a flunky, an underappreciated young man who was in need of a come-up. Now he was sitting on a safe full of money and more respect than any of the young men who used to punk him before. Now he was the gatekeeper, and he helped to determine who got money and who didn't. Coincidentally, everyone who used to give him a hard time was either dead or locked outside the gate. There was no way he would let old adversaries board his cocaine train.

As he looked around at the plush nightclub, everyone was having a good time. There was only one person missing. The man who had started it all, Indie, was locked behind bars, but no one seemed to notice his absence, not even YaYa. Liquor flowed freely, and the celebration was live, as if he were sitting there amongst the crowd too.

Fucked up. The game don't love nobody. Chew ya up and spit ya out, he thought, realizing that this was not a forever profession. He had to get the dough and get out.

He noticed YaYa sitting by the bar, and he made his way across the room to her.

She smiled when he neared her.

"All eyes are on you, ma," he said as he kissed her left cheek.

YaYa graciously nodded as she replied, "There's not much to look at. I'm just out trying to get my mind off of things."

The eight weeks that had passed hadn't healed any of her scars. Chase could see the sadness in her eyes.

"You been good?" he asked. "Indie has been asking about you. I'm going up to see him next week. You should make that trip with me. I know he'd want to see you."

YaYa shifted from foot to foot uncomfortably. "Can we just change the subject?" she asked. "I'm not trying to see him. We don't have much to say to one another."

"He has a lot to say, YaYa. You might want to find the time to listen and watch the way you move. The way that you and Khi-P acting might get people thinking the wrong thing," Chase said.

YaYa looked across the room and noticed Khi-P watching her. He lifted his glass of Dom to acknowledge them.

"It doesn't matter what people think, Chase. It is what it is," she replied. "I'm not looking back to Indie. I can't even begin to explain how that man hurt me."

Chase watched her walk away and knew that he had the burden of being the bearer of bad news. Indie had to know what was going on. YaYa was vulnerable. Her entire life had changed in the blink of an eye, so Chase couldn't fault her. Any type of affection was enticing to YaYa after what she had been through, but Khi-P knew better. There was no excusing his actions. There was nothing worse than disloyalty. If Khi-P was bold enough to court YaYa, he had no code. There would be no limit to what he would do. If he was willing to sleep with his man's chick, then he would be willing to turn snitch if and when the time ever came.

As Chase watched Khi-P wrap his arm around YaYa's shoulder, he gritted his teeth. He would definitely be making the drive to see Indie. As he gripped his waistline, he felt the burner that he had concealed on his hip. He was about his gunplay, and he wasn't above laying his murder game down on Khi-P if the time ever came.

YaYa was lit by the time she left the club. Khi-P had bought out the bar in his attempt to prove that the city had a new dictator. Usually her conscience talked her out of becoming intimate with Khi-P, but tonight she was too drunk to care.

Her body was on fire. For months she hadn't felt a man's touch. She was tired of suffering. It was time for her to experience satisfaction. Her actions were wrong, but she was tired of hurting. All YaYa wanted was to feel good again. She desperately needed Khi-P to take her away to another place, a place of bliss, even if it was only a temporary getaway.

As YaYa waited for Khi-P to enter the room, a funny feeling filled the pit of her stomach. She almost wanted to vomit. A part of her was sick at what she was about to do.

This is so foul. Indie doesn't deserve this. He didn't know about Leah, but I know that Khi-P is his peoples, she thought, trying to reason with herself. She pushed the thoughts to the back of her mind as she convinced herself that she was doing the right thing. Although she was mad at Indie, she still felt a sense of loyalty to him. She wanted to get even more than anything. It wasn't the fact that he had been with another woman that hurt. She had come to Houston with that knowledge. It wasn't like he had lied about that, but the fact that the other woman was Leah was crushing.

She shook her head from side to side as she mulled over her circumstances. It was true: life really was a bitch.

Some things just have to be done, she thought.

Mekhi entered the room, still tipsy from their night of partying. He was really relishing the idea of being boss, and now that YaYa had come around, he was sitting on a throne so high not even God could reach him. He was untouchable—the kid to see. If a bitch didn't like him, she had to be gay, or so he thought. His ego was that inflated.

As he walked over to her, he held a bottle of rosé wine in his hand. He drank straight from the bottle as he looked at her through lust-filled eyes.

"How you feel, ma? You a'ight?" he asked as he noticed the uncertainty in her stare.

She could barely look him in the eyes as she thought of what she was about to do. It wouldn't be pretty. She was taking the biggest risk of her life, making the ultimate sacrifice. Mekhi had no idea the thoughts that were racing through her mind. She was ready to back out, but felt that she was in too deep. It was now or never, sink or swim. It was time for YaYa to shit or get off the toilet.

She nodded toward the bottle in his hand. "You sharing?" she asked.

"With you, ma, whatever. I can give you whatever," he said.

"Are you sure about that?" she asked with a coy smile.

"I'm positive. My paper too long to short you on anything," he bragged.

YaYa had to admit that his arrogance was slightly attractive. It turned her on to know that he was so drawn to her. She was flattered. There was something intriguing about a rich nigga—not a rich man, but a gun-toting, tattoo-riddled, hood-respected, rich nigga. When a man could have his choice of any woman and he chooses you, it makes you feel like a queen, and Disaya Morgan had been chosen twice; once by Indie, and now Khi-P was voicing his intentions. He was trying to throw his hat in the ring. Now she had to decide if she was looking for a new contender.

The weight of Khi-P's body caused the luxurious bed to sink in slightly as butterflies filled her stomach. His expensive cologne enveloped her, causing her womanhood to contract in pleasure. There was nothing like a good-smelling man.

YaYa tensed up from his touch. His fingertips were foreign to her. Her nerve endings knew Indie's embrace. Khi-P was something new, something different, not even close to being comparable to Indie; but at least he was there. If Khi-P thought he would fill Indie's shoes, he was mistaken. It was simply the timing. He was in the right place at the right time.

"You sure you want to do this?" he asked as he kissed her collarbone.

YaYa fixed her mouth to say no, but instead she nodded yes as he skillfully caressed the nape of her neck while planting kisses on her cheek. She wasn't looking to make love, however. She wanted Khi-P to fill a void, to fulfill a physical desire.

She maneuvered herself so that she was in control and straddled him. Flashes of Indie popped into her mind, but she forced him out. Life had taken her and Indie in two completely different directions. He had disappointed her in the worst way. She knew that Leah had been the manipulating force behind it all, but it hurt all the same. It didn't matter who initiated what. All she knew was that Indie was no longer hers and that Leah was responsible for dismantling her life and killing her daughter. Payback was all she wanted, and in a way, sleeping with Mekhi was get-back for Indie becoming involved with Leah.

So, as she slid down on top of Mekhi, she rode her way, all the way to ecstasy . . . and the entire time, tears of regret fell down her face. There was no turning back now. The book of Indie had ended. She had just closed the last chapter. It was time to weave a new story for her life, and this tale would be filled with nothing but retribution.

Khi-P had stalled each time she had asked him to help her find Leah, but now he wouldn't be able to refuse her. If he wanted YaYa, that was the price he would have to pay.

Chase already knew that once he opened his mouth, things would get hectic, and as he sat in the waiting room of the prison, he was fully prepared for Indie's reaction. The messenger was always the bad guy, but if he didn't tell Indie, no one ever would.

Khi-P had Indie looking like a clown. He was on an ego trip and was publicly courting YaYa to denounce Indie's reign over the streets. They had all gotten money together, so his succession wasn't unexpected. It was the disrespect that was out of order. He could have picked any chick in Houston to take up time with. YaYa was clearly off limits. Chase and every other hustler in town knew that and dared not cross the line. Khi-P was making himself the exception to the rule because he thought that Indie couldn't touch him. What he didn't know was that Indie's reach was long. There wasn't a jail in the world that could hold him. Life was a game of chess, and Indie had conquered it all before the age of twenty-five. If he wanted to move, he had pawns that were more than willing to do it on his behalf.

When Indie emerged through the security door, Chase stood to greet him. The few months that he had been locked down had really changed Indie. There was something about his spirit that had diminished. Before his arrest, the love of a woman had kept him strong, but since parting ways with YaYa, he had become introverted in an attempt to conceal his strife from the world.

The two men embraced before they sat down.

"How you holding up?" Chase asked.

"It's not your job to worry about me, fam. You're my young wolf, my shooter. How are you holding up? You holding things down out there? Your paper up?" he asked.

"I'm good. Paper's nice, you know. Khi put me on, gave me a little bonus or whatnot . . . but you can't buy loyalty. I'm on that real nigga shit, nah mean?" he asked. "And your boy . . . he ain't real. He ain't built like us. Shit is starting to stink around him, if you get my drift."

Indie knew that Chase was subtly trying to warn him about Khi-P, but he wasn't for deciphering riddles. "Speak your mind, fam. You don't gotta sugarcoat it. What's good?"

Chase sat back in his seat and rubbed his hand over his mouth before he blurted out, "He's with YaYa."

"What, nigga?" Indie exclaimed as his jaw locked and his forehead frowned in anger. He was enraged, and his heart felt as if it would fall out of his chest.

"Khi-P has been seeing your girl, fam," Chase repeated, wishing that he had not been the one to break the news.

Indie was hot, and wanted nothing more than to break through the walls of the prison and get at Khi-P, but he was shackled. He was down. There was nothing he could do to stop them. They were both grown, and as much as Indie wanted to believe in YaYa, he knew that she betrayed him. Bars and steel were known for making a woman turn on her man.

He took a moment before he spoke because he needed to calm himself down. If he spoke too soon, he was afraid that an incriminating threat might fall out of his mouth.

Indie went numb as redrum took over his mental. He didn't flinch or even blink as he absorbed the information. He only had himself to blame for trusting YaYa. He knew the type of woman that she was when they first met. He had hoped to change her, to teach her how to love him, but obviously she hadn't learned much. A part of him already knew. He didn't want to admit the truth to himself. The anonymous picture he had been sent marked the beginning of the betrayal. Chase was only confirming what he already knew.

He appeared indifferent because he didn't want to show his cards, but his insides had turned to mush instantly. His stomach turned, and his heart ached mercilessly. The news was really tearing him up, fucking up his head. It definitely wouldn't make his time behind the wall any easier.

"Nah, can't be right. He's helping her out. I asked him to put her up in her own place and to throw her some dough," Indie said as he tried to convince himself that what Chase was speaking was false. He was a firm believer that he could control his own universe, and in his world, YaYa would never stray from home.

"I know you don't want to hear this, but she's still living with him. They hugged up in clubs and shit. I'm telling you they fucking with each other tough, and your man Khi-P is doing everything he can to make it known. He's real disrespectful with it, my dude," Chase informed.

Chase waited for the blow-up, but to his surprise, Indie was silent. For a long moment he just sat there, but Chase could see the wheels turning in his head.

Indie wanted to be mad at Mekhi and send the young gunners to his front door, but he knew that this was his own fault. YaYa was a grown woman, and she was choosing this path for herself. He hadn't expected her to wait, but he did expect her to show him some respect. After all that they had been to one another, he would have never anticipated this. He knew how she used to get down before they met, but time had changed her—or so he had thought. Indie nodded his head surely as he bit his inner cheek. His temple throbbed as he saw red. He was ready to put his murder game down. He ate niggas like Khi-P for lunch under normal circumstances, but there was nothing he could do from where he was sitting.

"What is she doing?" he whispered as he shook his head in disbelief. "I know her. She don't even fuck with small niggas like him."

"Nigga ain't small no more," Chase informed. "He got put on in a major way. I'm talking a killer connect, fam. Khi-P is on the rise."

Chase may as well have been speaking Chinese, because Indie just couldn't understand. He grew tight at just the thought of the two of them together, and he didn't believe for a second that Khi-P had been put on. Indie knew the game too well to believe that Khi-P had become connected out of the blue. "He was moving that bullshit-ass work before he linked up with us. Where is he getting his work from now?" he asked.

"I don't know. He won't say. All I know is he's been making it snow in Houston, and the streets are eating it up," Chase replied.

Indie thought of the bricks that had supposedly been stolen from him. Something wasn't right. Two plus two wasn't adding up right, and he was determined to get to the bottom of it. He stood from the table.

"Bring YaYa up here. I want to see her. I need to see her the next time you come up."

He knew YaYa too well. There was more to this story than met the eye, and he wanted to hear it from her.

Chapter Nineteen

Leah rocked slowly in the wooden chair as she sang to Skylar. Her eyes were distant as she watched the baby girl sucking gently on her bosom. Leah had gone beyond the realm of insanity; she was delusional.

Her own failed pregnancy had allowed her body to begin the process of making milk, and to keep up her production, she pumped her breasts daily, sometimes until her nipples bled. In her head, breastfeeding Skylar was the perfect mother/daughter bonding experience, and it would be as if Skylar were her own child. As she breastfed another woman's child, she felt no remorse.

"This is how it's supposed to be. Just me and you," she cooed.

The longer she kept Skylar away from Disaya, the less she cried. Baby Sky was adjusting to her new environment, and it wouldn't be long before she forgot her real mother completely. She was young enough to assimilate to a new mother, and to develop a new maternal attachment.

Baby Sky was healing to Leah's soul, but what Leah didn't realize was that nothing could erase the ghosts of her past. Her childhood had imbedded hatred so deep within her that she had no empathy for other people's pain. She thrived off of hurting others. She got off on their misery. Seeing others hurting made Leah feel a little bit better.

As she looked around her new suburban home, she laughed in triumph. She had won. She had beat YaYa, and now she was a half million dollars richer.

Leah began to cough violently and shiver. Sweat rolled down her forehead, but it wasn't from the Texas heat. She didn't know what was wrong. She had been almost positive that her womb would heal itself, but the more time that passed, the more her health failed her. Her entire body hurt. She stood and laid Skylar in a bassinet as she made her way to the bathroom. Standing in front of the mirror, she lifted her shirt and saw the deep red streaks on her abdomen. It looked like she had been beaten with a sledgehammer.

She grimaced as she rubbed her belly—the same belly that was supposed to be swollen and flourishing with life. Instead of growing a miracle inside of her womb, it was rotting out slowly. She was in desperate need of a hospital, but refused to go. If she took Skylar near any type of authority, they may take her away. Skylar's picture had been plastered on the news and in the local papers for months. Leah couldn't take the risk of going to the doctor, so she thugged it out.

She pulled out a bottle of Tylenol and emptied practically half the bottle into her hand. Hoping it would take the pain away, she swallowed them down and then went back to a sleeping Sky. She forced herself to will away the pain. Nothing was going to ruin this for her. Nothing.

As she scooped Skylar up in her arms, she rocked her back and forth. "Mommy loves you. We'll die together before they tear us apart. I promise."

Without a consistent coke connect, Khi-P knew his reign wouldn't last long. Eventually the bricks he had gotten from YaYa would run dry, and when that happened, he would need to re-up. He knew he would never be able to match the quality drug that Indie possessed, so he planned to mix whatever coke he was able to acquire with the bricks he had left in his safe. He had set up a meeting with a hook-up out of Miami, and was on his way out on the next flight.

"You sure you don't want to come with me, ma?" Khi-P asked.

Under normal circumstances, she would have jumped at the chance to shop on Collins Avenue, but she had other obligations. All week Chase had been asking her to accompany him to visit Indie. At first YaYa declined, but Chase called YaYa every day until she finally agreed to go with him. She knew exactly why Indie was summoning her. Chase was his li'l man, so she never doubted that he had been reporting her actions back to Indie.

During the entire drive, Chase didn't speak, as if she weren't even present. The radio crooned Jay-Z as Chase nodded his head to the beat. The three-hour drive was filled with awkward silence, and as they neared their destination, YaYa breathed a sigh of relief.

The barbed-wire electrical fence that surrounded the prison made her feel trapped before she even stepped foot inside. It was the first time she had been to see Indie, and she couldn't help but feel as though she had helped to put him there.

I should have never gotten the police involved, she thought.

"You ready?" Chase asked.

YaYa nodded because the lump that had formed in her throat stopped her from speaking. She walked into the prison with a grieving soul as she thought of Indie being locked away from everything and everyone he loved. Just off of what they used to be to one another, she felt sad. The streets had lost a good one.

She gripped the manila envelope in her hand. A confrontation between lovers was inevitable. She wanted Indie to come out of his mouth about Khi-P. At least she had a motive for messing with another man. Mekhi had the power to help her get the revenge she so desperately needed.

When they walked into the gates and into the dreary building, it felt like the life was instantly sucked out of her. She couldn't imagine what Indie was going through. The prison guards searched her thoroughly, invading the most private spaces of her body. She felt as if they owned her, but that's what prison was anyway—a different form of slavery, modern day inhumanity—especially when it was afflicted upon men like Indie Perkins.

Chase had paid a guard on Indie's behalf to have their visit outside where the prisoners roamed during their down time. They didn't need their conversation on wax. As YaYa sat on the top of the picnic table, she was so nervous she almost forgot to breathe.

"Relax," Chase said.

She nodded her head, and the clanging of the back prison door caused her to look up just as Indie emerged. His presence was so powerful.

She stood to her feet, fidgeting nervously as Indie walked toward them. As her heart quickened, she breathed heavily. She had forgotten how deeply she had loved him. For a brief moment, all of her animosity toward him dissipated. She didn't want to, but her feet began to move toward him.

Indie had plans to shun YaYa, to stop fucking with her, to keep his feelings indifferent during her visit, but when he saw his baby girl, all of his plans went out of the window. She ran to him, arms outstretched, and he received her with a warm embrace.

"Indie," she whispered, burying her head in his shoulder as he held her tightly. They hated each other so much that it could only be love. No one gave that much energy to another unless there were deep roots, and it got no deeper than their bond.

As Indie gently caressed her back and rubbed the nape of her neck, he felt mixed emotions. They belonged to each other. They would always be soul mates, but their pure love had been tainted by so much bad blood that it was hard to ignore. Like two elements, they mixed perfectly; they were cohesive, a perfect combination. Their hearts beat to the same drum, and when they finally pulled away from one another, they could feel the invisible wall that was growing between them, interrupting their connection.

"How we get here, baby girl? You fucking with Mekhi? How did shit end up like this?" he asked.

YaYa didn't respond verbally, but her head fell to her chest in shame. She couldn't look him in the eyes.

"What's down there, ma? Look at me," he said.

YaYa lifted her head. "I did what I had to do, Indie. You're not out there. You don't know what it's like. Khi-P is the only person I had to go to for help."

"You could have gone anywhere but there, ma! There's a million niggas in Houston. I never asked you to wait because I know how bitches are cut," he said harshly. "But I never knew you would get down like this, fucking a nigga in my circle."

YaYa could feel the disappointment as Indie stared at her. He had a way of looking at her that made her squirm. There was no use in lying. She knew what he wanted to know. He had already drawn his own conclusions just based off of her body language, but he wanted to hear the words come out of her mouth. He noted the jewels and clothes that she wore. None of them were from the collection he had gotten her. Everything was new, from the diamonds that graced her fingers and ears to the large Hermès bag she carried. She looked like new money. Indie could practically smell Khi-P's scent on her.

YaYa wasn't exactly happy to see Indie. She was glad that he was well, but she had harbored resentment toward him. "Bitch, huh?" she scoffed in disbelief. "You know what, Indie? Fuck you! You're not innocent in all of this. Yeah, I'm fucking with Mekhi to get the bitch that you fucked. To find the bitch that you gave a baby— the bitch you came down here and replaced me with! He's the only person that I can trust! So yes, I fuck with him. He's not you, but he's there for me, Indie. He is going to help me find the bitch that killed our daughter! The bitch that you chose!" She shoved the envelope into his chest and began to storm back to the picnic table where Chase was waiting.

Her rant was incoherent to Indie, and it didn't faze him, until he opened the envelope and saw the pictures that were inside. He frowned when he saw the photos of him and Leah. When he pulled out the ultrasound photo, he knew that YaYa and Leah had crossed paths. He couldn't put the pieces together by himself. YaYa was trying to tell him something, but he just couldn't connect the dots on his own.

"YaYa!" he shouted, causing her to stop midstride. She turned around, standing twenty feet away from him. "This shit is obviously your way of telling me something, so say it. How did you get these?" he asked as he closed the space between them.

"She gave them to me. The bitch you got pregnant is the same bitch that killed Nanzi, and I think she killed Sky too," YaYa said heatedly.

"What?" Indie said in disbelief.

"You heard me, Indie. She came to visit me in the hospital! She made them think I was loony, and she practically told me that she took Sky. So yeah, I'm fucking Khi-P. With his help, I can get to her."

"Are you sure?" he asked as he processed the information. His head was spinning as he came to the realization that he had been sleeping with the enemy all along. How could he blame YaYa for being with his man when he had fucked the girl who had ruined her life?

"Yes, I'm fucking sure, Indie! It's her, and I'm tired of letting her control my life. Khi-P—"

Indie gripped YaYa's shoulders in frustration as he finished her sentence. "Ain't gonna help you do shit, YaYa! Open your eyes, ma. You've been fucking with him for two months, and has he done anything to help you find her?"

The look on her face told him all he needed to know.

"He don't give a fuck about Leah or you, ma. He's using you. You're a trophy to prove to the hood that he's come up. Let me ask you something, and I want you to tell me the truth," Indie said. "You gave him the bricks out of my safe, didn't you?"

"Yes. I sold them to him for the other half of Skylar's ransom," YaYa admitted without remorse. "He gave me the money for them, though. He came through on his end. I didn't have any other choice. It was the only way for me to come up with the rest of the ransom."

"He didn't come through, YaYa; he came up. The nigga got over on you. He used you because he knew you didn't know shit about the game. That was four million dollars worth of cocaine, ma! The bricks were given to me on consignment. I still owe for that work," he whispered as he pulled her arm to draw her near. "Ain't nobody came knocking at my door yet to collect that debt, but trust me, they're coming. It's only a matter of time before they get a nigga in here to send a message to me, and at that point, it's going to be a wrap, because I'ma body him, and that's twenty to life, fuck an appeal."

YaYa's eyes grew big. "I didn't know. I thought he was being a good guy by taking them off of my hands."

"Do he have any of the bricks left?" Indie asked.

"Yeah. He has half of 'em. There's still a hundred kilos left. He wanted to keep half so that he could re-up with a different product and mix the two," YaYa informed.

"It's time for you to get on your hustle then, ma. Those are your bricks by right. I owe a bitch named Zya the paper for those joints, and I need you to step up and get them off for me," Indie said.

YaYa felt like a fool for being so naïve. Tired of being used by those around her, YaYa broke down. "I'm not a drug dealer, Indie. I can't do this by myself."

"It's time for you to stand on your own two feet, Disaya. The people I owe ain't taking no shorts. If I don't come up with that paper, shit will get real bad for me in here. They'll kill me, ma. Now I'm not afraid of no man, because every nigga bleed the same as me, but there's only so long I can hold niggas off. I need you on this, ma.

"If you get the bricks off, you'll have a lot of paper left over. My connect only want what she's owed. The rest will set you up, YaYa. You need money to get the power, ma. After you get your paper up, the sky is the limit. That's when you go for your revenge," he schooled.

"I can't," she whispered.

"You have to," he answered. "I'ma make sure you're straight. Chase will hold you down. I need the old YaYa back right now. The get-money chick I met in New Yitty. Where you at, ma?"

YaYa nodded her head unsurely. "I'm sorry. I'm so sorry about everything. You don't deserve to be in here. All we ever wanted to do was be together."

"I'm down, but don't count me out yet. My day in court will come, and when it does, I hope they set me free. But until then, you have to hold me down . . . hold us down, YaYa," Indie said. He kissed her forehead and tapped her on her backside as he pushed her away, urging her to leave him behind.

"I'm sorry, ma. I didn't know about Leah. I would have handled her a long time ago if I had known who she was. If she hurt my daughter, she deserves everything she has coming her way. She was staying at the house that I built in the country. Ask Chase to take you there. Be careful. I don't want to lose you too."

YaYa blew him a kiss and said, "You can't lose me. I'm yours. I'ma always come back to you."

Chase and YaYa pulled up to Indie's country home. No fear dwelled within YaYa as she looked up at the beautiful house. She was ready to get it popping. Her quest for Leah had been like a hunt, and she was eager to go in for the kill. She hopped out of the car before Chase could park the car good.

"Leah!" she shouted as she stormed up to the plantation-style wraparound porch. She pounded on the door as she shouted Leah's name again. She was ready to go hard, to go all in, but her anger tapered off when she realized that no one was home.

Chase stood back with his hands on his waistline as he watched YaYa spazzing. He couldn't really blame her. He knew that she had cracked from all of the detrimental things that had happened to her. All she wanted was Leah's head on a platter. Once she got that, she would start the healing process; until then, she would be stuck in this limbo.

YaYa reached for the door handle and turned it. To her surprise, the door squeaked open. She crept in cautiously as she observed her surroundings. The place was in shambles, as if a tornado had ripped through it. YaYa went from room to room until she had searched the entire house.

"It looks like she's been gone, ma," Chase said as he leaned against the kitchen countertop. He peered out of the window that looked into the back yard, and he frowned in concern. "Fuck is that?"

"What?" YaYa asked eagerly. She peered out of the window, and when she saw the makeshift grave in the ground, she shot out the back door.

YaYa didn't realize she was crying until her knees hit the dirt in front of the homemade grave. A wooden cross had been placed at the head of it, and she could tell by the uneven grass that the grave was only big enough for a baby to fit inside . . . her baby.

"No," she moaned in agony as she began to dig with her hands. "No, no, no, no!" she cried. Chase couldn't sit back and watch the pitiful scene. He wished that he had a mother who loved him the way that YaYa clearly loved baby Sky. He had never known a love so deep. The woman who had birthed him was in love with crack cocaine. The high state she lived in didn't allow her to love anyone, not even herself. Chase silently commended YaYa for her mothering ability. Sky's kidnapping wasn't her fault, yet he could see her placing the blame on her shoulders. He walked over to her and lifted her from the ground.

"She buried my daughter. She buried her here!"

Chase didn't know what to say. He wasn't a big fan of speaking just to hear himself talk, so he opted not to say a word. Instead, he embraced her as her legs gave out from beneath her.

Chase sat beside her on top of the grave for almost an hour as she sobbed heavily. She took her time because this was the last pity party she was going to throw for herself.

"How could she do this to her? She was just a baby," YaYa whispered. "I'm going to murder that bitch if it's the last thing I do. She isn't going to stop. She'll never stop making my life hell, and I'm tired. I'm the only one who can stop this. I have to become like her. I can't have limits, because that bitch has none."

After seeing the grave behind Indie's house, something inside of YaYa snapped. She lived for only one thing—revenge.

As she sat across the table from Mekhi, her mind raced. She was silent and had been distant for days. Khi-P had noticed a change in her. Just when he thought he was establishing a place in her life, she withdrew. She was pulling away from him, and he wanted to know why.

She nodded her head and tried her best to behave normally as she plotted out her next move in her head. Khi-P's life was on a countdown. Indie had ordered his execution. Chase was supposed to be the one to handle it, but YaYa felt that she should be the one to do it. She had allowed Khi-P to disrespect Indie, and she knew that Indie was bitter about the fact that she had dealt with his man. Killing him and retrieving Indie's bricks was the only way for her to prove to her man that she was loyal to him. She was back on team Indie, and the act that she was about to commit would show him that there was nothing she would not do for him.

You can do this, she thought.

"Is everything okay, YaYa?" Mekhi asked, interrupting her thoughts. "Ever since I've been back from my little business trip, you've been different."

"I'm fine," she assured as she picked at the full course meal that sat in front of her. She thought about the cocaine that he had put up in a storage facility. He had just re-upped, so now was the perfect time to make her move. She needed him out of the way and out of her life.

At first she was flattered by the pedestal that he had placed her on. After all the anguish she had been through, it felt good to be courted by Khi-P, but now it disgusted her. He didn't want her; he wanted the status that came along with having a woman like her. He was a great actor, the ultimate pretender. The nigga deserved an Academy Award he was so convincing. He always made it seem like his feelings for her were so genuine, so pure and uncontrollable, when really it was all a visage, a twisted web of manipulation that she had gotten caught up in. His feelings were faker than a knock-off purse, and now that YaYa saw the light, she was offended by the way he had flaunted her like a possession for the entire city to see.

If he cared so much, he would have never shorted me on those bricks, she thought. The more she sat and silently fumed over it, the more she wanted to call him out on his bullshit. If she had to kill him, she wanted him to know why he was going to die. She was about to lay her cards down on the table.

"I know that you shorted me on those bricks, Khi." She finally built up the nerve to let the words fall out of her mouth, and while her heart was racing on the inside, outwardly she appeared collected. "That work was worth four million easy. You saw me struggling. I didn't have a dollar to my name, and you still got over on me."

Her statement seemed to take him off guard momentarily. He knew that somebody had planted that bug in her ear. "Who told you that? Indie?" he said nonchalantly, continuing to eat his food while staring her in the eyes. But she didn't need to respond. He already knew whom she had been speaking with.

He was hard to read. The passive-aggressive expression on his face revealed nothing.

Khi-P had wanted to keep YaYa dependent on him. She didn't need her own money. "Have I ever told you no, YaYa? Don't let that jailbird make you think you're missing out on anything. Tell that mu'fucka to concentrate on not dropping the soap and to stop worrying about what's mine."

"Yours?" YaYa shot back incredulously.

This nigga is real cocky with his shit.

Khi-P stopped eating and wiped his mouth with his white linen napkin. "Yeah, mine, YaYa," he spat. "Don't play games, ma. Let's keep it one hunnid. You're a material girl, and I let you live in my material world. You belong to me now. I'm Daddy. I get you everything you need."

"Except independence, Mekhi! I'm stuck here under your thumb. I don't got no real paper of my own. I'm sponging off of you. Now, if you want to play the game, let's play it. Every nigga got to play to pay, and I'm talking big paper, not these little ghetto-girl shopping sprees you been doing. That little shit don't impress me. That's little nigga shit," she said as she rolled her eyes, insulting his manhood.

"So you a ho now? Huh, trick?" he asked, vexed because he felt she was comparing him to Indie.

"Tricks are for kids, Khi-P. I'm a business-woman. You want the perks, but you don't want to put in the work that it takes to court a chick like me. The money you spend on me is rightfully mine anyway. You parade me in front of the city like I'm your bitch. I'm not, Khi-P! If Indie wasn't locked up, you would've never had a chance," she said, speaking honestly as she sipped her wine calmly. She smiled, slightly amused by the look of anger that flashed across his face.

"You ungrateful bitch!" he seethed as he stood. He flipped the entire dining table over, sending their dinner flying everywhere. But he was in for a surprise when he saw the gun that Disaya had been pointing at him the entire time underneath the table. Her hand rested on the trigger.

"You gon' shoot me now because I took some bricks from you? You wouldn't even had known what to do with 'em. I gave you the money to get your daughter back, and this is what you do? This is how you gon' play it?" he asked.

Mekhi was appealing to her conscience. He had been the only person in her corner after Indie was arrested. Even if he did have ulterior motives, without him she wouldn't have had the money to even attempt to make the ransom drop. He could sense her indecision, and in the split second that it took her to think about her actions, he was across the room.

Mekhi grabbed her wrist and bent it back, forcing her to drop the gun. The slap that he delivered to her face sent her flailing to the floor. YaYa crawled as fast as she could to the gun, but he bent down and picked it up right before she could get to it.

He smirked as he rubbed his goatee while pointing the gun at her. "You should have just stuck with the program. I would've treated you like a queen, ma." He bent down and grabbed her hair and snatched her up.

"Oww," she protested as she tried to pull away from him. He only gripped her hair tighter. She could feel some of her hair being torn from the roots, and her scalp burned.

"Now I'm going to treat you like the bitch that you are," he said. "Take off your clothes."

"What?"

Khi-P aimed the gun at her head and said, "I didn't stutter. You should've shot me, bitch."

YaYa's nostrils flared as she removed her shirt and threw it at him. She was so enraged as she kicked out of her jeans. The sight of YaYa's voluptuous body instantly made his dick hard. He removed his jeans and boxers while still pointing the gun at her.

"You're going to rape me?" she asked incredulously.

Mekhi took a seat in one of the dining chairs. His manhood was ready, and he wasn't taking no for an answer. YaYa had challenged him and disrespected him. He had to punish her into submission.

"Come get on this dick," he said. The tone of his voice was so threatening that YaYa knew she didn't have a choice. He would shoot her if she disobeyed. She hesitated, but when she heard him click the safety off, she urged her feet to move. She had slept with Khi-P before, but this time the thought of him inside of her turned her stomach. This time he was forcing her. It wasn't her choice, and as she straddled him, her legs shook.

"Get on it, ma," he said as he put the gun directly on her heart. "You better ride this dick good, YaYa. If you don't, it could just cost you your life."

"Please at least put on a condom," she whispered.

"Nah, bitch. I'ma put a baby up in you. Maybe then you will let that nigga Indie go," Khi-P stated harshly. "You daughter's dead, so make another one."

His words stabbed at her emotions, and she bled tears as she lowered herself down onto his girth. She was stiff with fear and hatred.

"Ride my shit right, before I put a hole in your chest," he threatened.

YaYa forced herself to find her rhythm, rotating her hips while he was deep inside of her. He gripped her backside with one hand as he pulled her hips into him forcefully, making her ride it harder.

"Shit, ma," he moaned as his eyelids began to flutter.

"You the best." Seeing that he was becoming distracted, she grinded harder onto him. Sex noises filled the air as she began to moan loudly. She needed to get that gun out of his hand. She needed him to feel so good that he forgot he was forcing her to do this.

"Ooh, shit, Khi," she whispered, laying it on thick. She couldn't lie; Mekhi always put it down, and she couldn't stop the orgasm that was building between her legs. But it was a physiological response to pleasure, nothing more.

She was putting down her best to distract him, riding him so hard that he had to remove the gun from her chest so that he could put his other hand on the side of her ass and guide. Up . . . down . . . up . . . down. She bounced her juicy behind on him and winded ferociously, all the while eyeing the gun that he was loosely gripping in one hand.

"Damn, ma, I'm about to nut. Keep going," he whispered through pursed lips.

YaYa's eyes widened as his closed, and as soon as she saw his finger move away from the trigger, she knocked the gun from his hand. She jumped off of him and scrambled for the gun. As soon as her fingers wrapped around the trigger, she turned around and fired.

The silenced shot pierced Khi-P's stomach, and he gripped his side as blood seeped through his hands.

Breathing heavily, YaYa backed up as Khi-P lunged forward, grabbing her by the neck. "You shot me," he mumbled in weak disbelief. He wanted to tighten his grip around her neck, but the more effort he put into it, the looser his hands became. His blood was all over her, and as his eyes grew wide, she pushed him forcefully. She watched as he lay dying on the floor.

"YaYa, help me," he whispered as he gasped for air while reaching out for her.

YaYa bent down close to his ear and looked into Khi-P's desperate, weakening gaze. "Fuck you, Khi-P. I hope you rot in hell."

YaYa stood to her feet and put on her clothes. She hurriedly removed the storage unit keys from his key ring and took one last look at a struggling Khi-P. She didn't even wait for him to take his last breath before she walked out the door.

"Damn," he groaned. It was the last word he spoke. It wasn't the way that he had seen himself going out, and as the life left his body, he couldn't help but feel lonely. He bled to the death, spending the final moments of his life alone on his dining room floor.

Chapter Twenty

Bang! Bang! Bang! Bang! Bang!

The sound of guns rang out as YaYa, Trina, Miesha, and Sydney blasted off at Chase's command. If they were going to do this, it was going to be done right. Chase wasn't going into shit blind. As the last real nigga standing, he knew that he would need shooters behind him.

YaYa had a lot to learn, but the most important lesson was the art of war. The sound of the gun intimidated her, but just as Indie had schooled Chase, Chase schooled YaYa. She had to learn how to pop off without flinching. Chase was so used to the act of murder and gunplay now that he didn't even hear the blast after he pulled the trigger.

"Pop off before you get popped," he preached, sitting on the ledge at the gun range while the girls reloaded time after time. Chase made them shoot until their trigger fingers grew blisters. He needed them on point, and most importantly they needed to know that the weapons were not for show. If a gun was pulled, a bullet should follow—no exceptions. There was no room for hesitation.

It was nothing for YaYa to pull a trigger. Imagining Leah's face on the target in front of her made things so much easier. YaYa was determined to end up on top, and in order to do that, she needed to stay focused and put her emotions to the side. It was grind time. She was staying in Indie's home, and the bricks were waiting to be moved.

Miesha, Sydney, and Trina would all run their own blocks and move the work on the street level. They were the cook-up queens, so they were used to moving work. By breaking down a few bricks and setting up trap spots, they would maximize their profit.

Only YaYa would handle the major transactions. With Chase's help, she already had a few buyers lined up, but YaYa had a hundred bricks to get off. She didn't know a hundred hustlers, but she could easily locate a hundred hustlers' wives. She would get her product off through them. A network of bad bitches was always handy to have, and she was about to locate Houston's elite.

YaYa rented out a club and hosted a Prada Party, for which she hired vendors to come and sell their products at a discounted rate. She had designer purses, shoes, perfume, diamonds, and even Indian Remy for sale, knowing that it would attract every get-money chick in town. She sent Trina and the girls to every beauty salon in town to promote. Ten thousand flyers went out over the entire city, radio spots were purchased, and word of mouth spread like wildfire.

On the day of the event, her venue looked more like a luxury department store than a popular nightclub. YaYa played the perfect hostess as she mingled with the large group of women. Over two hundred ladies had shown up, and she was busy taking mental notes, attempting to weed out the real from the fake. As her eyes scanned the crowd, she could spot the big wigs in the game.

YaYa could tell by the type of purse a chick was carrying if her guy was getting money. Knock-offs were for small-timers. YaYa was looking for the chicks that were carrying Berkin bags, Coach, and Hermès. The key word was authentic.

She walked around giving out special invitations to a brunch the next morning. Only the elite were invited, and the next day when the

Acuras, Lexuses, Bentleys, and Mercedes pulled up to the restaurant, she knew that she had chosen the right ladies. All that she had told them was that she had a business opportunity for them. Under the pretenses of making money, every girl showed up. Inside, every hustler's wife was a little gold digger. Every woman liked to make a little money of her own on the side, and YaYa was about to use that to her advantage. First class was the only way to describe the women at the brunch—divas in their own right, they had arrived.

"Thank you for coming, ladies," YaYa announced as she took her seat at the head of a long dining table. "I handpicked you ladies because I feel that we could form a very beneficial business relationship. I know about the company you keep and the men you share your beds with. We're all in love with the same thing, chasing the same dream. I want you to convince your men to purchase their weight from me. For every kilo they buy, I'm willing to cut you ten percent of the take, so everybody eats."

YaYa could tell from the skeptical looks and the silence in the room that everyone was on edge. Nobody wanted to discuss that type of business. They were hesitant because they didn't know YaYa from the next bitch, and loose lips sunk ships every day. They feigned ignorance.

"I know no one wants to vocally say anything. I'm not a cop, and I'm not wearing a wire. I play the same position as all of you. I was in love with a man who got swallowed up by the game. Now I'm out here alone, and it's time to make it happen on my own. Don't end up like me. Don't be left with nothing when the dust settles. Make your own paper. Make it now and save it. I'm giving you all the opportunity to have your own."

YaYa sat back in her chair and motioned for Trina and the girls. They passed each girl a small giftwrapped box. "Please deliver these to your men with a message from me. Please tell them that business will be lucrative if they buy strictly from me. It will be worth their while. You all know how to reach me, so when it's time for business, you let me know."

YaYa had gift-wrapped an ounce of cocaine for each girl to take home. There wasn't a doubt in her mind that the fish scale would hook each and every one of their men. She would become the bird-lady in no time with the crystal white that she was holding.

The girls ate and chatted briefly before clearing the room. One by one the ladies left until there was only one left sitting in the room.

"I am very impressed by the way that you handle yourself, YaYa. I thought that my money would be in naïve hands, but I think there is a natural born hustler behind your glamour and Fendi," the girl said as she remained seated and sipped at her mimosa.

YaYa was taken off guard. The compliment was odd, and she spoke as if she knew her. As she peered closer, YaYa realized that this girl had not been one of the women she had invited to the brunch. Her heart quickened as she suspected that the lady was an undercover cop.

"I'm sorry, but I don't remember you from last night," YaYa said.

"That was another ingenious thing to do," she said as she sat back comfortably in her seat. "A woman has a lot of influence over her man. You capitalized off of that. Impressive. You remind me a lot of myself when I first got started in the game."

"Who are you?" YaYa asked. "I'm Indie's connect. I'm the woman you owe two-point-five million dollars," she said. "My name is Zya."

YaYa looked at the strikingly beautiful girl and her stomach turned to knots instantly. She was immediately insecure. She would have never expected a woman so beautiful and young to be his connect. In fact, she would have never suspected a woman at all. Instantly, her mind recalled all of the trips out of the country, all of the late night calls, all of the shipment pickups . . . everything. All along, Indie had been going to meet Zya. She was so pretty that it made YaYa uncomfortable and sick to her stomach at the thought of Indie fucking with the girl.

"You can inhale, Disaya. I don't want your man," she said with a slick smile. "I have my own. Trust."

YaYa laughed nervously, trying to play it off, but she was admittedly relieved. "Why are you here?"

"I'm here to let you know that you have thirty days to pay your debt. Please tell Indie that it is not my choice to play my hand this way, but I represent a bigger influence. I have held them off on my end for as long as I can, but now it's time to pay up. My respect and admiration for Indie means nothing to them. Well, not enough to pardon this unsettled business. I am sincerely apologetic for all that you guys have been through, but the fact still remains that you owe me money. It is important that I get my money, Disaya. It's not impossible. I used to move birds like they were going out of style.

"And as added incentive, I will help you out. I know about this girl Leah that you have beef with. If you get me my money, I'll give you her location," Zya promised. She extended her hand

and YaYa just stared at it for a long time. "Do we have a deal?"

YaYa shook Zya's hand, and no other words were spoken. Zya arose and put on her Prada glasses before walking out of the restaurant, escorted by two burly bodyguards who had been waiting just outside the entry.

YaYa shook her head as Chase stormed into the room appearing flustered. "Who the fuck was that? I went to piss and came back and the fucking door was being guarded!" he exclaimed.

As YaYa looked out of the restaurant window she saw Zya's Brazilian blowout whipping in the wind as she walked to the town car that was waiting curbside for her.

"YaYa. Ma. Who was that?" Chase repeated.

All YaYa could do was shake her head in admiration as she looked Chase in his eyes and said, "That's a bad bitch."

Zya had that effect on people. She usually left both men and women breathless.

Chase was his own one-man army. His violent reputation already preceded him, so it wasn't hard to gain control of most of the blocks in the city. Whoever put up protest was quickly silenced by his .45; consequently, no one objected as he restructured Houston's underworld.

YaYa served everybody from the fiends to the corner boys, all the way to the top of the food chain to the heavy hitters that were pushing real weight. The few hustlers who did buck only did so because YaYa was a female. They underestimated her, and it was a mistake that cost them dearly because when Chase came through, it was curtains for them.

At Indie's request, Chase ensured that YaYa was untouchable. One would have thought an entire goon squad was behind YaYa. Against a million enemies, Chase was one soldier with a million guns. When you looked at it like that, Chase could take on whoever, whenever, and he never had a problem putting in work on YaYa's behalf. Her hands stayed cleaned because Chase did the dirty work.

After killing Khi-P, she knew that the murder game wasn't for her. She didn't have it in her. Leah was the only person she wanted to see dead, and that kill she could justify. That murder would be the only easy one, but until their paths crossed again, she stuck to the script and played her position. Chase caught the bodies, he transported the goods; all she did was sit on the throne, make the connections, and count the paper.

She was a queen pin in the making, but wasn't in it for the street fame. YaYa had a specific goal in mind—relieving Indie of his debt and getting to Leah. After she accomplished those things, the game could kiss her good-bye.

Chapter Twenty-one

YaYa took to hustling like a plane to the friendly skies. Within three days, every single woman who attended the brunch had given her a call to set up a meeting. YaYa didn't sleep. She met with each couple personally. YaYa wanted to read the men who she was doing business with, and only after both she and Chase gave the nod of approval did she change the forecast and make it snow.

Since she was the only one in Houston with real weight, she set the market value. Indie had told her to price her bricks at $22,000, but YaYa sold them for thirty a pop. The fiends got high off the dope, but the money was her narcotic. Once it started pouring in, there was no stopping it. She was swimming in dough, and with Chase as the muscle behind her operation, her confidence was at an all time high. She wasn't willing to take any losses, and the hustlers she chose to deal with agreed to the price without protest because the quality was on point. She was their only connection to raw, unstepped-on product, and they worshipped the ground she walked on.

YaYa was no longer lost in Indie or Khi-P's shadow. She had come into her own, and just as she had admired Zya, every chick in Houston now looked at her the same way. She was getting it, and she made no apologies for it. Money wasn't her motivation, but it was an added perk to the game. Even after she settled all debts with Zya, she would walk away with a pretty penny.

It wasn't long before word got out and she had buyers from out of town trying to cop from her. With YaYa in charge, everybody ate. Nobody went without, which kept the streets peaceful. Niggas were too busy spending money to beef. Everything was good, and her operation was so low key that it was flawless. She wasn't flashy like Khi-P, or treacherous like Indie. She was smart. She didn't need any unwanted attention.

Hustling gave her something to focus on. She had been so consumed with the pain of Skylar's death that watching the bricks go out as the money came in was relaxing for her. The dedication and attention that she put into it separated her from the masses. She was out to get it, and since she had already lost everything that mattered to her, she was fearless. A woman with nothing to lose was the last person who should be handed power. The world was in her hands, and she could do with it as she pleased.

Unafraid of the repercussions of her actions, she would do whatever it took to get to Leah, and she felt sorry for anyone who stood in her way. No price was too steep, and nothing was off limits. Not even death could stop her. In fact, death was a part of the plan.

Leah held the scalpel-like knife as she meticulously sliced around the picture of Disaya, removing her face from the family snapshot of Indie and baby Sky. She concentrated as if she were performing open heart surgery.

"You never belonged in this picture in the first place," she mumbled as she thumped Disaya's face out. She grabbed the picture of herself and began to cut out her face. "I'm a much better fit." She tried to cut the same shape around her face so that it would fit perfectly into the altered photo. She was careful as her steady hand sliced along her jaw line. Her mouth fell open in anticipation as she neared completion.

"Almost done," she whispered. "Al . . . mo—"
Waaa!
The sound of Skylar's crying caused Leah's hand to shake, inadvertently slicing the cutting tool in the wrong direction and causing her to destroy the picture.

"Damn it!" she shouted in frustration. She stood from the table and pushed back with so much force that her chair toppled over. The incessant crying was driving her insane. "Ugh!" With the sharp blade gripped tightly in her hand, she walked toward the crying infant.

It would be so easy to shut her up. Just the slice of a blade would stop this bullshit, she thought as her nostrils flared.

She loomed over baby Sky, gripping the blade so tightly that it cut into her own skin. She stood as if she were in a trance as Skylar screamed her tiny heart out. It was as if the child could sense that danger was near.

Leah stared directly at Skylar, but she didn't really see her. She saw herself and the many times that she had cried for help. She remembered feeling afraid, helpless, and lonely as a child; as she listened, Skylar's cries became her own. She dropped the blade from her hand as blood dripped freely to the floor. Just as quickly as she had snapped into her daze, she snapped out of it and rushed to pick up baby Sky.

"Oh, I'm sorry, Sky. I'm sorry, honey. Mommy's right here," she crooned softly in her ear. "I forgot I can't hurt. Mommy doesn't want to hurt you . . . not like they hurt me."

YaYa made her way into the upscale restaurant. She was so shaky that she could barely stay on her feet. With every step, her five-inch heels threatened to fail her. She had no idea what she was walking into. Indie had made it perfectly clear that Zya was not to be underestimated. She was meeting with a major player. Zya may have been a woman, but she was just as ruthless as any of her male counterparts. YaYa definitely didn't want to see her. This meeting was the most important one of her life.

The usually busy establishment was empty, and YaYa couldn't help but wonder where the lunch rush had disappeared to. What she didn't know was that Zya had rented out the entire establishment so that they would have privacy. No one needed to hear their conversation. Whatever arrangements they came up with would be for their ears only. No one else needed to know.

Although YaYa wanted Chase to be there, she came alone, and as her heart beat out of her chest, she wished that she had at least come strapped. Firing a gun was not something she looked forward to doing again, but at least it would have secured her safety. As she looked around nervously, she felt naked.

"Relax. If I wanted you dead, you would already be somebody's memory."

YaYa heard Zya's voice above her, and she looked up to see Zya on the second floor balcony.

"Come up," Zya instructed as she nodded toward the spiral glass staircase. "You can leave the money down there. My people will take care of it."

YaYa looked down at the two oversized duffel bags she carried. It had taken her a month of sleepless nights to hustle up that paper. There was no way she was just handing it off to Zya's men. She looked up at her and replied, "If you don't mind, I would like for you to count it now . . . in front of me."

Zya smiled. It had been a long time since she had counted that much money. Her days of shoebox stacking were long gone. She had people to keep her finances in order now, but she knew why YaYa wanted her to count it personally. She had a lot at stake, too much to leave the count up to men she had no affiliation with. It was only because of that Zya agreed.

"You might as well take off them shoes and grab a drink then. We'll be here for a while."

After three bottles of the finest champagne and four hours of counting, then recounting, they counted a total of $2.5 million, and the women had established a newfound respect for one another. Zya didn't know many men who could pull off what YaYa had in only four weeks. That alone impressed Zya.

"You should really think about staying in the game. You're good at it," Zya said.

"Only because I had to be," YaYa responded. "I would have done anything to get the information you promised to deliver."

"Speaking of which," Zya said. She pulled an envelope from her handbag and handed it to YaYa.

YaYa stopped breathing as she received the envelope. That one piece of paper was all she lived for. Now there would be nothing stopping her. She had Leah's location, and it was time to get it popping.

Chapter Twenty-two

For a week, YaYa didn't even open the envelope. She just sat inside of Indie's home and drank wine as she stared at it, mentally preparing herself for what she was about to do. As she sat at the kitchen table, she gripped the tape of Nanzi's murder tightly in her hand. It was the same tape that Leah had set her up with. It displayed the night that had ruined her life and shifted the way the winds of misery blew by her.

It was all packaged up and ready to be mailed off. She knew that she would need some type of insurance. The tape was it. She had written a letter inside, giving away the identity of the shooter. Just in case her plan to kill Leah failed, she was going to mail the tape to Detective Norris. She knew that he would not turn down a case like that one.

YaYa had it all planned out. The only thing that was stopping her at this point was herself. So, she secluded herself to mentally prepare herself for the battle of a lifetime. She accepted no visitors. Neither Chase nor Trina and the girls could contact her. When they knocked, she didn't answer. When they called, she sent them to voice mail. She didn't even accept phone calls from Indie.

There was one person that she couldn't ignore, however, and when she came knocking at her front door, YaYa had to answer.

"Elaine?" YaYa said in surprise as she opened the door.

"Indie sent me, YaYa. No one has been able to reach you for days. You have a lot of people worried about you, sweetheart. I flew all the way down here from New York to make sure you were okay. Indie told me a bit about what's going on . . . not too much, though. You know he can't speak freely in there. You never know who might be listening. So, you fill in the blanks," Elaine demanded.

Shocked to see her, but grateful for Elaine's presence, YaYa didn't object to her being there. She simply walked over to the table and grabbed the envelope with Leah's location and then the envelope filled with pictures of Leah and Indie together. She handed them to Elaine. "This is what's going on. This is the bitch that killed your son Nanzi, the one that I told you about. She kidnapped and killed Sky, too."

Elaine's mouth fell to her chest as she opened the first envelope and viewed the pictures. She immediately placed the face. It had been a long time, but Leah was the spitting image of her mother. As her mind took a walk down memory lane, Elaine remembered Leah. She recalled the little girl and her nutty-ass mother, Natalie.

"I know her. She . . . her mother . . . oh my God!" Elaine gasped as she put a manicured hand over her mouth. She opened the other envelope that contained Leah's address.

"What?" YaYa asked. "Elaine, what's going on?"

"I . . . I think I know why all of this is happening. I know where it all started," she whispered in disbelief.

"I don't give a damn how it started, but I know how it will end. I just have to get my head together. As soon as I think I can handle it, I'm going to find that bitch," she said.

"YaYa, I have to go. I know what this girl is after. I know what she wants," Elaine said urgently.

"How do you—"

Elaine held up her hand to interrupt YaYa before the question could even come out. "Just trust me. I have to go, but promise me you won't make a move until I get back."

"I can't promise that, Elaine. You're not telling me enough," YaYa responded.

"Just trust me," she said.

Elaine rushed out with one picture of Leah still in her hand and the address where she could be found memorized in her head. "It's been more than twenty years and this madness is still going on," she whispered as she pulled away.

She knew where to go to stop it. She had to go where all of the envy had begun. She had to go to the source. Only he could stop it. Unbeknownst to everyone but herself, she had kept up with him after all these years, and now it was time for her to be heard and seen. This craziness had to come to a conclusion.

Elaine sat reserved with her legs crossed and her manicured hands placed delicately on her knee. As she looked around the waiting room, she saw the young girls who were there. Each of them had a story to tell; no doubt, one that she was sure was quite similar to her own.

Twenty-five years ago, she was just like these girls: a ride-or-die for a man who would never return the loyalty. She, too, had once been in love with a man who was no good for her. Too foolish to realize it, Elaine had been stuck in a redundant relationship for years. Pimp and prostitute was her relation. Seeking love, but receiving control, Elaine became lost in Slim. It wasn't until she realized that Slim was incapable of giving her the love that he constantly promised that she left.

So, she could relate to the girls sitting in the prison, waiting to visit boyfriends, husbands, and even pimps. She knew their strife. She was a seasoned vet in the street game they were playing.

Buchanan Slim had been a gift and a curse to her. It was the bad times that she had endured with him that taught her how to recognize and appreciate true love when it came her way. Her days of working street corners had been long, dark, and hard, but they had not been in vain. The streets raised her and taught her more than any textbook could ever do.

She had let Slim go long ago. He had led her straight into the darkness. Lost in love, she had committed murder over him, and she had not seen or spoken with him since that tragic night. She knew that he had been blamed for her sin. They had locked him away, and a part of her felt that it was vindication for every young girl that he had ruined.

She had not seen him in years, and today she sat nervously, waiting to reunite with him after so long. As she sat patiently, a thunderstorm of emotions wreaked havoc on her insides. Nervous energy caused her red-bottom heel to bounce off of the floor, and her breath caught in her chest when she saw Slim walk into the room.

She couldn't bring herself to approach him. Elaine sat, breathing shallow bits of air as she watched him search the room for his visitor. When his eyes settled on her, she knew that he recognized her. She waited for his reaction. Expecting anger or resentment, she braced herself, but when he approached her and she looked deep into his eyes, all she felt was forgiveness and humility.

"Hello, Lai," he greeted.

She hadn't been called that in years, but hearing her old nickname fall off of his lips brought back so many memories. Some she was fond of and others ashamed of, but they all made up her past—a past that she had accepted and learned from.

"Hello, Slim," she replied.

"After all this time, you wait until the day before I'm about to be paroled before you bless me with a visit, huh?" he asked playfully.

His tone held no fury, and Elaine could sense a change in him. The superficial, self-centered, selfish pimp no longer existed. Instead, he had been replaced with a man so spiritually full that his faith glowed through his skin.

"I wouldn't have come if it wasn't important," Elaine said. "You're different."

"As are you, my sister," he retorted.

"You found Allah?" she asked, surprised.

Slim nodded and gave her a hearty laugh as his eyes smiled at her genuinely. "You say that as if I was a lost cause."

Elaine didn't respond because they both knew the type of scum he used to be.

The moment of silence allowed just enough time for tension to sneak into the room. She could feel him staring at her, and she avoided his gaze as she motioned for him to sit. "Please. There's something I need to speak with you about."

Slim sat down. "What can I do for you, beautiful?" he asked.

Elaine's eyebrow rose and she pointed a warning finger at him. "Don't start, Slim. Don't even try it. That charm doesn't work on me anymore. I'm not the same girl I used to be."

Slim chuckled, not used to being stood up to. "So I see."

"First I want to tell you that I'm so sorry. I am the only person who knows that you don't belong here. I apologize for taking your freedom from you. I had two boys to raise. I couldn't admit to killing Dynasty," she explained.

"I forgave you a long time ago, Elaine. I know you didn't come all this way to say that. What did you really come for?" he asked.

"I came because I need you to right one of the wrongs that you committed, one that has ruined the lives of two young girls," Elaine said.

Slim didn't respond, but the fresh pools of tears that accumulated in his eyes expressed his remorse.

"YaYa is in trouble, Slim. Her daughter—"

"My baby has a daughter?" he asked as he realized how much he had missed. His green-eyed angel had been put in the back of his mind for so long. He never wanted to think of her or of what her life must have been like growing up without a mother or father, but now Elaine was making him face it.

"Has she been with you all this time?" he asked.

Elaine shook her head, crushing the tiny hope that he had mustered. "No. I wish that she had been, but I didn't take her. I couldn't look at her every day knowing what I had done.

"She and my son met about a year ago. They had a daughter together. That's how I reunited with her. I felt horrible about letting her go to the system, but I was bitter too, Slim. You played with a lot of people's emotions . . . fucked over a lot of good women."

"I know," Slim admitted.

"I don't think you do, Slim. Those women were my friends. I knew them. I slept, shit, and ate with those women twenty-four hours a day."

"You say it like it was prison." Slim chuckled.

"It was your prison. We were locked down by you, and now YaYa is suffering because of the games you played," Elaine explained.

"Don't say that to me, Lai. I have enough regrets. Don't add to the pile," Slim pleaded, his strong baritone cracking under pressure.

"I wouldn't tell you this unless it was absolutely necessary. YaYa's daughter was kidnapped and killed, Slim," Elaine explained. "And I believe that all of this happened because of you."

Slim felt a mixture of anger and indignation, feeling as though Elaine was trying to place blame on him that he didn't deserve. Little did he know, YaYa's situation with Skylar and Leah was directly related to him.

"You remember Natalie?" Elaine asked.

Slim flipped through his mental Rolodex. He had encountered so many women in his day that it took him a minute to recall her exactly.

"Crazy bitch was always trying to pin a baby on me," Slim said with a chuckle.

"Well, the crazy bitch has a crazy daughter . . . a daughter who you denied . . . a daughter who believes that you are her father, and one who has a lot of resentment towards YaYa because of the way that you treated her. Natalie's daughter, Leah, kidnapped YaYa's daughter." Elaine placed a picture of Leah on the table for Slim to see.

He frowned because he remembered the little girl. He had always had sympathy for the child. Slim shook his head in disbelief.

"I feel horrible, Lai, but I don't see why that girl would even think I'm her father," Slim whispered as he leaned into the table intently.

Elaine looked at him in exasperation. "Slim, you played with a lot of people's hearts. We all loved you. We all worshipped you. We all wanted to be the lucky lady to tie you down with a baby. You made a lot of promises to a lot of women, knowing that you never meant any of us any good.

"You planted this seed, Natalie watered it, and now it's grown into a problem named Leah that no one knows how to handle. She has a lot of hate and jealousy in her heart. She feels like YaYa had the life that was meant for her. This could end very badly, Slim. You're the only one who can fix this," Elaine said firmly. "You have to right your wrongs, Slim."

"What do you want me to do, Lai?" Slim asked as he sat back defensively in his chair. "Yeah, I talked a good game back in the day, but that girl isn't my child. I know the seeds I left behind, and Nanzi . . . he was it."

"And Leah killed him," Elaine shot back. "She shot my baby in the head because of you, damn it!"

"What?" Slim said in shock.

"That little bitch is doing a lot of damage all because she feels like she is lacking something that you gave to YaYa. She's lacking a father's love.

"Little does she know a love like yours isn't worth much. Poor child didn't miss out on anything, but jealousy is the devil's puppet. It can help breed a lot of hatred. She was on the outside looking in, and that crazy mother of hers had her thinking that you were a giant when in actuality, you were this big." Elaine held her thumb and index finger slightly apart as she showed Slim what she thought of him.

"That's not fair, Lai," Slim stated.

"But it's true," Elaine said. "YaYa needs your help. She's thinking about going after this girl. I can see it in her eyes that she's going to kill her. She has already lost everything. I don't want to see her lose her freedom behind this thing, but I also don't want that crazy girl hurting YaYa again.

"When you get out of here, you fix this mess, Slim. Do it for the little green-eyed girl you used to worship. If you ever loved her like you claimed to, then you will make this right, because she needs you now more than ever before."

Slim nodded, knowing that his selfish and womanizing ways had led to this chaos. He hadn't seen YaYa since she was a little girl, but she still held the keys to his heart, and knowing that she was suffering because of his foolish behavior . . . For a man who had been deemed heartless, he still felt the nagging tear on the left side of his chest that indicated heartbreak. He had destroyed a lot of lives, and now it was time to be accountable for his actions.

Slim knew when he walked out of the prison gates that very soon he would be returning. He had a choice to make. He could go and help his baby girl, the only lady he had ever truly given his heart to, or he could leave his past behind. By going to Houston, he would be violating the conditions of his parole and would undoubtedly be sent back to finish the rest of his bid. Any sane man would have just let Disaya be, would've moved on and let the past go, but as Elaine's car pulled up to the prison gates, his insanity was proven. He could not allow YaYa to suffer at the hands of Leah. He had to go to her aid.

He climbed into Elaine's vehicle and they took off without speaking. They both understood the risk that Slim was taking, but neither of them felt the need to vocalize it.

As Elaine hopped onto the highway, she prayed that they made it back to Houston in time. She had been calling YaYa nonstop, but she always got sent to voice mail. Elaine felt in her heart that YaYa was going after Leah. She had a long, twenty-four-hour drive ahead of her. Slim had no ID, so he couldn't take a flight. As they settled in for the long haul ahead of them, Elaine spoke up.

"Pray for her, Slim. She's going to need it. She's going to need us. Pray that we get to her on time."

Chapter Twenty-three

YaYa hid behind the tinted windows of the Acura LX as she sat outside of Leah's home. Nothing was moving inside. She had been there all night, and not a single light had popped on. This was the moment she had been waiting for.

For weeks she had put in work, hustling endlessly, sleeplessly, recklessly, hopelessly. She had to earn her stripes and get her money up so that she could touch Leah and get away with it. The quest for revenge had been a hard one, a long one, but as she sat up the block from Leah's home, she knew that it was all worth it.

Headlights off, the Acura blended into the dark night. The street lights that Disaya had busted helped to conceal her as well. She had everything all planned out. The showdown of a lifetime was about to occur.

I'm not leaving here until she's dead. I won't leave her any room to hurt me again. Fuck her apology; I want to hear her eulogy.

YaYa's hands shook as she loaded the bullets into the magazine of her gun. She wasn't cruel, so the thought of taking a life terrified her, but it didn't scare her enough to change her mind. Leah had destroyed her life one too many times. The bitch had to go. Murder was the ultimate sin, but there was no other alternative. It was YaYa or Leah. The entire world knew it.

They couldn't co-exist. The earth wasn't big enough for the both of them. Leah's obsession with YaYa was too great to ever let it go, and as long as there was air in her lungs, Leah would terrorize her.

As YaYa sat, her eyes never left the house. She was more focused than she had ever been in her life. She kept replaying the many times that Leah had fucked her over. She had set her up and made it seem as if she had killed Nanzi; she had fucked her man and gotten pregnant by him; she had kidnapped and killed her daughter. The things that Leah had done were unforgivable, and now her fateful day had come.

Despite the passing midnight hour, YaYa refused to close her eyes. She had no time for fatigue. She fought sleep until finally she saw the sky fade from black to orange. Dawn was illuminating the horizon, and YaYa was tired of waiting. Patience was a virtue that she did not possess. She opened her car door and tucked the gun in the waistline of her True Religion jeans as she approached Leah's home. She looked around the neighborhood to make sure that no one was watching her. The early morning hour kept the other residents at bay as they slept comfortably in their safe suburban homes.

Gunshots were not a common occurrence around those parts, but YaYa didn't give a damn. She wore no mask, no gloves. She was going in as she was, and with no silencer on her pistol, she was about to wake the entire neighborhood.

Just as she was nearing Leah's house, the garage door began to lift. YaYa quickly lowered her head and pulled the hood of her Fendi jacket over her head as she kept walking past Leah's home. To the naked eye, she appeared to be a random passerby.

As Leah pulled out of the driveway, YaYa peeked over at her. Just the sight of her face made YaYa boil with contempt. As the garage door began to go back down, YaYa thought, *Hurry up and pull off, bitch.*

Leah put her car into drive and sped away.

Once the coast was clear, YaYa hurriedly sneaked beneath the garage door. She barely made it inside before it closed shut. She walked inside the home. She didn't need to look around or snoop. YaYa and Leah had played this cat and mouse game once before. They knew each other well—too well. This dance was well rehearsed, and it was time to tango.

YaYa checked for weapons in the house before blocking the garage entry, pulling a large baker's cabinet in front of it.

Now she has to come through the front door, YaYa thought.

She looked around the pristine, luxury home where Leah dwelled, and a deep hatred made her heart pound in anticipation.

I'ma burn this bitch to the ground. She bought this with my money. Made her happiness from my misery. We'll both die in this bitch before I let her walk out of here alive, she thought.

YaYa took the canister in her hand and began to pour the liquid inside all over the room.

"You dirty bitch!" she mumbled as she poured it violently over everything. "I hate you! I'ma hand deliver what you have coming to you!" she fussed as the smell of gasoline quickly overtook the room. It burned her eyes and nostrils as she made her way from the kitchen to the den to the office, checking to make sure that she would have the advantage and that Leah had no surprises in store for her.

She made her way to the living room and doused the entire room, because it was where the grand finale would take place. If she had to go up in flames to make sure that Leah got it, then so be it.

She sat down on the couch, crossing her legs prissily. She pulled the gun out and clicked it off of safety. She cocked it back and wrapped her finger around the trigger as she placed it on her lap. Facing the door, she was fully prepared to put a bullet through Leah's head as soon as she walked inside. Her trigger finger was itching.

All she wanted was to get to the end of this thing. Leah had been in control of her life for way too long. Ever since the day she met Leah, her world had been in a downward spiral. The end was near.

I can't wait to finish this bitch, she thought anxiously. The hairs on the back of her neck stood straight up as a haunting feeling came over her, but before she could turn around, she felt cold steel pressing against the back of her neck.

"So you found me?"

The sound of Leah's voice startled YaYa, yet she didn't move. Leah had caught YaYa off guard, but she would never let her know it. Instead, YaYa was cool as a cucumber on the outside as she felt her anger rising inside. Images of Mona popped into her brain. Skylar . . . Indie . . . all whose lives had been taken one way or the other as a result of Leah's antics. YaYa gripped her trigger.

"I will blow your top off, YaYa. Don't test me," Leah threatened.

YaYa laughed as she stood to her feet.

"Did you not hear me?" Leah shouted. "Sit the fuck back down before I kill you!"

YaYa raised her free hand and held a closed fist in the air. "I don't think you're going to do that, Leah."
She opened her balled fist and let the contents of her hand fall to the floor. "You need bullets in order to do that," she mocked as she dropped the ammunition to Leah's gun.

All twelve shots bounced off the carpet, rendering Leah helpless. YaYa smirked. There was no way she would be caught slipping. She had found that gun and emptied the clip the moment she had come through the door. She knew that Leah would recognize her and loop back. It wasn't her face that Leah had spotted. It was the red-bottom high heels that YaYa wore. The $1,000 pumps looked odd on a woman walking down the street in the early morning hour, and when she saw Leah do a double take before pulling off, YaYa knew that she would soon be back.

YaYa had waited too long for this to blow it by being careless. All of her *i*'s were dotted and *t*'s were crossed. She was leaving no stone unturned.

Leah dropped the gun, knowing that it would be of no use to her at this point. She could see the determination in YaYa's eyes, and she scoffed in disgust. "You fucking bitch. You always come out on top, don't you, YaYa? You're like a fucking cat with this nine lives shit. How many times do I have to destroy you?"

"What the fuck is wrong with you?" YaYa shouted. "Why me? Why the fuck are you so fucking obsessed with me, bitch? Damn, I have a pussy just like you! I put my pants on one leg at a time like everybody else! What the fuck did I ever do to you?" YaYa asked emotionally as she stabbed her gun in the air for emphasis. "Poor little YaYa," Leah teased. "Poor little light-skinned, green-eyed YaYa. Poor little daddy's girl. Poor little spoiled bitch!" The more Leah went on, the more crazed she became. "You stole my life! You stole my father. My daddy couldn't even see me because he was so blinded by you and your bitch of a mother!"

"What?" YaYa gasped. "I don't even have a father! You're so fucking delusional. What the fuck are you talking about, Leah? Listen to yourself.

You killed my daughter! A baby! Because you're a jealous bitch! And for what? For nothing!"

"Buchanan Slim," Leah whispered as tears she wailed became acquainted with the snot that was running from her nose.

YaYa's eyes widened as her chest heaved up and down and she wrinkled her brow in disbelief. She hadn't heard the name in so long that it was like a slap to the face. She had almost forgotten about him. She had labeled herself a parentless child after Slim and Dynasty had been taken from her. It had been easier to just pretend as if they never existed.

"No father, my ass," Leah scoffed as she noticed the drastic change in YaYa's facial expression. "You took him from me, YaYa. He was my father . . . my daddy . . . and all he wanted was you. He had his own daughter! He didn't have to adopt you as his own!"

"This is what all of this is for? For Slim?" YaYa asked loudly as she frantically grabbed her hair and walked around, fuming. "You stupid, stupid bitch! You killed my daughter and took my life away from me over him. He was my daddy, not my father! He was a pimp! Yes, I was his favorite girl, Leah, but why do you think I never visited him in prison? Huh? Why do you think I've let all of these years go by without reaching out to him?"

Leah was too focused on YaYa's gun to answer her.

"Because he wasn't my father. He was my pimp. He was grooming me for the game! From the very day I was born, I was being groomed. He didn't love me! You could have had him! The gifts, the attention . . . it was all manipulation. I just didn't realize it until I was a grown woman!

"Eventually he would have raped me. He would have had to. That's what the job entailed. He didn't love me. He saw a dollar sign when he looked at me. And that's the man that you worship?

"I loved him because he was all that I knew, but he was a grimy mu'fucka, just like all of the rest!" YaYa shouted. "That's the man that motivated all of this bullshit?"

"That's the man that made me, bitch! Don't talk about him like that! He gave you what he was supposed to give me, and you still talk about him like he's shit under your shoe!" Leah's tears mixed with her black mascara and made trails of misery down her cheeks. "You're ungrateful! I would have taken the attention he gave to you in a heartbeat. He might not have been perfect, but he was yours. Do you know what I had to do to try and get him to love me? Do you know?"

YaYa had heard enough. She pointed the pistol directly at Leah's face. YaYa didn't care what Leah's motives were. She hated her, and there was no erasing the devastation that she had caused.

"Don't do this, YaYa. Don't. You don't know how I got this way. It's not my fault," Leah pleaded. She hoped to appeal to YaYa's soft side. *The bitch doesn't have it in her to kill me,* she thought smugly.

"I'm sorry for everything, YaYa. I'm so sorry," she said. Her performance was convincing, but there wasn't a bone in her body that felt true remorse. She just needed that gun out of YaYa's hands so she wouldn't be at such a disadvantage. *She's soft,* Leah thought. "You don't know the full story. I'm not evil, YaYa. If you knew—"

"I don't care to know. It's too late for all of that. You're going to die today," YaYa said as she stepped directly in front of Leah's face and put the gun in the center of her forehead.

Leah dropped the "I'm sorry" act as anger passed over her. She was livid that YaYa once again had the upper hand. Her facial expression changed from pleading to enraged.

"Do it, you bitch! I've already taken everything from you anyway. You have nothing left," she said in a low, hateful tone as she stared Disaya in her eyes. "Skylar deserved a better mother than you anyway. I did her a favor."

YaYa's heart did a double take. Leah's words cut her to the core. YaYa felt her body temperature rise as her nostrils flared. She nodded her head as she stepped back from Leah, removing the gun from her head.

"That's right. You're a weak bitch. I win, YaYa," Leah taunted with a laugh that made the hairs on YaYa's arms stand tall.

YaYa nodded her head as she popped the ammunition clip out of the gun. She cocked it back, and the bullet that was in the head went flying into the air.

Shooting this bitch will be too quick. A bullet is too good for her. I want her to feel my pain, she thought as she pulled her hair back into a ponytail. She grabbed the pistol by the barrel and walked up to Leah.

Whop!

She struck Leah with all her might. Leah's head snapped as it went to the side sharply. YaYa had hit her so hard that Leah could feel her neck crack as blood flowed out of her mouth. Stunned and dazed, Leah lifted a shaky hand to her face. Seeing all of the blood that covered her fingers sent her over the edge.

"Aghh!" she screamed as she charged YaYa.

It was the faceoff of a lifetime. They both harbored so much hatred for one another that they knew this could only end in death.

YaYa sidestepped and slapped Leah on the back of the neck with the gun, sending her crashing into the dining room table. This time YaYa didn't give her time to rebound. She pounced on Leah.

"You fucking jealous, evil bitch!" YaYa shouted as she hit Leah with all of her strength. With every word she delivered, her hand went up and down in the air as she pummeled Leah's face with the unloaded pistol. There is no better way to say—YaYa was beating the shit out of Leah.

"You took my baby away from me! You set me up!"

YaYa delivered deadly blows, and she wasn't giving nothing but headshots. She hit Leah so hard that the gun was busting up her own knuckles, but she didn't care. Blood flew everywhere as Leah tried to fight back, but YaYa was like a woman possessed.

"You should have . . . never . . . fucked . . . with me!" she shouted as if she were somebody's mama teaching a lesson. It was undoubtedly the worst ass-whooping that Leah had ever received.

Knowing that she was falling into unconsciousness, Leah lifted her leg in a desperate effort to defend herself. She kicked YaYa as hard as she could in her kneecap.

Pop! The sound of YaYa's bone shifting out of place was sickening.

"Agh!" YaYa yelled in excruciating pain as she lost her balance. She stumbled because she could no longer put weight on her injured leg, and it was the perfect distraction for Leah. It gave her just enough time to regain some composure.

She pushed YaYa to the ground, causing her head to crash into the floor. YaYa grimaced and closed her eyes. The impact was enough to make her dizzy. She was so disoriented that she didn't feel Leah's hands as they wrapped around her neck. Leah straddled YaYa and choked her out. The intense pressure was almost unbearable, and YaYa clawed at Leah's hands as she desperately gasped for air.

"Die! Just fucking die already," Leah said menacingly through gritted teeth. She squeezed, digging her fingernails into YaYa's skin as her own blood fell onto YaYa's neck.

YaYa's lungs burned with desperation. She couldn't believe what was about to go down. She couldn't go out like this, not after everything she had been through to find Leah. She struggled to free herself from Leah's grasp, but she had the strength of a lunatic. It was as if she were fighting with a grown man. Leah was so strong, and the sick look in her eyes frightened YaYa.

She's killing me, she thought as her eyes bugged wide in fear.

Leah's forehead broke out in a sweat as she used all of her energy. She could barely see through the blood in her eyes, but she could feel YaYa weakening beneath her. She jerked YaYa's neck violently until she felt her stop moving. She lowered her face to YaYa's mouth, and when she didn't hear her breathing, she smiled in satisfaction.

"She's dead," Leah whispered as if she couldn't believe it. "She's dead."

The Last Chapter

Heaving in exhaustion and sweating profusely, Leah loosened her hands. She began to laugh as tears of relief and happiness came over her. She had wanted to rid the world of YaYa for so long, yet she never thought she would actually see the day. She laughed directly in YaYa's face, mocking the dead woman.

Leah stood to her feet and looked around her home. It was in shambles. Furniture was overturned and blood was everywhere, but she didn't care. All of her broken possessions could be replaced. YaYa's death was all that mattered.

Now I just have to get rid of the body.

Crash!

Before Leah could finish her thought, she took a blow to the back of the head, sending her flying to the floor.

YaYa had stopped breathing. She knew that if she didn't give up and play dead that Leah would actually kill her. She didn't mind going, but she for damn sure was going to take Leah to hell with her.

Leah moaned as she weakly got on her knees and tried to crawl toward YaYa's gun. Just as her hand wrapped around the weapon, YaYa stomped on it.

"Shit!" Leah screamed as YaYa crushed every bone in her finger.

"Aghh!" YaYa shouted as she kicked Leah in her face. "Agh! Agh! Agh!" She stomped Leah's head, and it bounced off of the ground as if it were a basketball.

She backed away from Leah and rubbed her tender neck. Leah had choked her to the point where her skin was red and raw. Tired of the games, it was time for her to do what she had come to do. It was obvious that they both were all in. They were going hard, and each refused to allow the other to win.

"I'm never going to let you beat me, bitch," Leah said as she spit a few of her teeth out of her mouth and dragged her bloody body across the white-carpeted floor.

As YaYa loomed over Leah, she kicked her one more time for good measure. Panting, her chest heaved as she thought about what she had to do. "That is quite unfortunate, Leah. See, bitch, I know you will never stop making my life hell, and

I have accepted the fact that I will probably never stop allowing you to. We're stuck in this sick-ass cycle, me and you," she said as she reached into the pocket of her skinny jeans and pulled out a cigarette. Her hands shook as she removed a lighter. Placing the cigarette between her lips, she continued to speak. "That's why this ends today. This shit is over today."

"Only one of us can walk out of here," Leah shouted. "You know who that's going to be, don't you? You can't kill me, bitch! Even when I die, I'ma live forever through you. You won't have a choice but to think about me every day."

YaYa smirked and lit the cigarette. She took her time as she toked it long and hard, inviting the nicotine into her lungs.

"I know," YaYa said as she closed her eyes and hit her cigarette again slowly. "Neither one of us is going to walk out of here. I'ma burn this bitch to the ground with both of us in it."

YaYa was past the point of trying to piece her life together. Life was no longer worth living. Her revenge is what had fueled her for this long. Without Indie and her daughter, she didn't want to be here. Leah had pushed her over the edge, and now all she wanted was finality.

Leah could see that YaYa was limitless, and for the first time, she feared her. "Noo!" she shouted as YaYa grabbed Leah's legs and dragged her kicking and screaming across the floor. Leah's tender womb banged violently against the floor. The infection had set in to the point where she couldn't even touch her stomach without wincing in pain, and the feeling of all of her weight bearing down on that spot almost made her pass out. She screamed, as it felt like tiny bombs were going off inside of her.

"Shut the fuck up! Don't bitch up now," YaYa replied as she gave her another slap across the face. She held the cigarette between her lips as she manhandled Leah.

The gas had already been poured. Once YaYa tossed her cigarette, the house would go up in flames.

YaYa grabbed Leah by her long, luxurious mane and slammed her head hard into the end table, knocking Leah out cold. When YaYa thought it was safe, she let her legs give up on her. She sat on the floor beside the woman who had ruined her life and she cried. She just broke down, looking at Leah's motionless body while she smoked the square. It was a soul-wrenching cry, because she knew that everything, including her own life, would be over soon.

It seemed as though her entire existence had been one long journey that added up to this moment. She hadn't known that Leah had been in the shadows with envy in her heart from the very beginning.

I didn't start this shit, but I'm definitely about to end it.

YaYa pulled on the square one last time, and as she blew out the smoke, she tossed it into the air. As soon as it hit the floor, a bluish-orange flame erupted and spread instantly. YaYa sat back, mesmerized, hypnotized by the very fire that would take her life. Seeing the flames dancing before her reminded her of the fire she had started as a child, when she was being raped at her foster home. Back then, that had been her way to get revenge and to escape. Irony had come full circle, because again that was her reason for starting this blaze.

Waaa!

Waaa!

Thinking that she was going crazy, she began to speak to Skylar. *I know, baby. Mama's coming. I'm coming to be with you, Sky,* she thought.

She began to cough as the poisonous smoke robbed the air of any breathable oxygen. Her lungs burned as she closed her eyes and began to pray.

Waaa!

It wasn't until she heard the shrill cries again that she realized that they weren't coming from inside her head.

Oh my God. I completely forgot that Leah had a child. Her baby is inside this house!

YaYa climbed to her feet, and was hit in the face by all of the smoke. The sting from the thick fog of death tortured her eyes as she tried to see through the black cloud. Her conscience began to eat at her as she thought of Leah's baby being injured in the fire. She hated Leah, but did not have a cruel bone in her body. Leah's baby was Indie's baby, and she couldn't allow the baby to burn up in a fire that she had started.

Waaa!

YaYa finally located the door where the sound was coming from. Perspiration drenched her from the excessive heat. She could feel her skin frying off as the fire grew more monstrous with each second. She feared that even if she did make it to the baby, neither of them would make it out alive.

Waaa!

"Aghh! Damn it!" she shouted when her hand touched the doorknob. It was scalding, and took layers of skin off of her hand. Her skin stuck to the door handle, crackling as it cooked, causing her stomach to churn. The heat was overwhelming, but it didn't frighten her as much as the thick, black smoke that was clogging the air. She was suffocating, and although she was pushing herself to move forward, she realized that within seconds she would be dead. She held the hot door handle and screamed in agony as it burned her. She didn't let it go, however; she couldn't as long as that baby was on the other side of the door.

Pushing open the door, she staggered into the room.

Waaa!

The smoke had consumed everything, and all she saw was black. Following the sound of the cries served as her only navigational tool. She held out her hands as she roamed the room as fast as she could, until finally she felt the wooden edges of a crib. She reached down and grabbed the baby.

Cough! Cough!

When YaYa lifted the child to her face, she almost dropped her in disbelief.

"Skylar?" she said, thinking her instincts were playing tricks on her.

Although she couldn't see her, she could feel the rhythm of her heartbeat as she held her closely. Something inside of her went crazy as her stomach knotted and tears came to her. The hair on her neck stood up, and shivers ran down her spine.

Is this my baby? Is this my Sky? Can't be! Oh my God! Sky?

Waaa!

The sound of the cries were so familiar to her. Even the way the child clung to her was familiar.

This is my baby, she thought. Oh my God! Oh my God! This is Sky. Thank you, God! She thought as she cradled Skylar to her chest.

"It's okay, Sky. Mommy's here. Mommy's right here," she soothed as she frantically looked around the room. "Mommy's going to get you out of here," she promised as she cried and kissed the top of her daughter's head. She didn't have time to waste.

I have to get out of here, she thought with renewed determination. Her heart swelled at the thought of holding her daughter in her arms. For so long she had grieved, only to find her alive. Now she had to keep her alive.

Her heart began to beat out of her chest as she cradled the screaming baby to her body, wrapping her as best she could. The blaze was uncontrollable as it jumped and burned in the hallway. There was no way she could get out of the room without being burned.

She went to the windows in the room and saw that they were barred from the outside. It was the only room in the house with bars. It had been Skylar's prison. Leah had made sure that no one could come in and take away the little girl.

YaYa broke the glass with her elbow and attempted to break through the bars. She wrapped her hands in Skylar's bed sheets and pushed on the black security bars with all of her might, to no avail. That wasn't her exit.

She had no choice but to go out the same way that she had come in. Fear paralyzed her, but the diminishing wails of her daughter pushed her forward. She could hear Skylar growing weaker by the second. She quickly wrapped the bed sheet around her daughter's tiny body. She had nothing to protect herself from the flames, but she didn't care.

Huddling over Skylar like a running back moving a football, YaYa ran through the fire. She gritted her teeth as it bit at her, charring her to the bone.

"Aghh!" she yelled. The pain was unbearable, but she refused to stop moving.

I have to get Skylar out of here. She can't die in a fire I started. God, please!

YaYa could see the sun shining through the living room windows, and she knew that she was close.

Without warning, it felt as if the floor had been taken from beneath her. She fell with her daughter in her arms.

"You're going to burn in this fire, bitch!" she heard Leah scream. "You're not going to take Skylar away from me. You'll never take anything away from me again. I'm her mommy now!"

YaYa kicked her foot and felt it connect with Leah's face. She couldn't see her. It was too dark inside, but she could hear her crazed rants.

"I'm going to kill you, bitch!" *Cough! Cough!*

YaYa held onto Skylar for dear life and crawled on the floor. The air was lighter down there, allowing her to breathe a bit easier. She saw the outside light underneath the front door frame, and she crawled in that direction.

"Bitch, where are you?"

Leah's voice was behind her as YaYa desperately crawled toward her escape. She was moving as fast as she could, but when she felt Leah's hand grab her calf, she knew that it was over. There wasn't enough air in her lungs to put up a good fight. She released Skylar as Leah pulled her back into the depth of the blaze.

The two tussled as they weakly flipped over, Leah on top, then YaYa. Scratching, biting, nothing was off limits, but neither of them could get the upper hand. The sound of splintering wood caused them both to look up, but by then it was too late. The last thing that they saw was the second floor as it came tumbling down on top of them.

Epilogue

As the fire chief stepped through the remnants of the house, he shook his head in disgust. There was no stopping this blaze. The amount of gasoline accelerant that had been used was enough to burn down an entire suburb. He had recognized right away that it was arson.

"You're a very lucky little girl," he said as he held baby Skylar in his arms. They had recovered three bodies from beneath the rubble, but Skylar was the only one who had come out of the blaze unscathed. As hot as the blaze had been, Skylar was blessed. Nothing short of God could have spared her. She had a few minor burns, but when they uncovered her, she was conscious, screaming and kicking from fear. Undoubtedly, if they hadn't found her when they did, she would have suffocated.

Walking past the EMTs on the scene, the chief said a silent prayer as he watched one of the bodies being zipped up in a body bag. Burn victims were always the worst, because their families usually didn't have much to bury when it was all said and done. His job was a hard one, but as he held the screaming baby in his arms, he knew that it was rescues like this one that put a silver lining around his dark cloud.

He handed baby Sky off to an EMT, knowing that she would be in safe hands.

"Chief? We have a live one over here!" he heard one of the firefighters yell out. He looked up in disbelief, surprised that anyone else had survived such a ferocious blaze. He dropped his heavy fire resistant jacket and ran over to the gurney.

"We have a pulse. It's faint, but it is there," the EMT announced as they prepared to move the victim to the hospital.

The fire chief turned to the other set of EMTs, who were transporting the victim who unfortunately hadn't survived. He looked at the female paramedic that was pushing the gurney and said, "Make sure no one sees that body." He nodded toward the media cameras that were just arriving on the scene. "We don't need our burn victim all over tonight's broadcast. Let's respect the family."

The woman nodded and then put the body in the back of the ambulance. Sirens filled the air as it drove away.

At that moment, Buchanan Slim and Elaine came racing through the crowd. They were stopped by the police officers that had arrived on the scene.

"Wait a minute. My daughter was inside that house!" he protested. Despite what Disaya thought of him, he had truly looked at her as his child. Yes, he was a pimp, but she had stolen his heart from day one. He would have never inflicted any pain on her. "Let them through," the fire chief yelled.

Slim and Elaine rushed over to the gurney.

Please, don't let this be YaYa. I don't want to have to tell Indie that she is dead, Elaine thought as she clasped her hands together tightly in desperation.

When Elaine saw the charred body that the EMTs were working on, the contents of her stomach came up in her mouth. "Oh my God!" she shouted as she heaved uncontrollably. The body was unrecognizable. Her face, body, hands, even her hair: it was all black. Only small pieces of pink flesh showed through, and the smell was horrendous.

"Is she alive?" Slim asked.

"Barely," the chief replied. "We are going to take her to the hospital now. There were two women in the house at the time of the blaze. I know it's hard, but can you identify this woman at all?" he asked.

Elaine stood to her feet and gave the body a once over. There was nothing left to assign identity to. She was about to give up, until she saw the sun bouncing off of the diamonds in YaYa's ring. "It's her. It's YaYa," Elaine choked out. "That's the ring that my son gave to her. That's Disaya Morgan. Will she be okay?" she asked as she watched the paramedics load her into the ambulance.

"Only time will tell, but they will do all that they can to keep her alive. Now, there is the issue of the baby . . ."

"Baby?" Elaine asked in shock. It was then that she recognized the sounds of a screaming child. She turned toward the noise and took off running when she saw her granddaughter's face.

"Thank you, God! Thank you!" she cried as she retrieved Sky and rocked her gently in her arms. "Oh God, thank you!" She held the baby up in front of her face as she examined her injuries. She was so grateful that Skylar was in one piece that all she could do was cry.

Slim came up behind her and put his hand on the small of Elaine's back. "Is this YaYa's daughter?" he asked.

Elaine handed Skylar over to him and watched as his eyes pooled with emotion. "This is Skylar."

"I've missed so much," he whispered. "I just hope that YaYa pulls through and gives me the chance to make all of this right. I have so much making up to do."

Beep! Beep! Beep!

The sound of YaYa's heart monitor was deafening as Elaine, Bill, and Slim sat around her bed. Skylar lay in her grandmother's arms as they all anxiously waited for YaYa to come to. The white bandages that covered her from head to toe made her look like a mummy. Her appearance would be forever altered. Many surgeries lay ahead, and cosmetic procedures would be the only thing to ever fix the damage to her features, but still she was blessed to be alive.

Days had passed and her vitals had been improving every day, but the doctor explained that it would take time for her to come to.

"YaYa, you have to be strong, baby girl. It's me, Slim. I'm here now," he said. The sound of his voice caused her eyelids to flutter wildly.

"She can hear you," Elaine announced in surprise. "Keep talking. I think she's trying to wake up."

"I'm so sorry for leaving you out here alone. I'm going to make it up to you. You just have to be strong and come back to us. We are all waiting for you. Skylar's here. She's safe. Just wake up, YaYa," he said.

"Oh my Lord," Elaine gasped as she stood to her feet. Slowly, YaYa's eyes began to open. "Bill, go get the doctors! Hurry!"

Bill rushed from the room, and Slim kept talking. The more he spoke to her, the more she came back to the land of the living.

A team of specialists rushed into the room.

"Can you tell us your name? Do you remember anything?" the attending physician asked as he shined a light in YaYa's eyes to make sure that she was coherent.

"Disaya . . . Disaya . . ." She moaned, still too weak to speak.

"Take your time," the doctor coached. "Tell me your name."

"Disaya Morgan," she finally said. "The baby. Where is she?"

Elaine stood up and held Skylar so that YaYa could see. "She's right here, YaYa. She's safe. You just get better, you hear?" Elaine turned to the doctor. "She sounds different."

"Her larynx was badly injured from the smoke inhalation. She will sound different for a while, if not indefinitely, but the important thing is she is alive. After being trapped in a fire like that, she is very blessed to even be here. Yes, her features will never be the same, but you have to look at this optimistically, for her sake."

YaYa lay back and closed her eyes as she thought about the moments just before she had blacked out in the fire. . . .

Leah tried to lift up, but the weight of the house on her back was too heavy a load. YaYa lay dead right beside her as the smell of burning flesh invaded her nose. The sounds of sirens could be heard in the distance.

All I have to do is hold on. They're coming for me, *she thought.*

"Is anyone alive in there? Please, call out if you can hear my voice!" she heard a fireman say.

The only response he got was the sound of Skylar's cries, because Leah was too injured to speak. Her body was burning like hot coal. YaYa was dead. Finally her mission had been accomplished. Now Leah could do what she had always wanted to do—take her place. She used the little bit of strength she had left and removed YaYa's ring from her finger. She slipped it onto her own.

She could feel her skin frying off of her face. Just from the sight of YaYa, she knew that if she did make it out alive, she would be too badly burnt for her identity to be confirmed. The ring would be significant, and would help her become a new person. It would help her become YaYa. She could finally step into the shoes she had always wanted to fill.

Despite the pain that she was feeling, Leah smiled slightly. Just as she heard the firefighters burst through the door, she gave in to the pain, but the sick smile was still stuck on her face, because she knew that if she awoke, she would be a new woman—literally.

No longer would she be known as Leah Richards. She would be Disaya Morgan.

Leah opened her eyes, and the smile was still stuck on her face.

"YaYa? YaYa?" Elaine called as she frowned slightly from YaYa's odd behavior.

Leah jumped as she remembered to acknowledge her new name. She quickly wiped the smile from her face.

"Huh?" she mumbled.

"Are you okay? You blacked out for a moment," Elaine said.

"I'm fine. I just hurt all over," she whispered.

"Well, someone is here for you. Your father, Slim. He is here for you," Elaine said.

Leah gasped as Buchanan Slim came into her view. He was just as she remembered him, and more handsome than ever.

"Hey, baby girl. I'm right here with you. I'm always going to be right here with you. I'm so sorry for deserting you, and I love you."

Leah was too choked up to respond. Tears fell from her eyes, irritating her already burnt flesh, but she couldn't stop them from falling.

This was all she had ever wanted. Slim's acceptance was what she had been chasing her entire life.

Finally, he loves me. Finally I'm going to get what I deserve.

As Indie stood before the judge, he couldn't keep his focus. He grimaced as a painful shudder wracked his body. He could feel the universe shifting; his center of gravity was off. His intuition told him that something was wrong. Sweat formed on his brow as his pulse quickened. He could hear his heart beating in his head.

"Mr. Perkins, it seems as if the officer in your case . . ."

Indie could see the judge's lips moving, but he couldn't hear the words that came out. The courtroom was hazy as his anxiety level arose to an all-time high.

He turned his neck and looked at the crowd. Through his blurry vision, he saw Chase and Trina sitting in the crowd. He adjusted his tie as he attempted to gain some composure. He didn't know what was wrong with him, but all of a sudden it felt as if the thermostat had been turned up a hundred notches.

"It's hot . . . it's . . . it's . . . hot. Can I get some wat—" Indie gripped his chest in agony. He could feel it in his soul that something was awry. It was as if he were sharing in YaYa's death. He could feel the flames as if he were right there with her, as if he were suffering her fate. Her face flashed through his mind as he closed his eyes.

"Mr. Perkins, are you okay?"

Indie could hear his lawyer speaking to him in concern, but he couldn't respond as he gripped the wooden defense table. He could see her clear as day, as if she were standing right in front of him.

I love you, Indie.

He heard her voice in his ear. God had connected them in her final fleeting moments, and whether he knew it or not, his dear YaYa was no more. His insides felt as if they were being twisted torturously as he doubled over.

"Call . . . a . . . doctor," he managed to gasp. "I think I'm having a heart attack."

A small crowd gathered around him, and despite his health, he was immediately cuffed. Chase hopped up and walked into the front row.

"Indie, you good, fam. They're calling for an ambulance," he said. "Hold on, big homie. They're on the way."

"YaYa," Indie choked out as his face scrunched in excruciating pain. "Something's wrong with YaYa. Find her."

It was the last words that left his mouth before he fell to one knee and the court workers frantically went to his aid.

Chase approached the hospital room with Indie's attorney, and they were stopped by the armed police officer that stood at the doorway. "You can't go in there, boy," the officer said as he put a forceful hand onto Chase's chest. "Boy?" Chase huffed with a smirk and laugh as he calmly removed the officer's hand from his chest. He ignored the officer and walked through him, shoving him slightly with his shoulder as he entered the room.

The officer put his hand on his pistol to show his authority, but before the situation could escalate, Indie's attorney stepped in.

"Indie Perkins is no longer under your detail," Stanzler informed.

"I'm just doing my job," the officer replied.

As the sound of hard-bottom shoes echoed against the tiled hospital floor, Stanzler turned to see the U.S. District Attorney coming down the hall, along with Agent Norris.

"They will explain. Now, move. This man is no longer government property," Stanzler said. "Stand down, officer." The authority in his tone was enough to make the cop step to the side unsurely as Stanzler entered the hospital room behind Chase.

Indie was awake and speaking to his doctor about his condition when his company entered the room.

"You had a heart attack, Mr. Perkins, a very mild one, but an attack nonetheless. I'm not sure what brought this on. All of your test results came back favorably, but I am still concerned. I suspect it is stress that caused it, and there is no medical remedy that I can prescribe for that."

"Perhaps your freedom will do the trick?" Stanzler said as he folded his hands behind his back and stepped toward Indie.

"What?" Indie asked.

At just that moment, the D.A. and Agent Norris burst into the room. The sour look on both of their faces caused an arrogant smirk to spread across Indie's.

"Your indictment has been thrown out. Due to your incoherency during your apprehension it was warranted as an unlawful arrest. The warrant wasn't even presented to you or Ms. Morgan before the officers entered your home. They messed up Indie. When you get out of here you're a free man," Stanzler explained.

The D.A. cleared his throat and gritted his teeth as he said, "You slipped through the cracks this time, Mr. Perkins, due to some amateurish police work." He looked at Norris sternly before continuing. "It won't happen next time."

"I won't let it," Norris added as he stared Indie in the eye.

Indie held Norris' stare and then nodded his head toward the exit. "Gentlemen, you can see yourselves out."

"Fuck out of here!" Chase mumbled as he held open the door.

Indie began to pull the IV out of his arm.

"No, Mr. Perkins, you must rest. Please. You are not ready to leave."

Indie grabbed his Armani suit off of the chair that sat beside the bed and headed toward the bathroom. "I can rest when I die, doc. I've got a young lady waiting for me," he said.

He emerged from the hospital shining like a new penny as Chase walked by his side. He couldn't wait to get to YaYa. She had been holding things down on her own, but now that he was out, he could relieve the burden.

Leah was in his crosshairs. Now that he was free, the bitch definitely had to get it. He could easily forgive the lies she told to him, but the hurt she had dished out to YaYa would be what caused her death.

"Have you heard from YaYa?" he asked.

"Nah, kid. She said that she had something to take care of and that she needed to do it alone," Chase said.

Indie knew that she had gone after Leah. He only hoped that she could handle herself and get in and out without any repercussions. He had a nagging gut feeling that the attack he had experienced in the courtroom was directly linked to YaYa. Something just didn't sit right with him. The energy in his heart was all wrong.

"Find her. I need to get to her ASAP."

Trina rushed him as soon as he stepped foot outside. He was like a second brother to her, and she was so relieved to see that he was okay.

"Indie!" she called out excitedly as he picked her up. She handed him his phone and he powered it on. Within seconds, it rang loudly in his hand. His mother's name flashed across his screen, and he answered it immediately.

"Ma, I'm out. The case was dismi—"

"Indie," she said, interrupting him. He could hear the heavy sadness in her voice. "It's YaYa."

Indie's labored breathing could be heard through the phone. "Don't tell me this, Ma. Don't tell me this. My heart can't take it. Where is she?"

"She's in the hospital, Indie. Things went bad . . . real bad. You need to get here quickly. She's hurt and she needs you."

As Zya sat in the back of the ambulance, she pulled off her disguise and unzipped the black bag where YaYa's body lay inside. She was barely breathing and was holding on for dear life.

As Zya's team of private doctors surrounded YaYa, the ambulance raced through the streets. They weren't headed for the hospital, however; they were headed to a secluded residence that was owned by a friend of Zya's, a business associate named Anari.

After giving YaYa the information on Leah, Zya had a feeling that things would go badly. She liked YaYa, and felt as if she could be an asset to her. It wasn't long ago that Zya had been mentored herself, and now she was passing on the knowledge she had learned—that is, if YaYa survived.

Zya had tried to grab Skylar as well, but the fire chief had gotten to the baby before her.

As she looked at YaYa, she could barely recognize her. Half of her face had been completely seared off.

"We're losing her," one of the doctors called out.

"Do everything you can for her," Zya said. "I pay you enough money to pull off the impossible."

When Zya had given YaYa the challenge of paying back the debt, she never thought that it could be pulled off, especially under the strict constraints of a thirty-day time limit. Her efficient hustle had impressed a lot of people, a round table full of very important people, which is why Zya was asked to retrieve her. There wasn't a lot of people who could make birds fly the way that YaYa had. Someone like her would prove valuable to an organization like the one to which Zya belonged. YaYa had to live. She had to survive.

As they pulled into the immaculate estate, YaYa's life hung in the balance. Zya didn't know if YaYa would live or die. In fact, her chances were slim. But the young girl was a hustler, and if she did survive, Zya had a job for her.

The End . . . Or is it?
You tell me. If you want to read more of this saga, please be sure to let me know.
www.ashleyjaquavis.com
www.readordieonline.com

BOOK CLUB DISCUSSION QUESTIONS

1 Did the book conclude the way you thought it would?

2 Were Leah's actions justified by her gruesome childhood?

3 Was Slim to blame for all of the drama in books 1 and 2?

4 Who was your favorite character?

5 Was YaYa wrong for messing with Khi-P after Indie went to jail?

6 Are Indie and YaYa true soul mates? Will they ever end up together?

7 Will Leah get away with taking over Disaya's identity?

8   Did Buchanan Slim really love YaYa, or was she right? Was he simply grooming her for the pimp game?

9   Do you think YaYa should have listened to Indie and not gotten the police involved with Skylar's kidnapping?

10 Did you know that the crying that Leah was hearing was actually baby Skylar, or did you think it was her dead baby?

11 Is Leah as crazy as you thought she was, or do you feel her plight?

12 Is there room for a Part 3, or is this the end?

Notes

ORDER FORM
URBAN BOOKS, LLC
78 E. Industry Ct
Deer Park, NY 11729

Name: (please print):_____

Address:_____

City/State:_____

Zip:_____

QTY	TITLES	PRICE
	16 On The Block	$14.95
	A Girl From Flint	$14.95
	A Pimp's Life	$14.95
	Baltimore Chronicles	$14.95
	Baltimore Chronicles 2	$14.95
	Betrayal	$14.95
	Black Diamond	$14.95

Shipping and handling-add $3.50 for 1st book, then $1.75 for each additional book. Please send a check payable to:
Urban Books, LLC
Please allow 4-6 weeks for delivery

ORDER FORM
URBAN BOOKS, LLC
78 E. Industry Ct
Deer Park, NY 11729

Name: (please print):_____

Address:_____

City/State:_____

Zip:_____

QTY	TITLES	PRICE
	Black Diamond 2	$14.95
	Black Friday	$14.95
	Both Sides Of The Fence	$14.95
	Both Sides Of The Fence 2	$14.95
	California Connection	$14.95
	California Connection 2	$14.95

Shipping and handling-add $3.50 for 1st book, then $1.75 for each additional book.

Please send a check payable to:

Urban Books, LLC

Please allow 4-6 weeks for delivery

ORDER FORM
URBAN BOOKS, LLC
78 E. Industry Ct
Deer Park, NY 11729

Name: (please print):_____

Address:_____

City/State:_____

Zip:_____

QTY	TITLES	PRICE
	Cheesecake And Teardrops	$14.95
	Congratulations	$14.95
	Crazy In Love	$14.95
	Cyber Case	$14.95
	Denim Diaries	$14.95
	Diary Of A Mad First Lady	$14.95
	Diary Of A Stalker	$14.95

Shipping and handling-add $3.50 for 1st book, then $1.75 for each additional book.
Please send a check payable to:
Urban Books, LLC
Please allow 4-6 weeks for delivery